Death in the Setting Sun

Death in the Setting Sun

DERYN LAKE

This edition published in Great Britain in 2005 by
Allison & Busby Limited
Bon Marché Centre
241-251 Ferndale Road
Brixton, London SW9 8BJ
http://www.allisonandbusby.com

A catalogue record for this book is available from the British Library.

10 9 8 7 6 5 4 3 2

ISBN 0 7490 8365 4

Printed and bound by
Bookmarque Ltd, Croydon, Surrey

DERYN LAKE is the pen name of the popular historical novelist Dinah Lampitt. Born in Essex and raised in London, she trained and worked as a journalist on a variety of magazines (most notably *Woman*) as well as on Fleet Street. She married and had two children before writing her first book. Fascinated by history, she researches her subjects thoroughly and packs her books full of accurate details. She currently lives close to the famous battlefield of 1066.

For my special Amelia – with Grandy's best love

Acknowledgements

My thanks, first and foremost, to Beryl Cross who introduced me to Gunnersbury Park and showed me the two houses which now stand there, together with the Round Pond, The Temple and the Bath House. Princess Amelia's house was destroyed years ago but the Rothschild family built two mansions on the site which I found fascinating. I hope others will too. Next, thanks are due to Keith Gotch, now retired to Devon, but still an expert on bodies. His help with the drowned victim was terrific, as usual. I would also like to thank my editor, David Shelley, always ready to laugh, and my agent Vanessa Holt. Finally come Henry, Elliot and Fintan, whose visits make my day; and Susan Carnaby and John Elnaugh, who brighten my life.

Chapter One

Like many seasons that are destined to be severe, the winter of 1764 started moderately enough with mild evenings, crisp leaf falls and a lot of fine clear sunshine in the daytime. A golden October thus gave way to a misty November, though the fog itself was warm and vaporous. But round about the beginning of December the wind changed direction in the night, blowing from the north, with a hint of snow on its breath, so that John Rawlings, closing his shop in Shug Lane and hurrying home to Nassau Street, found himself almost running to keep out the cold. Bursting into the hall, blowing his hands, he thanked the footman who helped him divest his greatcoat and hat, and hurried to the library where he knew the fire would have been lit.

The room was empty as he had half expected but indeed there was a great blaze in the hearth and John held his hands out to it before pouring himself a sherry from a decanter that stood on a side table. Then, having taken two small sips, he braved the chill once more and hurried upstairs to the nursery where his daughter, Rose, who had been born two and a half years before, awaited him together with John's wife, Emilia.

He paused in the nursery doorway, they as yet unaware of his presence, and looked at them with much fondness. Emilia still had that angelic quality which had so attracted him: fair hair and blue eyes and a slim, slight figure unaltered by childbearing. At present she was three months pregnant with her second child but nothing of this showed as yet and, with the candles and firelight reflecting in her hair and on her skin, she looked young and untouched. Rose, however, had been born with ancient wisdom, though only her father was aware of this, but as he looked at her now she sensed his gaze and smiled at him, lighting up like a flame. Her hair was a deep rich red, curling round her small face in spirals. Dominated by a pair of huge dark blue eyes, fringed by black lashes which brushed against her creamy skin, it was an exceptional face that one day would grow and mature into true beauty.

Emilia, seeing the child smile, followed her glance and saw her husband leaning against the doorframe. She stood up straight.

"John. I didn't know you'd come in."

"I was watching the two of you. It was a pretty scene."

She wrinkled her nose at him. "Come and join us. We've missed you."

He entered the room and Rose ran into his arms as he bent to pick her up. "And how are you, lovely girl?"

"I am very well, thank you Papa."

Her speech, like the rest of her, had a curious maturity which was extremely charming.

John, gathering her into his arms and holding her against him, felt the spring of her mop of hair and buried his nose in it.

"What's in there? A little mouse?"

Emilia remonstrated. "Oh, sweetheart, you'll frighten the child."

But Rose was laughing, wriggling in John's grasp, and shouting, "Yes, yes. Do you want to see?"

He peered into her hair then closed the whorls of red again quickly. "I mustn't disturb him. He's sitting at supper."

At this the child exploded with mirth and John gently placed her on the floor. Crossing to where Emilia stood, he gave her a kiss, then put his arm round her. "And how have you been today, my dear?"

"Reasonably well. And you?"

"Well, I don't know if I am geting old but my new apprentice seems incredibly slow-witted."

"Why, what has he done?"

"It's rather what he didn't do. I had left two packets on the counter, one of Saxifrage root, finely chopped, for an old man with toothache. The other was for another old boy suffering with piles. I'd given him oil made from infusing the flowers of

Mullein. Anyway, while I was out calling on a patient he gives the wrong packet to the wrong chap, if you follow me."

Emilia giggled naughtily and John tightened his grip on her, thinking how much she meant to him, how much they had grown together.

"Can you imagine the confusion? One fellow wrestling with the root, the other staring in horror at the oil. God's life, my reputation will be in shreds at this rate."

"But he's a willing boy."

"Yes," John answered thoughtfully, "he's that all right."

He stared into space, thinking how sad it was that Nicholas Dawkins, known as the Muscovite because of his exotic ancestry, had finally left him and had now himself been made free of the Worshipful Society of Apothecaries. Yet 'left him' was hardly describing the case. For Nicholas had gone to Kensington and was running a shop into which John and his adopted father, Sir Gabriel Kent, had invested money in equal shares. Though Nicholas was still without a bride, John imagined that this state of affairs would not continue for long, in view of the Muscovite's weakness for the female sex. However, at the present time the Apothecary was labouring in the company of one Gideon Purle, who was, as Emilia said, willing but lacking in flair.

John sighed aloud. "No doubt he'll learn in time."

"What did you do about his error?"

"I sent him on the run to the house of the man with piles lest he try to put the root of Saxifrage up his..."

"John! Not in front of the child."

"Sorry. I momentarily forgot her presence."

He bent down to Rose guiltily but she was already absorbed in playing with a wooden horse and had not heard him. Straightening up, John looked at Emilia over her head, then he winked. Emilia gave a delighted laugh and said, "Husband, you're incorrigible. Come, let's hand Rose over to her nursemaid and sit together awhile. Rose, say goodnight to your father."

The child looked up from her play, then got to her feet. "Goodnight, Papa."

He bent to kiss her once more, pulling her close to him with a sudden urgency, almost as if they were going to be separated. Rose's deep blue eyes looked slightly startled but she kissed him none the less, her cool lips against his cheek.

"You're rough, Papa."

John laughed, fingering his chin. "I need a shave, Rose, that's all."

Just for a moment he had a vision of himself with several days' stubble on him, and he shivered slightly despite the fire that glowed in the nursery. Fortunately Emilia had turned away so did not notice but John, standing upright, felt an inexplicable finger of melancholy. He quite deliberately fought it off and forced a smile at his wife.

"Are you ready?"

"No, give me a moment or two. You go down. I'll join you shortly."

"Very well."

He hurried down the stairs, not totally warmed by the fire in the hall, and back into the sanctuary of the library. But still the dark mood was upon him and, finishing his sherry, he poured himself another one and sat down.

It had been two and a half years since he had last been called to assist Sir John Fielding, the famous magistrate known to the mob as the Blind Beak. Two and a half years in which Rose had grown from a newborn baby into a delightful little girl, whose powers of speech were well-advanced. Sir Gabriel Kent, her grandfather, was now aged eighty, having celebrated his birthday last summer in tremendous style. He had returned to London, to Nassau Street, and invited the whole of the town to feast and play cards and dance. It had been a sumptuous occasion and John had been amazed at how many important people came to celebrate with the old man, who still dressed to the inch in stunning ensembles of black and white, all topped by a very old-fashioned wig of three storeys in height.

One of the guests had been John's childhood friend Samuel Swann, now quite definitely putting on weight, the thinness of his wife, Jocasta, fortunately hidden by the fact that she had been *en ceinte*. The Apothecary had to admit that marrying an heiress had given Sam a certain portly air of self-satisfaction which he found fractionally irritating. But all had been forgotten when he had looked at Sir Gabriel's aristocratic face and seen it glowing with pleasure.

Other guests had included Sir John and Lady Fielding, together with their adopted daughter Mary Ann, actually a niece of Elizabeth Fielding's. John had been highly amused to observe that the arrival of Lord Elibank, an old friend of Sir Gabriel's, had the young woman preening like a cat while Milord had been covered with confusion. The Apothecary guessed at once that there had been some previous connection between the two, one which had presumably ended in tears. Still, he could hardly blame his lordship, for Miss Whittingham – or Fielding as she called herself these days – at the age of eighteen was gorgeous to behold indeed. And wasn't the girl aware of it, casting her predatory eyes round the room and getting into conversation with the richest and best-connected men there.

"She's after a fortune," John had whispered to Samuel – and somewhat to his surprise his friend had blushed, conclusively proving that once upon a time he, too, had had a fancy for her.

But the little temptress was still unmarried and, as far as John knew, had not received any firm offers for her hand, which only went to show something or other, though the Apothecary was not quite sure what.

A log shifted in the fireplace and John went to throw another on, wondering what had caused his earlier dark mood. Imagination, he told himself, though he had to admit that these strange feelings often prefaced a disaster of some kind. Yet again he shrugged the presentiment away, glad that Emilia was coming into the room to keep him company.

They had been married five years, very happily. So happily indeed that he rarely thought of Elizabeth di Lorenzi, a woman he had met on honeymoon with whom he could have fallen in love had circumstances been different, and hardly at all of Coralie Clive, his former mistress. In fact, he had grown to love Emilia more in that time and now could say he was truly content.

Yet there was something in him, some basic part of his character, that longed for adventure and excitement. So much so that he often found himself wishing that he could be like other men who settled into a life of routine and regularised living. Like Samuel Swann, for example. But the very idea made him smile. Dear Samuel, the most affable of all his friends, was within a hair's breadth of growing pompous and prematurely middle-aged, a route down which John had no intention of going.

"What are you thinking?" asked Emilia from the doorway. "You're smiling."

"I was actually dwelling on Samuel. Do you not think he's changing?"

"Well, he's getting older."

"Obviously. But I actually meant in himself. He's growing rather important, don't you agree?"

Emilia giggled. "He's getting fatter certainly."

"And by contrast Jocasta is so thin. Which reminds me, when is her baby due?"

"In early January, just after Christmas."

"Dear Sam. He's been wanting a child for years. Perhaps its arrival will bring him to his senses."

Emilia drew her chair closer. "Oh come on, John, you're being unkind. Just because he's growing middle-aged in a different way from you there's no need to pillory the man."

"Pillory? I'm doing no such thing. I merely said that his sudden wealth and his enhanced status are making him self-important."

Emilia laughed. "Perhaps you might have got that way if you had married money."

John shook his head vigorously. "Never. I quest adventure too much." His face fell. "Am I middle-aged? I rather thought that didn't happen till forty."

She gave him a beautiful smile. "My darling, you will never be middle-aged, even if you live to be ninety. You have about you the eternal youthful spirit. And I think it is all the adventures you've been involved with over the years that has brought this about.

"Do you?"

"Yes. And you're missing them now, aren't you? There's been a restlessness about you recently."

John put out his had and took hold of one of hers. "Sweetheart, you know me as well as my father does. Yes, I have been longing for a call from John Fielding. But all's quiet. Though mind you, that last affair, riddled with bodies as it was, was enough for me for many months."

"So I should think." She stood up. "Come along, Husband. Dinner will be served at any moment. Let's go to the dining room."

"Not before I've given you a kiss."

"If you insist," said Emilia, but she made no move to get away from him.

The dining room was on the first floor and they made their way there, Emilia's arm linked amiably through his. Then they sat down at opposite ends of the table and John, hungry indeed after a day with Gideon, ate his way through three courses without conversing. It was while they were on the fruit and cheese that Emilia spoke again.

"I forgot to tell you that I had a letter this morning from a girl I was at school with."

"Oh yes?" said John, sipping his wine.

"It seems that she contacted my mother to find out where I

was and was surprised and pleased to hear that I was married."

"It has been some time since you saw her then?"

"Yes. We drifted apart after we left. But she has tracked me down and wants to come and visit me. She is dying to meet Rose – and you of course."

"Of course," said John with a serious expression, and was shot a look of reproof. "Anyway, go on."

"Her name is Priscilla Fleming and she is a year younger than I. Apparently she has got a rather a good occupation as a companion to one of Princess Amelia's ladies-in-waiting."

"A fine post indeed."

For George II's daughter, Amelia, unmarried but with a lively reputation regarding certain peers of the realm, was known to live a life of luxury and indulgence, wintering in Cavendish Square and spending her summers at Gunnersbury House. Her parties were considered quite the thing and an invitation to one of them meant that socially one had arrived.

"Which lady-in-waiting employs her?" John continued, genuinely interested.

"Lady Theydon. Apparently Priscilla is distantly connected with her – third cousin or somesuch thing. Anyway, when Priscilla's mother died shortly after the girl left school, Lady Theydon wrote and offered her the post – which she gladly accepted."

"Quite a step up for her."

"It certainly was. In any event, I wrote back immediately and invited her to come and see me as soon as she has some free time. She is in Cavendish Square at the moment so that shouldn't prove too challenging."

"No," John answered, but he was no longer concentrating, his mind already wandering off, wondering how long it would be before Gideon Purle began to think sensibly and act accordingly. In fact he was so deep in contemplation that he jumped when Emilia spoke again.

"...you will be sure to come home promptly, won't you?"

"When?" he asked, forcing himself back to reality.

"Oh John, you haven't been listening. I said I was going to invite Priscilla to visit next Tuesday and stay to dine. Then she can meet both you and Rose."

"A good plan, my dear. Carry on."

She gave him a reproachful look. "You don't care, do you?"

"Of course, I do," he answered. Then he looked at her most sincerely and said again, "You know I care about everything you do."

"Oh John," she answered, and smiled her special smile at him.

The minute he set eyes on her he knew that he had met her before somewhere, though where that had been for the moment eluded him. While he was thinking, he gave his best bow then kissed her hand. Priscilla fluttered a little in response and made another small curtsey.

He looked at her and just for a fleeting second had the impression of a porcine face staring back at him, though when he looked again he realised that this was somewhat unfair. A pair of blue eyes set slightly close together and a flattish nose were what were creating the effect, though the rest of Priscilla Fleming's face was pretty enough. A fine head of blonde hair was drawn back beneath a large befeathered hat, while the lashes surrounding the somewhat small eyes were thick and dark. She also had a wide smile, displaying a set of gappy teeth. Yet she was so well dressed, such a belle of fashion, that she had the air of a truly attractive woman. And so convincing was this demeanour that John found himself believing it.

"Mr. Rawlings," she said in a cultivated voice that had just the hint of another accent in its depths, "it is truly a pleasure to meet you."

As she moved, a strong waft of perfume came from her clothes which John found particularly appealing.

"It certainly is, Miss Fleming," he responded, "but, forgive me, I feel that we have met before somewhere."

Priscilla laughed lazily. "Of course we have. I have been in your shop several times, little realising who you were."

John raised his brows. "But surely Shug Lane is a long way from Curzon Street, where I presume you reside."

Priscilla continued to smile. "Ah, my dear Sir, there is a simple explanation, though one which I would desire you to keep confidential. Fact is that the Princess tried some of your Restoring Elixir and has sworn by it ever since. As one of the lesser servants I am sent to purchase same at regular intervals. So there's the answer."

Emilia came in. "Good heavens, what a small world it is to be sure. To think you have seen John frequently but never knew who he was."

"Well, I do now," Priscilla said, and laughed once more.

She was very jolly and, considering everything, most attractive in her way. John found himself warming to her. Escorting the two ladies into the library, he poured them sherry and listened to them chattering.

"Of course, the Princess bought Gunnersbury House three years ago but has done a great deal of restoration work. She has started work on a garden folly and is turning it into a Bath House. It is such fun, you really should see it." Priscilla clasped her hands together. "Yes, dearest Emilia, you must come and visit me there. It would be a splendid opportunity for you to have a look at Gunnersbury which is really quite magnificent."

John turned. "But that wouldn't be until the spring, surely?"

Priscilla's face continued to smile widely. "We often go there in the winter months to make sure that the servants are doing things properly. I shall invite you as soon as possible." She looked at John. "Will you come, Sir?"

"Certainly, if I can get time off from my shop."

"But surely you are your own master. After all, the place is yours is it not?"

"Yes, Madam, it is. But at the moment I have a new apprentice, not fit to be left in charge as yet. I'll have to see how he shapes up."

"Oh, please allow yourself a day off."

"I'll have to see."

Priscilla turned to Emilia. "But at least you can come, my dear friend. Gracious, I am so glad to have found you again. What a long time to have been apart."

"Yes, indeed it is. So tell me, Priscilla, do you have a beau?"

There was an infinitesimal pause before her friend answered, "Oh, several. Princess Amelia keeps an open house and I have met one or two comely young men amongst her guests."

"But nothing serious, I take it?"

"You take it correctly. I am a hawker when it comes to love. I take mortal pains to remain single, I'll have you know."

John asked, "But surely that is just a phase you are going through?"

The small eyes flashed in his direction. "Of course. When I meet the right man I promise you I shall settle down and become an exemplary wife."

Emilia laughed. "You haven't changed a bit, Priscilla. I can remember you saying much the same at school."

There was a toss of fair curls and the feathers on the hat bobbed in response. "Well, there you are then. Let us speak of something else."

John sat back silently, leaving the coversation to the two women, trying to recall exactly when he had first met Priscilla Fleming. He had a vague recollection of her coming into his shop some six months ago, hesitating, as he remembered, in the doorway. Then, as he had walked out of the compounding room, she had looked him up and down and broken into a wide-toothed smile. At the time he had thought her flirtatious but could see now that this was simply her manner, her way of conducting herself. In other words, she was an extremely confident young woman who refused to let anything stand in her way. He eyed her now, thinking how she had turned rather unappealing looks to her advantage.

"...I find your little girl adorable," Priscilla was saying, smiling charmingly.

Emilia wrinkled her nose. "Yes, she's remarkable, at least we believe so." She leant forward confidentially. "Actually, I am expecting another child soon."

"Really? And when is the baby due?"

"In June."

"How wonderful for you. Oh my dear Emilia, to find you so happy and so settled. It is all I could ever have wished for you." She turned to John, eyes alight. "Thank you for making my friend so happy, Mr. Rawlings. You are clearly an ideal husband."

"I would hardly say that," the Apothecary answered truthfully, thinking of the times he had left his wife to her own devices while he had gone in pursuit of villains and blackguards.

"Nonsense," Priscilla answered gaily. "You are everything that a woman could desire."

She was flirting with him, gently so, and John could not help but respond.

"You flatter, Miss Fleming. I assure you that the reality is nothing like as good as you would have me. Is it, Emilia?"

"No," she answered honestly, "it can be pretty dreadful when he is involved in some skullduggery and leaves me alone."

The piggy face frowned. "Oh? What skullduggery is this?"

Emilia immediately looked contrite, as if she had said too much. In fact she even went so far as to glance at her husband and say, "John?"

"I occasionally assist Sir John Fielding," he answered smoothly.

The effect on Priscilla was astounding. She clasped her hands together, her cheeks went pink, the little eyes opened wide.

"I vow and declare I adore a mystery," she said. "Do you really work with the Blind Beak?"

"Occasionally, yes."

"You must tell me all about it. I simply can't wait to hear every detail."

Fortunately at that moment the door opened and a footman announced, "Dinner is served." Miss Fleming stood up, removing her hat to reveal masses of golden curls. "Why, Emilia," she said, "how like you to choose a truly exciting husband. I envy you, I really do."

Emilia smiled, somewhat nervously John thought. "Yes, he's commendable in most things."

Priscilla linked her arm familiarly through the Apothecary's. "You must tell me everything over dinner. Promise?"

"Yes, I promise," he said, and led her upstairs to the first floor dining room.

Chapter Two

The meal was a great success, most of the talking being done by Emilia's long-lost friend. John felt by the end of it that he almost knew Princess Amelia and her entourage and that he could have found his way round Gunnersbury House without a guide, so vividly did Priscilla describe them. She certainly had a way with words and it occurred to the Apothecary that the girl might have some talent as a writer. So much so that he asked her outright. Priscilla blushed modestly.

"Well, I have written one or two stories to amuse my friends. And this year the Princess has asked me to organise the Christmas celebration."

"Oh?" John was interested. "And what form will it take?"

Priscilla blushed again. "It is a masque and the cast will consist of the Princess's court, together with a professional actor."

"And where is he coming from?"

"From the Theatre Royal, Drury Lane."

John felt a slight plunging of his heart. The woman he had once loved to distraction, the celebrated Coralie Clive, was now taking all the leads at that very theatre. He covered the moment by asking another question.

"And where is the play to be performed?"

"That's rather a delicate matter. You see, when I first envisaged it I set it in the large saloon at Gunnersbury House, which is absolutely ideal for the purpose. In fact I adapted the plot to suit the building. Then it was to be a summer extravaganza. But now the Princess has decided that it is to be done at Christmas so it will have to be in Curzon Street, which will not be as good."

"Why must it be there?" asked Emilia.

"Because Princess Amelia winters in London. So that is that."

"Could she not be persuaded to go to Gunnersbury?"

"The house will be freezing. Particularly in view of the current cold spell. I think it would take too much effort to remove the court and get Gunnersbury House warmed up."

"None the less," Emilia persisted, "it would be a shame to spoil the play. Perhaps you should speak to her."

Priscilla looked downcast, an expression that temporarily enhanced her porcine cast of features. "I, personally, would not dare ask Her Royal Highness. It was through Lady Theydon that I was approached to write the masque in the first place."

"Then let Lady Theydon be your messenger. Explain that in your opinion it would quite spoil the production if it were not performed where you originally intended."

Priscilla appeared dubious. "Princess Amelia is a very determined woman. Once she has made her mind up nothing will shift her."

"Well, you could at least try."

"You're right. I promise that I will ask Lady Theydon to speak on my behalf." She turned to Emilia. "But, my dear friend, wherever it is to be performed, I shall try and get you to be a member of the audience. And you, John, of course."

Imagining himself wedged in amongst a great press of people, John made a mental note to be otherwise engaged should the invitation materialise. Emilia, however, brightened.

"I should enjoy that. Thank you."

Priscilla glanced flirtatiously round. "My pleasure will be enhanced by your company."

John paid particular attention to the grape he was peeling, thus avoiding her bright-eyed gaze.

It was as they were getting ready for bed that Emilia let out a sigh and said, "Poor Priscilla."

"Why?" asked John, genuinely surprised.

"That is all a cover up, you know, about wishing to remain a spinster. I feel I should have invited someone else to partner her this evening. It would have pleased her enormously."

"Who? Most of our friends are married."

"Oh, I would have thought of someone," Emilia answered vaguely. She snuggled into bed, pulling the clothes up under her chin. "Oh, it's cold. Hurry up."

John jumped in and pulled his wife close to him. "You like your new friend, don't you?"

"She's not new. I knew her for about five years. And, yes, I do. Why?"

"No reason," he answered, and went to sleep.

The next morning a messenger came with a large display of flowers and a note from Priscilla, full of effusive thanks.

"She invites me to take tea with her in Curzon Street," said Emilia, scanning it at breakfast.

"Then go, my darling. Enjoy yourself," John answered, wiping his mouth and standing up.

Emilia glanced at him. "Are you off to work? Why so early?"

"Because I don't trust Gideon to turn up on time. Until I can get it through his fat head to open up, I have to be there to watch him."

Emilia sighed. "Oh, poor John. I do hope the boy is going to come up to snuff."

"So do I," her husband answered heavily.

A few minutes later he left the house and turned into Gerrard Street, his greatcoat pulled well round him, his hat firmly on his head. It was bitterly cold and he thrust his gloved hands deep into his pockets, gazing ahead of him, determined to get to Shug Lane as quickly as possible. As he walked he found his thoughts turning to last night's guest.

The Apothecary reckoned her to be about thirty years of age and, despite her slightly piggy face, attractive enough to have caught the attention of several males. So the story of her waiting for the right man was probably true. John hoped for her sake that the man did not take too long to enter her life, particularly as Priscilla had mentioned having a family.

Deep in thought he turned into Shug Lane and made purposefully for his shop, which was situated about halfway up. Somewhat to his surprise he saw that Gideon had arrived and was busy sweeping out, prior to opening.

"Good morning," he called cheerily, and tapped on the door.

Gideon looked up. "Good morning, Sir."

While the boy unlocked, John studied him.

He was sixteen years old; a stocky, red-headed creature with eyes the colour of gooseberries and a great grin on him. In fact it was difficult, despite the overwhelming reasons to be annoyed, to get very angry. He had a winining way of looking alarmed and going pale, then smiling nervously, which completely disarmed John, however furious he was. Once, when he had been on the point of beating him, Gideon had given him that frightened smile and the Apothecary had ended up dropping the cane to the floor.

"Spoil the child, spare the rod," Samuel had said, shortly after Gideon had signed his indentures.

"And how often do you beat your apprentice?"

"Once a week, regular as clockwork."

"I don't believe a word of it," John had answered, and Samuel had been forced to admit that once a year was nearer the truth.

Now Gideon gave his master a bright grin and said, "I was just about to take the covers off, Sir."

"Then away you go. But Gideon–"

"Yes, Sir?"

"Be careful not to break anything. Lift them gently, there's a good chap."

"Very good, Sir."

The Apprentice then proceeded to lift the covers off as carefully as if they covered the crown jewels, each one being treated with exaggerated care.

"Not that carefully," said John, slightly irritated.

"No, Sir," Gideon answered, yanked at the next one and, sure enough, an alembic smashed to the floor in smithereens.

Shaking his head, John vanished into the compounding room to make himself a cup of tea.

The morning passed much like any other, ladies coming in for a variety of cures, everything from megrim to flux; elderly gentlemen concerned with gravel or gout; bucks and blades either buying condoms or urgently seeking a cure for the clap. However, remembering Gideon's recent error, John insisted on serving everyone personally and had just bidden farewell to a regular customer, a winsome woman of fifty years ripe, seeking something to restore her faded youth, when the door burst open, setting the bell jangling. An elegant figure stood there, clad in a green and black striped coat, a silver waistcoat, green breeches and stockings of the same emerald hue.

The figure bowed and said in an Irish accent so broad that it sounded phoney, "Good morning to yeez. Would you be after having anything for a pain in my hypochondrium? I sustained a recent injury and it's hurting me to hell."

Gideon gave an audible gulp and it was left to the Apothecary to say, "Take a seat, Sir. Can you tell me how you came by this injury?"

The Irishman sank into the chair vacated by the lady, who had stopped in the doorway to gaze on the newcomer's handsome face.

"Sure and it was on stage. We were fighting, d'ye see."

"Ah, I take it this was a mock fight. Done in pursuit of your profession perhaps?"

The Irishman nodded wearily. "That is so. But, blessed saints, the other bugger hadn't practised the moves and wasn't I the one to suffer for it."

"Would it be possible to examine you? You can step into the back for the sake of decency."

"Decency be blowed. It's only me chest."

And with that the Irishman removed his cloak, ripped his shirt out of his breeches and hauled it upwards, displaying a great deal of muscular upper body. The Apothecary pressed and prodded gently, to the accompaniment of groans of varying strengths, finally saying, "Yes, Sir, you have sustained a broken rib in my view."

"Great God, I'll have the fellow's neck, so I will."

"It really isn't anything to worry about. I'll prescribe you a strong decoction of Madder. That will relieve the bruising both internal and outer."

"But me rib, what should I do about that?"

"Nothing," John answered calmly. "It will heal on its own. I wouldn't recommend that you continue the stage fight, however."

"Ah, there's me job gone. I'll be honest with you, Apothecary. I'm at the very early stages of my career, though one day I hope to play the leads, mark you. But the fact of the matter is that now I'm only employed to brawl and crowd, if you take my meaning. So, I'll be hanging round the other theatres to see what they've got. Ah, 'tis a terrible life, so it is."

He looked at John ruefully, his good-looking features creased into such a sad expression that the Apothecary found himself offering comfort.

"I take it you were at Drury Lane, my friend?"

"I was indeed, Sir. I was a fighting Capulet until last night."

The next question was out before John could help it. "Do you know Miss Coralie Clive?"

"Not to speak to, no. However that has not stopped me worshipping from afar. But she is in the realm to which I aspire, mark my words."

"Then why not go to David Garrick and explain that you are temporarily *hors de combat* and ask if you may just crowd for the time being?"

"He's abroad at the moment and will continue to be so for some time." The Irishman finished tucking his shirt back in and pulled his coat back into position. "Now, Sir, if you'll give me the decoction I'll be on my way."

John searched along the counter until he found a bottle of the red liquid. "Take twice a day, but not at night, unless you want to be up and at your chamber pot."

"Thank you, Sir." The Irishman searched in his pocket until he found a card which he presented with a flourish. "My ticket."

"Thank you." John solemnly handed him a card in return. "That will be one shilling."

"Expensive but worth it if it does the trick. Good day to yeez."

And he was gone, cramming his tricorne on his head and leaving the shop with a further jingling of bells.

"Quite a character, Sir," said Gideon, watching his retreating form through the window.

"Yes."

John studied the card which read, 'Michael O'Callaghan, Thespian and Artiste.' Beneath this bold inscription there was printed an address off Fleet Street. John suspected that it was probably somewhere rather seedy.

"Strange to think of him being on the same stage as Coralie," he said to himself, then felt a rush of self-annoyance that such a thought should even have presented itself.

The next day found Emilia in a state of extreme nervousness. "John, before you go to work you must advise me on my wardrobe," she announced at breakfast.

He looked up from *The Daily Courant*. "Wardrobe?" he asked.

"Yes. It is today that I go to take tea with Priscilla. I really am determined to cut a dash fashion-wise. Supposing I should run into Princess Amelia."

"Why? Does she wear cutting styles?"

"I have no idea but one must be prepared. The train has made a comeback, you know. Do you think my open robe with the small train would be suitable? That is if I can get into it."

John smiled at her, thinking how excitement became her, transforming her into someone far younger than her actual age.

Indeed, Emilia almost looked childlike as she gazed at him earnestly.

"Let's go upstairs and have a look at your selection," he said, cramming a piece of beef into his mouth and chewing hastily.

"Oh good," she said, clasped her hands together and practically ran up the flight in front of him.

Several of her favourite dresses were lying on the bed and before he could say a word Emilia had slipped off her nightrail and was trying the first one on. After fitting them all they eventually decided on a sacque-backed gown in heavy woven silk, trimmed with lace and flowers, the saque falling in a slight train as fashion decreed. The stays beneath meant that it could be laced as tightly as ever.

"Phew," said Emilia, holding her breath.

"You won't get away with this much longer," John remarked, noticing the flush in her cheeks.

"Nor would I wish to. I feel like an oyster crushed by its shell."

"Well, breathe in today and after that, loosen your stays."

"Yes, Apothecary," she said cheekily, making a face at him.

John felt another rush of love for her and pulled her close. "Enjoy yourself," he said, "and remember that you will be one of the most beautiful women there. There's no need for all these alarms, you know."

"But I enjoy them," Emilia said, and kissed him on the cheek. He responded with a proper kiss, a kiss which left them both feeling rather flustered, and it was as much as he could do to tear himself away and walk through the cold to Shug Lane. Which, however, he forced himself to do, slowing his gait as he spied Gideon, running and breathless and somewhat ill-attired, but ahead of him just the same.

Chapter Three

After his day's work, knowing that Emilia would be late, John made an appointment to see his tailor, a man he held in high esteem. He had been attending the same fellow, whose name was Josiah Bentham, for several years, and now he made his way to Ludgate Hill, where Josiah resided next door to a linen drapers, with whom he had connections. Usually, of course, Mr. Bentham attended to him in his home but tonight, because John had firmly insisted, the client was making his way to see the tailor.

Taking a hackney coach, John travelled with a sense of enjoyment. Not that he needed a new suit, nor even workclothes, his clothes press bulging with garments. But styles were changing. The flared coat skirts which he had been sporting were being cut back, waistcoats were flaunting small stand collars. Indeed, he looked forward to a half hour in which he could talk about fashion with an expert and, if necesary, call Josiah in to alter some of his existing clothes.

The night was extremely cold, the moon frosty and covered by a hazy layer of cloud. As the coach proceeded down The Strand, John was struck by the fact that few prostitutes were out, preferring to lose a night's trade than to brave the elements, no doubt. Fleet Street, where lay the notorious Fleet Ditch, an open sewer with an indescribable stench, was not as noxious as usual. John noticed as they passed over Fleet Bridge that the Ditch had frozen over, trapping the worst of the stinks within. None the less he applied his handkerchief to his nostrils and did not remove it until they had climbed further up Ludgate Hill.

The hackney drew to a halt outside the linen drapers and John, paying the man off, knocked on the door beside the shop. It was opened by a boy, who bowed and said, "Mr. Josiah is waiting above, Sir." Cautiously, John ascended the steep flight of stairs.

He entered a scene of high activity. Despite the lateness of the hour cutters and stitchers were working feverishly on a whole medley of cloths, while the tailor himself, tape measure round neck, flitted from place to place, overseeing all. He turned as he heard John come in and gave an extraordinary bow.

"Mr. Rawlings, my dear Sir. I do hope your journey here was not too hazardous."

"No, I took a hackney."

"Just as well. Far too far to walk, particularly on such a freezing night." He paused, said, "Excuse me a moment if you would," and hurried over to one of his assistants.

John looked round him. The room was very long, presumably stretching over the linen drapers shop underneath, and had exposed timbers. There was a large grate in which a coal fire licked halfway up the chimney, throwing out a goodly heat for those nearest to it. In the far corner of the room, however, where the boy who had answered the door sat with a couple of others, there blew a draft which felt as if it had the ocean on its breath. Yet it was the activity in the room that John found exhilirating. For everyone, old and young alike, was working full pelt to finish the garments that lay on the tables stretched out before them. It was like a scene depicting merry dwarves at toil and the Apothecary felt a smile cross his somewhat tired features.

A table near the fire boasted various provisions together with some bottles of wine. Mr. Bentham, without enquiring whether his visitor would like a drink or not, proceeded to pour out a reasonable claret.

Handing it to John, he said, "And now, Mr. Rawlings, let us discuss fashion."

John took a chair. "What are the latest trends, Mr. Bentham?"

The tailor, who had not partaken, put his fingertips together. "Well, as you will have no doubt observed, the side seams of the coat are increaingly curving backward, bringing the hip buttons closer together, the effect, of course, is to narrow the back. The flared skirts are, alas Sir, going out."

"Oh dear," said John, alarmed by the fact that he had several fully flared coats in his press.

"Your present collection can, of course, be modified."

"Thank heavens for that. What else is going on?"

"Well, the stock has replaced the cravat. But I see you are already aware of that." He cast an approving eye at the Apothecary's neckwear.

"Yes. What else?"

"Heels, my good Sir, are getting lower." He paused once more and refilled John's glass. "And now, Sir, let me show you quite the finest piece of material that it has been my pleasure to handle in many a long year." He clapped his hands and one of the boys in the corner immediately got to his feet. "Jarman," called Mr. Bentham, "bring me a sample of Midnight in Venice."

"Yes, Sir," and the boy went rummaging amongst bales of cloth and pulled out one which he carried reverentially towards his master.

It was indeed very fine, made of midnight blue with a design of small silver stars. John picked it up and felt the quality between his fingers. "Does it come from Venice?" he asked,

"It does, Sir, it does. It is quite the latest style of fabric. Can you not see it with a shot silver waistcoat embroidered in petit-point with deep blue flowers, thus contrasting with the upper garment?"

"Unfortunately," the Apothecary answered, clearing his throat, "I can."

Josiah looked roguish. "Can I tempt you, Sir?"

"I don't think so. I am a family man now."

"Of course, of course. Now, when shall I call to remove your flared coats?"

"Tomorrow perhaps."

"Tomorrow at six?"

"That would be splendid. Now, can you send a lad to the hackney coach point for me?"

"Of course, Sir. At once. Do have some more wine."

It was a little after seven-thirty when John began the journey home. London was freezing and there were few people about. Staring out of the window, wishing that he was already in his house, the Apothecary saw that the streets were almost empty. Then there was a hold up as he drew level with the King's Theatre in The Hay Market, into which one or two souls were still hurrying. He stared, feeling he recognised one of them, then as she turned her face was caught by light so that he saw it quite distinctly. It was Priscilla Fleming. But it was to the person accompanying her that John's eyes were drawn. For it was none other than the Irishman who had come to his shop earlier that day. Michael O'Callaghan was, surprisingly, taking a young lady of some standing to the theatre that night.

"Did Priscilla mention a man called Michael?" he asked Emilia, who was sitting opposite him in the study, reading a book.

She looked up. "No, I don't think so. Has he a second name?"

"Michael O'Callaghan. He's an Irish actor who came to my shop earlier today. He was slightly injured in a stage fight but making heavy weather of it. Anyway, I saw them going into the King's Theatre together."

Emilia stared. "How odd. When I left she said she was going to retire early; that she was feeling fatigued."

"She obviously revived," said John drily.

"Clearly," Emilia answered, and gave the smile that her husband adored. "She seems very taken up with theatre people so perhaps she felt she should risk going out."

"I wouldn't have thought he was her type somehow."

"Why?"

"Because, frankly, he's down-at-heel. He only crowds and

fights. He seems ambitious enough but as yet certainly hasn't made the climb to better things."

"Perhaps he's a secret admirer."

"Obviously he is. But I'm surprised she didn't mention it to you."

"Oh, she has a lot on her mind," Emilia answered vaguely. "This theatrical presentation she is putting on for the Princess is quite an undertaking. She has even asked me to take a part."

"Really?" John lowered his paper and stared at his wife.

"Yes. It is apparently to be held at Curzon Street because that is where the Princess wants it. Anyway, poor Priscilla can't get hold of enough young women. In short, she's desperate for them. So, Husband, she has asked me if I will consider it."

"And will you?"

"Yes. That is if you don't mind."

"My only worry is that you are three months pregnant."

"Well I shall have to be wedged in a little longer. May I do it?"

"My darling, you may do as you wish. You knew that when I married you. I am not a man to follow convention and you have total freedom – within limits of course."

She got up and crossed over to him, lowering herself onto his lap and giving him little kisses round his eyes and nose.

"And what limits might they be?"

"That you go on loving me and don't take a fancy to anyone else."

Emilia wound her arms round his neck. "How could I when all I ever wanted is here, now."

It was an unforgettable moment and one that he would treasure. "Darling Emilia," he said, and gave her a kiss full of the sudden rush of an inexplicable emotion which beset him.

Waking suddenly in the middle of the night, John realised that he had been dreaming of Midnight in Venice, of all things, and had to admit that it was the most wonderful piece of material he had

seen in an age and fit to dream about indeed. And now, he
realised, he had the perfect excuse to order a suit made from it,
cut on the most fashionable lines. As Emilia was to take part in
the royal entertainment, the theatrical performance organised for
the benefit of Princess Amelia, it would be beholden on him to
attend. And what better to wear than a coat and breeches fashioned in that divine material.

Cautiously, John lit the candle by his bed. Emilia stirred but
did not wake. Taking a paper and pencil he kept handy on his
bedside chest, the bottom half of which contained a chamber pot,
the Apothecary did some sums. He could afford it – just – without depriving Rose and the forthcoming child of anything. But
he would have to work hard. And Gideon would have to pull his
weight. Deciding to put an advertisement in a newspaper to gin-
ger up business, John roughly drafted one. Then, at last, he blew
out the candle.

But sleep would not come. Memories of that uneasy sense he
had had when he had held Emilia close, together with a general
sensation of disquiet, plagued him to the point that he finally rose
and went downstairs to the library. Even this old, familiar, well-
loved room seemed eerie in the moonlight, which flooded in
round the shutters. Pulling them back, John stared out into the
garden. Then he froze. There was somebody out there, he felt
positive. He watched the shape, which stood quite still beneath
the trees, looking towards the house.

John felt his blood run cold. It stood so still he could almost
believe it was a ghost. But he must have made the slightest move
because suddenly the figure, voluminously cloaked so that it was
impossible to guess its gender, took off to the back of the garden
and must have climbed the wall leading to Dolphin's Yard where
the horses were stabled and the coach kept.

The Apothecary toyed with the idea of running into the street
and giving chase but realised, even as the idea came to him, that
the notion was doomed. Dressed only in a nightshirt and adding

the extra minutes it would take to fetch his pistol, he would have already lost the intruder. Deep in thought he returned to bed, having first checked all the locks, determining to say nothing to Emilia.

Chapter Four

Throughout the first week of December it remained just as cold, then, in the second week, snow fell on London and refused to go away. Ordering the path outside number two Nassau Street swept, John struggled down Gerrard Street on his way to work, then encoutered another snowdrift in Shug Lane.

"Come along, Gideon," he called and set to with his apprentice, sweeping for all they were worth, until he had cleared the alley a goodly way on either side of the shop.

Then, rosy-cheeked and blowing their hands, master and pupil went into the compounding room and brewed tea.

John stared mournfully outwards. It was very grey and the first few flakes were starting to fall again. "I doubt we'll get much custom today," he said. But even as he uttered the words a shopkeeper from next door appeared and, pushing his way in, set the bell jangling.

"Good morning, Mr. Rawlings," he said through chattering teeth.

"Good morning, Mr. Colville."

"Have you something for my apprentice? The boy has a streaming cold and today seems totally devoid of energy. Unless he's putting on an act, of course."

"I'll come in and see him as soon as I've finished my tea. Would you like some?"

"I'd appreciate a cup. Thank you."

They all three went into the compounding room and Gideon poured for Eustace Colville, whose shop John feared going in to for the temptation to buy was so great. Stacked almost to the ceiling with books, it contained ancient works as well as those of a more up-to-date nature, and had everything from heavy tomes of maps to the latest novel. It also imported books from Europe which were aimed at those emigres living in London, amongst whom Mr. Colville had a thriving clientele.

Tea drunk, John put on his greatcoat before walking the few steps to the next door shop where he found the apprentice in a sorry state. Eyes streaming, nose pouring, the boy had a fever and a distillation upon his lungs.

John turned to the bookseller. "This lad needs to go home to bed. He has a severe attack of ague and really should rest."

Mr. Colville looked slightly daunted. "Well, I can't leave my shop to walk him back. Oh dear!"

"I'll send Gideon to get a chair, if that's agreeable."

Eustace pulled a slight face but agreed and a few minutes later, looking terrible but clutching two bottles, one made from the fresh leaves of Colt's Foot to relieve his cough, the other a mixture of distilled water, again of Colt's Foot but mixed with Elderflowers and Nightshade for the ague, Mark the apprentice was on his way. Gideon stared after the retreating chair.

"I've a sore throat, Sir."

"Right," answered John. "Let's have a look."

He peered down the chasm but could see nothing untoward. However, he decided to play the game.

"Um, that will need watching. I recommend the juice of the leaves of Birch Tree. Every hour on the hour. Wash your mouth out with that and I'll keep an eye on you. Here's some. Start now."

He ran his hand along the shelves and handed the wretched boy the bitter-tasting concoction. Then he grinned as from the back room came the sounds of Gideon enthusiastically starting to rinse his mouth then hawking at the terrible taste.

The Apothecary's feeling that trade would be slow turned out to be justified and at three o'clock he shut up shop and walked back through the dying day, Gideon trotting alongside. As always, when he turned into Gerrard Street, John felt his heart lift, knowing that Emilia and Rose would be waiting for him, that the house would be warm and welcoming. Yet despite its obvious comfort there was today something slightly threatening about the place, a feeling caused by the strange sexless figure in the garden, staring so silently. He had almost thought it to be a spectre. Yet it had been human enough when it took off in fright towards Dolphin's Yard.

John slowed his pace. Who could it have been and what did they want? And had he been right not to tell Emilia about it? Yet what harm could befall her? She was surrounded by servants and lived the life of a young mother, protected and cherished at all times. He had told Axford, the head footman, about the incident and requested that he check every lock and bolt at night. Further than that, short of reporting the incident to Sir John Fielding, who had far more serious matters to occupy his time, there was nothing the Apothecary could do about it.

"You all right, Sir?" asked Gideon breathlessly.

"Yes, why?"

"You've slowed your pace."

"I was just thinking about something." And in a rush of confidence John unburdened himself to the boy.

Gideon looked defiant, his fair skin flushing with excitement. "Do you want me to keep watch, Sir? I can sit up all night with a blunderbuss. I'll blow the bastard's head off if he comes near."

John laughed. "It happened a few days ago. It's just that I was remembering it."

Gideon looked disappointed. "You know I would, Master."

John smiled. "I appreciate your loyalty. Perhaps you would double check the locks for me. Axford said he would do them but I think it would be as well for someone to have another inspection."

The apprentice looked pugnacious. "Consider it done, Sir. I shall check everything last thing at night. Woe betide the man if I catch him."

"I don't know that it was a man."

"But surely no woman would come into the garden late."

"Why should anyone, if you take my meaning. That's the puzzle. What did they want?"

"Um..." said Gideon, suddenly very serious.

Rose was up and rushed to the door at the sound of her father's footsteps. He swept her up into his arms, delighting in her presence, in the smell and feel of her. She would be three next April and was already advanced in speech and behaviour, filling him with intense pride. As yet she was unaware that she was to be presented with a sibling next June and considered John her property. For though she loved her mother, Rose's main love was for her father. Now she greeted him.

"Papa, I saw Miss Priscilla."

"Did you, sweetheart? When?"

"When I was out for my walk. She was walking too."

Emilia came to join them and John gave her a fond kiss. "I hear you've seen Priscilla."

"Yes. I was out with the basinette and ran into her. The poor thing is going half-demented with this production of hers."

John followed her into the parlour, where a good fire burned in the grate.

"What exactly is it she's doing?"

"Well, it's something on the lines of a masque, with singing and dancing and music. She has written the story and now it is up to us to act it."

"And who does she expect in the audience?"

"For a start most of Princess Amelia's ladies: namely the Countess of Hampshire, Lady Georgiana – she's in it and the only other young one so you will appreciate how desperate Priscilla is – Lady Feathstonehaugh and Lady Kemp, and Lady Theydon, of course. The men are mostly husbands and hangers on."

"Hangers on?"

"Well, you know what I mean. Then there's the young professional actor."

"Don't tell me, let me guess. Michael O'Callaghan."

"Yes, you're right. I asked her about the King's Theatre the other night and she admitted that she met him to audition him."

"Oh, is that what they call it these days."

"John, don't be wicked. She was genuinely seeking somebody."

"I'll wager she was."

Emilia looked reproving. "I don't know what is the matter with you." She paused, then said, "You don't like Priscilla, do you?"

He felt he couldn't lie. "Not a great deal, no. I find her somewhat concerned with herself and her affairs. But that is just me. The important thing is that you like her and she is a good friend to you."

"Yes, she is," Emilia answered, just a hint of defiance in her tone. "I am having a great deal of fun rehearsing for the show."

"Has she adapted it to suit the house in Curzon Street?"

"Yes, but it will not be quite so effective as it would have been at Gunnersbury House. She had planned to have it in the grand saloon there which is situated on the first floor, apparently with magnificent windows. We would have played in front of them with the audience in little chairs in front of us."

"I see. And is there no saloon as grand in Curzon Street?"

"Not really. It is nothing like as big. Still, the audience will just have to squeeze in tightly."

John sighed, the idea of being crammed amongst a jostling throng returning. He comforted himself with the thought of his new suit, already ordered, Then he felt guilty and remembered the pleasure the whole enterprise was giving to his wife, and took himself to task for being as self centred as he had earlier accused Priscilla of being.

He put his arm round Emilia. "Shall we go to the playhouse this evening?"

She blushed a little. "My darling, Priscilla has called a rehearsal for us younger people at four o'clock. Apparently Mr. O'Callaghan cannot get there until then."

"Oh, I see."

"Do you mind? I could cancel it, I suppose."

"Nonsense. Go and enjoy yourself. I'll be perfectly happy remaining here with Rose."

"Promise?"

"I do."

"Then in that case I shall go and change. Priscilla is always so well dressed and I would hate her to think me sloppy."

But John thought as his wife left the room that he had an urge to go out and wondered whether he might visit the Pandemonium Club. However, he felt slightly weary and not quite up to their activities. Perhaps, he considered, this could be the very night to call on Samuel and Jocasta and see how they were faring. But then came a better idea. A visit to Sir John Fielding, a man nearly always at home because of his disability. He could call on him at Bow Street and discuss old cases. Suddenly feeling cheerful, John went upstairs to change.

Had it really been ten years? John thought, as the hackney coach he had hired rumbled through the darkness towards the tall, thin house in Bow Street. Ten long years with almost as many cases of brutal murder to solve? Yet he knew it had for he had ended his indentures in 1754 and now a decade had passed since he had first glimpsed the house in Bow Street. Then he had been a terrified boy, taken in for questioning before the menacing Blind Beak. Now he was an established apothecary and had become a personal friend of the Fielding family. A great deal had changed indeed in those ten years.

It had been through that very first case that he had come into contact with Coralie Clive. She had saved his life, later he had saved hers, so in a way they owned one another. It had been inevitable that she would become his mistress and eventually marry him. But he had grown tired of her relentless ambition and had suddenly married Emilia Alleyn, never regretting his decision for a moment.

In the hackney's dark interior John felt himself grow hot, remembering Elizabeth di Lorenzi and the passion he had felt for her even while on his honeymoon. Once, very nearly, he had been on the point of possessing her. Then his marriage vows had stopped him, just as they would now. In fact he was more in love with Emilia today than he had been at the time of his wedding to her. He knew that some of those forced into arranged marriages who claimed it was possible to grow together, were right. He and his wife were becoming more united with the fullness of time.

Peering out through the gloom, John saw the thin house rise before him. Knocking on the roof with his great stick he brought the hackney to a standstill and paid the driver off. Then he looked up at the first floor salon. The curtains were drawn against the night but there were lights on. Sir John Fielding was at home.

Greeting the Court Runner who was manning the Public Office, the Apothecary enquired whether it would be possible to see the great man without an appointment.

"I should think so, Mr. Rawlings. He's nearly always available for you."

He whistled up the staircase and a servant called down, "What's going on?"

"It's Mr. Rawlings. He's called to see Sir John but he ain't got an appointment."

A face appeared. "Hang on, Mr. R. I'll tell him you're here."

The face withdrew again and John was left to look at the Runner, who was carefully examining a ledger.

"It's very cold," he ventured.

"Cold indeed, Sir. Not much crime about, actually."

"You mean they're all staying indoors."

"That's about it, Sir."

The footman reappeared. "Come up, Sir, and welcome. Sir John will receive you."

Gratefully John climbed the stairs to where the family lived above the Public Office and the Court, and was shown into the familiar first floor salon. Here everything was cosy and warm, the light from the fire and candles throwing a red glow over the furniture and walls. But all paled into insignificance beside the figure that sat in a high-backed chair beside the fire. Resplendent in a flowing wig, his powerful features throwing sharp shadows, his eyes covered by a black ribbon which concealed them from the gazes of the curious, sat the Principal Magistrate of London, Sir John Fielding himself.

John bowed as the Blind Beak rose. "Mr. Rawlings, what a pleasure. It has been a while, has it not? My dear fellow, how are you keeping? And your lovely wife?"

"We are all very well, Sir."

"I'm delighted to hear it. Take a seat, do. Have you dined? If not you must do so with us. I insist."

"How very kind of you, Sir. I'd be delighted."

"Meanwhile have some punch." And without waiting for an answer, the Magistrate rang a bell.

"And how are Lady Fielding and Mary Ann?"

"Both well, though the girl's a handful. We have more blades and bucks calling here than we have room for. Half the town is in love with her. But she, little madam, will have none of 'em. I reckon the girl's holding out for a high position."

Just as I thought, considered the Apothecary. He cleared his throat. "She is indeed ravishingly pretty, Sir."

"Old Lord Elibank fell for her and made a fool of himself," the Beak continued with a slightly hollow laugh. "Why, the poor fellow is old enough to be her grandfather. But that didn't stop him going for her, cap in hand."

"And Mary Ann? How did she respond?"

"Spurned him I imagine. Anyway he limped off, very sorry for himself." John thought that he had been right once more, that Lord Elibank had shown signs of being acutely uncomfortable at Sir Gabriel's birthday party.

The Blind Beak sighed. "Daughters are a trouble, I assure you."

John smiled ruefully. "I still have all that lying ahead."

"Yes. Well, let's hope that the next one is a boy."

"I would quite like that, I must admit."

There was a small knock and the door opened to reveal Elizabeth Fielding, carrying a tray on which was a jug of punch and two glasses.

"May I join you?" she asked.

John had risen to his feet and bowed. Now he said, "It would be a pleasure, Madam."

"I wondered if you might be discussing something."

The Magistrate turned his head in her direction. "Only daughters, my love."

Elizabeth pulled a face. "Daughters indeed. The little cat is out with her maid, gone to visit a female friend. I only pray that they don't get into any mischief."

Sir John laughed his tuneful laugh. "Might as well hope that the moon turns black. Anyway, enough of her. We'll bore our guest. What news from you, Mr. Rawlings?"

It was an odd thing but John, who had no intention of so doing, suddenly found himself telling the Magistrate about the late intruder in the garden.

Sir John listened in total silence, as did his wife. Eventually he said, "So this creature took off when he realised you were watching?"

"Yes. But what puzzles me is his motive. Why stand so silently and stare at my house. What could he hope to gain?"

"Perhaps it was someone from the streets looking for somewhere to sleep." This from Elizabeth.

Oddly, John found this comforting. "I hadn't thought of that," he said. "Do you know, you're probably right. So it was nothing sinister after all."

But for all that as he hired a hackney coach to take him home and dismounted in Nassau Street, he looked over his shoulder, full of sudden dread.

A coach was approaching and as it turned in from Gerrard Street he saw the familiar figure of Irish Tom on the box. Making a bow, John opened the door and pulled down the step and was rewarded with Emilia's spectacular smile.

"Oh John, I didn't think you were going out. Have you had a good time?"

"Yes, I dined with the Magistrate and his wife. And what about you? How did the rehearsal go?"

"Excellently." He could smell wine on her breath and smiled to himself. "But you'll never guess what."

"What?"

"Lady Theydon has managed it. She has persuaded Princess Amelia that the masque is to take place at Gunnersbury Park. In fact, the Princess is going to keep her Christmas there and is despatching servants tomorrow to heat the place up."

John opened the front door, feeling the warm air from the hall come to greet him. "But how will this affect you? And Michael O'Callaghan, come to that?"

Emilia's small face took on a slightly worried look. "Ah, that is where you come in."

"Me?" said John, helping her off with her cloak, then removing his greatcoat.

"Yes, you."

He took her hand. "Come into the library. Let's have a drink before we retire. Wine is good in moderation for pregnant women."

Her guilty expression made him chuckle to himself.

"Perhaps I shouldn't. I have had three glasses tonight."

"Well, one more won't hurt you."

He poured two glasses of claret then returned to his chair by the fire. "Now, how do I come into the grand design?"

Emilia smiled, a fraction nervously. "Priscilla has invited me to stay at Gunnersbury. Just for four days during which time she will rehearse as frequently as possible. Mr. O'Callaghan has also been invited. On the fourth day we will perform for the Princess. Oh, John, do say I can go."

"Well, of course you can. You have given enough of your time not to drop out now. When is this to be?"

"We, that is Mr. O'Callaghan and myself, are to arrive at Gunnersbury on the eighteenth. We will perform for the Princess on the twenty-second and then you and I can travel back in time for Christmas."

She looked so appealing, her face taking on the childlike look that had always so attracted him.

"And when do the full court go to Gunnersbury?"

"Some time next week. When the servants have got the place habitable."

"How nice, to walk in when everything is warm and comfortable I mean."

Emilia sipped her wine. "Well, you do."

John laughed. "You're right, of course. I have a very contented life, thanks to you." He paused, drank a little, then said, "I shall miss you."

"But it's only four days, John. For you will come and join me on the fourth."

"Yes, only four days apart," he answered, and stared into the flames.

Chapter Five

His advertisement having appeared in *The Daily Courant*, John's business did increase slightly. Firstly, ladies appeared in his shop, interested in his perfumes. Secondly, he was called out more to undertake medical duties. Every time he left he worried about leaving the place in the sole charge of Gideon Purle. But so far there had been no cause for complaint.

It seemed to the Apothecary, when he looked back, that during the third week of December he was hardly at home. Leaving the house before it was light and coming back well after the time to dine, sometimes quite tired if there had been a particularly trying patient, he rarely saw his daughter and little of his wife.

"But sweetheart, you cannot go on like this," Emilia complained.

"It will ease off, I assure you. It's only the first enthusiasm following the advertisement."

But they both knew he was lying, that his particular manner, combined with the most effective use of medicines, was finally building his practice up.

"If only Nicholas were still with me," he said with a sigh.

Yet that was impossible. The Muscovite was successfully running a shop in Kensington and had his own apprentice. That particular door was closed.

John worked on, hardly noticing which day was which, until eventually Emilia said, "You do realise that I leave for Gunnersbury tomorrow."

"What?"

John's attention, completely absorbed with a young woman with a terrible attack of loose teeth, snapped back to the present with a jolt.

"I said I am leaving for Gunnersbury House," Emilia repeated with just a hint of ice in her tone.

"My darling, I had no idea. Truth to tell I've been rather taken up with problems. I'm sorry."

She relented. "Oh, I hate leaving you like this. But I promised to take part and I can't let Priscilla down. You do understand, don't you?"

He suddenly, inexplicably, felt deeply depressed. "Must you go?" was out of his mouth before he had time to control it.

"Oh John! Yes, I must. I gave my word. Irish Tom will drop me then come back and be at your disposal. He will bring you down on the twenty-second. It is all arranged."

There was nothing he could say. "Very well," he managed, and spread his hands.

She went to him and stroked his forehead. "Darling, you look so tired. I shall miss you, you know that."

"Yes, I know," he answered wearily.

"Come, let us go to bed," said Emilia. "You look fit to drop."

"I am."

And he followed her up the stairs and got into bed where he fell asleep at once, determined to devote more time to his family and less to his work.

He woke unusually early and half sat up in bed, lighting the candle carefully. It was still dark and very cold in the room. Beside him Emilia slept, deep down in dreams. Raising himself on one elbow the Apothecary looked at her, studying her face. Sleep had etched out any lines she had so that she appeared no more than a girl and this, together with a natural innocence which she had always possessed, brought sudden tears to his eyes. He thought then about Coralie Clive and Elizabeth di Lorenzi and knew that he could never have married either of them. That both, in their individual ways, would have been too wild, too much to cope with. Emilia, though considered by some to be a strange choice at the time, had proved herself an ideal wife.

Watching her, keeping so quiet, John had never experienced anything quite like it, feeling tenderness, love, and a fierce urge to protect her against all harm. Very gently he leaned over and kissed her. She stirred but did not wake. He kissed her again and this time she opened her eyes. Her saw fear in them, saw it turn to recognition and fondness.

"John?" She was asking him a question.

"I love you, Emilia, and I always will."

"I love you too."

She put her arms round his neck and drew him close, and he responded quite naturally, swiftly removing his nightshirt and pulling her beneath him as they made love in the light of dawning.

Later that morning, Emilia set off, armed with a trunk and hat box. Irish Tom brought the coach round from the mews, promising his employer that he would be back the next day.

"...it being so snowy and all, Sorrh."

"Don't worry, take your time. And Tom..."

"Yes, Sorrh?"

"Go at a reasonable pace. Mrs. Rawlings must be looked after, you know."

"I'll be treating her as if she were the royal jewels, Sorrh."

John put his head and shoulders into the coach's interior where Emilia was settling herself before the journey began.

"Goodbye, darling. I'll see you on the twenty-second."

"Goodbye, Emilia." He was interrupted by a twitch on his leg and saw that Rose had come outside in the cold, pursued by a frantic nurse. "It's all right, Polly. She wants to say farewell to her mama."

"But it's freezing, Mr. Rawlings."

"I'll keep her warm."

So saying he scooped Rose up and held her beneath the folds of his coat. From this position she leant into the coach and kissed her mother goodbye, very fondly. Then she wriggled out of John's grasp and went back to her nurse, who took the child indoors.

The Apothecary held the coach a moment longer, taking

Emilia's hand and raising it to his lips. Then he waved farewell, shut the door and, telling Irish Tom to drive carefully, watched the conveyance until it disappeared out of sight, turning into Gerrard Street.

He went back into the house, put on his greatcoat and hat and set off for Shug Lane feeling strangely empty and, yet again, with that odd sense of depression which had so recently haunted him.

Irish Tom returned in the evening of the next day, cursing and swearing as only an Irishman could.

"By God, Sorrh, I wouldn't like a journey like that again."

"Well, you're going to have to do it in a day's time."

The Irishman pulled a face. "I most earnestly enjoin you to leave tomorrow, Sorrh, and put up for the night at Sir Gabriel's. It gets dark so early and it is impossible to travel fast in these conditions. If you want to get there on time you really must."

"But leaving the shop is the problem, Tom. Quite honestly Gideon is just a boy and somewhat forgetful."

"Then close it, Mr. Rawlings, do. I can't guarantee to get you there else."

"Very well, I'll compromise. I'll shut the place at noon tomorrow and be gone to Kensington at one. How will that suit?"

"That will suit fine, Sorrh. Now, if you'll excuse me, I'm off to get some sleep."

And he disappeared, still grumbling and muttering about the dangers of the road in bad weather.

True to his word, the Apothecary closed the premises in Shug Lane at five minutes past twelve, being delayed by a beau who came mincing in for his Christmas supplies of physick for the stomach, a potion for headache, suppositories, and two condoms of the cheaper washable variety. Having seen him leave, John sent Gideon off to see his parents, lit the lights in the windows and hurried back to Nassau Street to pack a trunk, which included his newly delivered suit. Then, puctually at one, Irish Tom appeared, looking smart and ready for the journey. Kissing Rose hastily, the Apothecary climbed in and they set off through the snowy streets.

It was a bleak journey, John wrapping himself in a fur coverlet to keep out the biting cold. The way to Kensington also took longer because of the bad conditions. Reaching Hyde Park as the sun was going down, a bell was ringing to warn travellers to band together before crossing the open space. Irish Tom duly halted the coach and talked to the other drivers until six conveyances had gathered, including the post. Then they proceeded slowly forward, one behind the other, their sheer weight of numbers being suffi-cient to scare off any highwaymen. Once through without inci-dent, Tom took the King's Old Road to Kensington, but beaten by snow turned off and went to the village via the main track.

It was dark when they entered the place, growing bigger as its popularity continued to increase, and made their way immediate-ly to Church Lane. Here, in the house on the end of the row, Sir Gabriel Kent, John's adoptive father, resided. Pausing outside the front door while Irish Tom saw to the luggage, John remembered his first encounter with the great man. He had been three years old, begging on the streets of London with his mother Phyllida Fleet. Even now he could recall the brief bleak pain as the carriage wheels passed over them, the moment when Sir Gabriel had lifted them up and carried them inside that same carriage and back to his home in Nassau Street.

At that moment the rest of John Rawlings's life had changed irrevocably. That Sir Gabriel would fall in love with and eventually marry his mother, that he should be taken on as a proper son, that he should sign indentures with an apothecary and himself become succesful, were things the child he had been could not have known. But now here he was, arriving at his country retreat unan-nounced, but certain of a great greeting as soon as he set his foot over the threshold.

John rang the bell and heard a pair of footsteps come to answer. Forestalling any short-sightedness on behalf of the servant, the

Apothecary called out, "It's me. John Rawlings. Is Sir Gabriel at home?" then paused, amazed, to see his father himself, bearing a candle tree, standing in the doorway.

They stared at one another for a second, John thinking how fine the octogenarian looked in his deshabille of flowing gown and turban fashioned, as always, in black and white. A glittering zircon, a vivid blue in shade, brought a little relief to the stark ensemble, but other than for that Sir Gabriel's rig-out was dramatic in its darkness.

"Father," said John and smiled broadly, seizing the older man in an embrace.

"My boy," answered Sir Gabriel, holding the candles high above his head. "What an unexpected pleasure. Are you alone?"

"Yes, Sir. I'm on my way to fetch Emilia. May I come in?"

"Of course. You are here for the night?"

"I most certainly am. That is if the bedroom is free and you expect no other guests," he added.

The door opened wide and all the warmth and comfort of the house flowed out into the dark lane. With a sigh of pleasure, John entered his second home.

A short while later he sat in the dining room, picking over a substantial supper. Sir Gabriel had dined at four as was the custom with the old-school, and had then settled down to an evening of reading, having given the footman the night off.

"So where are you going tomorrow exactly?" he asked.

"To Gunnersbury House. The summer home of Princess Amelia, who has decided, to be contrary, to celebrate Christmas there."

"Ah yes, I have played cards at her place a couple of times."

John stared. "You've been there?"

"Yes, dressed to the hilt I might add. The Princess, a strange lady, once small and elegant but now grown corpulent, is an inveterate gambler and likes nothing better than to give parties for the purpose of playing cards. Horace Walpole is a regular visitor."

"And what about her nephew, the King?"

"He goes from time to time, I believe."

"But not to play."

"Certainly not." Sir Gabriel laughed.

"But why were you only invited twice? Surely, Father, you did not commit a faux-pas?"

"My dear child, how could you even think anything so inelegant. Truth to tell, it's rather a journey from here and, quite honestly, now that I no longer have my own coach it was that which put me off. When the Marquis of Kensington is invited, should I receive an invitation for the same night, then I will gladly accompany him."

"And what about Walpole?"

"You know how much he enjoys socialising. But even he finds it a strain, I believe. On one occasion he had to send to London for a dress coat and a sword in order to be properly attired."

"Well, I shall meet the lady for myself tomorrow."

"She'll probably take a great fancy to you and add you to her guest list."

"I doubt it. An obscure apothecary will hardly come up to her dazzling heights." John was silent a moment, laying a hand on his father's arm. "Sir, you mentioned being without your coach. Do you miss it?"

"Not at all. Really Kensington is sufficiently small to enable one to walk about. Which I do as it is extremely beneficial to the health. I am much better than I was when in town, don't you know. I may be eighty but I feel good for another twenty years."

"At least," John answered, then impulsively hugged Sir Gabriel. "You are a most remarkable person, Sir."

The older man laughed. "My boy, you flatter me. You always do."

"I tell the truth," said John sincerely, and gave his father a kiss.

* * *

The following morning, much refreshed from a good night's sleep, he set off for his destination. They picked their way through the snow, sticking to the main tracks at which efforts had been made to keep the path clear. Leaving Kensington behind them they headed into the open country, passing through small villages as they went, and stopping to refresh themselves at an inn situated near the battlefield of Turnham Green. Then they pressed on, harried by the ever-present snow and the threat of more from heavy dark skies.

At exactly two o'clock they turned off Brentford Lane through a pair of impressive gates and up a short drive, and there, lying before them, was an early Palladian mansion, its exquisite outline made even more stunning by the winter day. It was a fairy palace, John thought, always a fervent admirer of that form of architecture. Calling to Irish Tom to stop the coach, the Apothecary got out to have a better look.

The house stood almost square in its design, a large pillared balcony on the first floor, the triumph of which was an arched window of enormous size standing between four others, two on either side. Above these pillars was an imposing decorated architrave bearing the design of a classical ribbon surrounding a central disc. The great window stood centrally over the front door which was reached by a short flight of steps, an altogether pleasing aspect to they eye. In short, John thought, it was the kind of house he would like to own but would never be able to afford. Getting back in the coach he instructed Tom to set him down then drive to the coachhouse.

A footman was on duty at the bottom of the entrance flight and, having heard John's name, lowered the step for him and saw him out, directing Irish Tom to go to the stables. At the top of the flight another servant took John's greatcoat and hat and bowed him into the water closet, a fact which he found a little obsequious. Having made use of the somewhat smelly facilities, the Apothecary emerged ready for the performance.

Before him a grand staircase rose up, peeling off in two directions at the top. Several fine people were slowly ascending, careful of their apparel. John followed two ladies who were mounting ahead of him, studying them as he went. Both had on elaborate white wigs and wore spectacles giving the impression that they were very alike. And, indeed, this illusion was continued in their general appearance, for both had lost their chin line, both were identically wrinkled, and both had hands which flew about like birds as they talked.

"Ah, my dear," said the bolder of the two, casting her eyes around and taking in the attractive man walking a few paces behind her, "when will this terrible snow vanish is what I demand to know."

"One could say that it is very picturesque, mark you," replied the other.

"Picturesque be blowed," said the first woman with spirit. "It is a wonder we have anyone in the audience at all. Only the most devoted will have undertaken such a journey."

She smiled at John who gave his best bow and smiled back.

The first woman dropped a very small curtsey. "Are you coming to see our masque, Sir?"

"I am indeed. Allow me to present myself. My name is Rawlings, John Rawlings, Madam."

She extended a hand with a grandiose gesture. "And I am Frances Featherstonehaugh. Lady Featherstonehaugh. I am one of the Princess's ladies."

He kissed the hand, managing to instil a certain reverence into the embrace. Lady Featherstonehaugh looked duly gratified. Not to be outdone, the meeker of the two introduced herself.

"And I am Lady Kemp."

John took her hand and kissed it with equal fervour.

"You are acquainted with Princess Amelia?" It was Lady Featherstonehaugh who spoke.

"Not as yet, I'm afraid. My wife is a friend of Priscilla Fleming and is taking part in the masque. She is Emilia Rawlings. Do you know her?"

Lady Featherstonehaugh gave a merry laugh and her face vanished in a sea of wrinkles. "I have seen her I believe but that is all. A pretty little thing."

"Yes, she is. Very."

"And where did you travel from this morning, young man?" Lady Kemp spoke.

"From Kensington. We have a small country place there which we share with my father."

"And who might he be?"

"Sir Gabriel Kent."

The ladies exchanged a glance, then smiled simultaneously, endorsing yet again the notion that they were very alike. Was it John's imagination or had the mention of his father's name made them approve of him a little more?

They proceeded up the stairs, the Apothecary walking a couple of steps behind. At the top the ladies turned to the left staircase and, having mounted this, made their way along a short corridor, done out in a deep compelling blue. Then they entered a salon in which quite a crowd was already gathered. John, thankful indeed that he was wearing his new suit in that dashing material called Midnight in Venice, surveyed the scene through his quizzer.

Everybody was dressed to kill, men and women alike. He had never seen such a sparkling array of people nor quite so many glittering jewels. John recognised the Prince of Mecklenburg, Lord Clanbrassil, Lord and Lady Southampton and Lord Pelham. Realising that he was in extremely distinguished company, he adopted a nonchalant expression and was just about to stroll amongst the guests when he felt a plucking at his elbow. He saw that it was Lady Kemp.

"My dear Mr. Rawlings, allow me to present you."

"I'd be honoured, madam."

She turned to a group of middle-aged ladies who were eyeing John with varying degrees of suspicion.

"Madam," Lady Kemp addressed one of them, presumably the most senior, "may I submit Mr. John Rawlings to you?" The woman, who had an extremely painful expression, as if her feet hurt, gave a curt nod. "The Countess of Hampshire, Mr. Rawlings."

"Chawmed," she said in an affected tone with an underlying accent.

"Madam, the honour is mine."

As he bowed before her John wondered about her origins, thinking that she had once been extremely pretty; indeed her eyes were still lovely. An inspired guess told him that she had been on the stage at some point in her life. But he had no time to study her further because he was being introduced to a name he recongised.

"Lady Theydon, may I present Mr. John Rawlings?"

"You may," said a plummy voice.

John looked up from a deep bow and found himself gazing into one of the most vacuous faces he had seen in an age. Eyes big and brown and cow-like were staring into his from a large doughy visage. Suddenly the woman simpered and everything crinkled except for the eyes which continued to look with the same fixed regard.

"How dee do?" she continued, and as she spoke the Apothecary saw that her lips were slightly slack, faintly bedewed with saliva.

"Honoured Madam," was all he could find to say.

The other member of the posse was Lady Featherstonehaugh who gave him a wintery smile. "We are all waiting for Princess Amelia, then we can have some refreshment before the masque commences. I trust you are staying in the house tonight. Otherwise travelling back will be a nightmare."

"I don't as yet know what arrangements have been made, my Lady. But I assure you I won't travel once darkness has fallen."

"Very wise. These great country houses are all very well but at night the areas surrounding them are riddled with highwaymen." She paused and looked at the doors at which a couple of liveried footmen had appeared. "Here comes the Princess now," she added in an undertone.

In company with everybody else John gave a deep bow, then looked up, though not daring to use his quizzing glass.

He was looking at a woman who had once been a beauty but had now grown stout, with something of a huddle about her stance and bearing. Her face had become full of chins, while her eyes, formerly so pretty, had grown heavy-lidded and baggy. Yet there was still a sparkle about her, an air of being important and privileged. She also seemed, unless her looks belied her, quite kindly. Dressed in an elaborate gown of lilac silk, heavily embroidered with a myriad of silver flowers with diamond sparklers at their centre, she most certainly glittered as she came into the room.

Once, John was aware, she had been the chosen bride of Frederick II of Prussia, known as the Great, but though Frederick had pursued her with fervour, corresponding both with Amelia and her mother, his tyrannical father, who loathed his son, had refused to give his consent to the marriage. Eventually the disillusioned Frederick had been forced to marry a German Princess, Elizabeth-Christina, but he had never loved her and they did not produce an heir. Princess Amelia had never married but had had several affairs, the most notable of which had been with the married Duke of Grafton who, in fact, had two mistresses simultaneously, one the Princess, the other the wife of the Earl of Burlington. These ladies, together with his wife, had presumably worn him out because he had died some seven years ago in 1757. Gazing at her now, the Apothecary thought about her past and could not help but smile.

The Princess clapped her hands together. "Good people," she said, her accent quite English despite the fact she had been born in Hanover, "the performance will begin shortly. Meanwhile please enjoy yourselves."

At this she waddled forward, smiling and gracious, obviously only too happy to have her house full.

Footmen bearing trays passed amongst the guests and John helped himself to a glass of champage, stealing a glance at the watch Sir Gabriel had given him for his twenty-first birthday. It was half past two and the masque was due to start at three.

"She's so full of life," said Lady Theydon, her moist lips creasing into a smile. "Of course as I said to my husband recently, we all look to the Princess for an example of how to grow old. She's so lively and full of fun. Don't you agree, ladies?"

There was a general chorus of yeses.

"It was quite a job to persuade her to come to Gunnersbury for Christmas but I managed it, with my dear husband. And I'm sure you'll agree that it is a lovely setting and looks so romantic under snow. Don't you think so?"

Another chorus of agreement.

John, excusing himself, crossed to the window leading onto the balcony he had seen from outside. The sun was at a low ebb, not yet tinting the snow pink but instead giving it a golden glow. The great trees of the park bore their white decorations with magnificence though the formal gardens, apparently very beautiful, lay hidden beneath their covering. The sky was grey, almost blending with the rest of the landscape and as if to echo its colour the two formal lakes had frozen, sending the swans and ducks to shelter on the land. It was a wonderful vista and the Apothecary found himself wishing again that he might one day own something like this.

How long he stood staring he couldn't tell but he was suddenly brought back to reality by a footman intoning, "Your Highness, my Lords, my Ladies, ladies and gentlemen, kindly take your seats. *The Masque of Christmas* is about to begin."

With a smile, John put down his glass and progressed through to the Great Saloon, taking his seat on a little gilt chair.

There was a general bout of coughing and throat-clearing and then the small orchestra, consisting of a violin, a viola, a cello and a flute, started to play, the violinist conducting with his bow. During this overture people talked as was customary, a habit of which John did not approve, preferring to listen to the music. However the experience was soon at an end and the handsome Mr. O'Callaghan, wearing tights and a draped shirt, appeared.

"*The Masque of Christmas*," he announced in a beautiful voice.

There was rapturous applause from the ladies. The performance had begun.

Chapter Six

Michael O'Callaghan, having said his few words, made an exit and several children rushed on dressed as snowflakes. They sang a merry song, somewhat tunelessly, then whirled round and round in the open space beneath the great window which had been designated as the stage area. John found his eye wandering to the landscape outside, struck again by the ever-lengthening shadows and how they made dark, mysterious pools beneath the trees.

The next scene brought his attention back to the masque for Emilia entered with the Irishman, declaring her undying love for him. She looked stunningly beautiful, he thought, her little face accentuated by theatrical make-up. She was also quite a good actress, speaking up loudly and clearly and remembering all her lines. Michael, on the other hand, had indeed the actor's great voice but could not lose his Irish accent which, John had to admit, added a great deal of charm to his performance.

He was extremely handsome, the Apothecary thought, with his strong, clearly defined features, his long black hair which, defying the fashion for white wigs, he wore tied back in a queue, together with his devastating green eyes. He would do well playing the role of a highwayman, perhaps Macheath, though this notion made John shudder, recalling the affair of *The Beggar's Opera* and its dire consequences.

The masque progressed, the basic story line being about the eternal triangle, represented by Emilia, Michael O'Callaghan and Priscilla. The snowflake children appeared again dressed as little cupids in pink tights and gold tops, firing make-believe arrows from golden bows. It was all very light-hearted and pleasant to look at but as to the writing, John did not care for it. Though to tell Emilia so would have been bad manners, he considered. The main theme seemed to be about a yule log brought into the house on Christmas Eve but nobody could find a fragment of last year's log to kindle it. It was superficial but pleasant to watch was his summation.

There was no interval, the whole thing lasting only an hour. Several people left the room during this time, gone to relieve themselves no doubt. But all were present as the piece drew to its close, Princess Amelia nodding and smiling and clearly delighted with the entire spectacle.

The finale came. Priscilla made her entrance in a vivid red cloak, a colour that almost hurt the eyes it was so glorious to look at. She triumphed over Emilia who was sent away, looking sad and drooping about the shoulders. The Irishman sang of love in a pleasant light baritone voice; the children danced; then every member of the cast came on and performed a Merry Andrew, amongst their number Lady Georgiana who had been relegated to a minor role.

John applauded wildly, thinking his wife to be the prettiest member of the ensemble, though run a close second by Milady, who really was exquisite. Blonde and blue-eyed, not disimilar to Emilia in type, she looked a true member of the aristocracy with her perfect figure and upright bearing. In a highly individual style she had a blonde ringlet, just one, hanging over her left shoulder, which John thought an utterly captivating fashion.

As the lady took her bow she caught the Apothecary looking at her and blushed in a most becoming manner, which he found quite delightful.

Princess Amelia stood up and addressed the entire cast. "My Lady, ladies and gentleman, please join us in this room as soon as you are ready. Refreshments will be served. I will retire for a few minutes. Ladies, attend me if you please."

Lady Theydon, Lady Kemp and Lady Featherstonhaugh immediately rose from their places and went to the Princess's side. The Countess of Hampshire, as befitted her station no doubt, took slightly longer to walk the distance. As soon as they had all gathered, the Princess trundled from the room, smiling at all who caught her eye. John was instantly reminded of the four Marys who had served Mary, Queen of Scots, as the quartet of serving women, walking two abreast, demurely followed her out.

No sooner had she gone than servants appeared, once more bearing trays. John took another glass of champagne and crossed to the great window, staring out into the gardens. From this observation place he had a fine view of the grounds, except where the trees grew thickly at some distance from the house. Nothing stirred below him but now the sun was blood-red and setting quite quickly. John turned away from the window but as he did so he saw Priscilla in her scarlet cloak run across the lawn and down the steps, past the ornamental lakes and into the shadow of the trees. Wondering what on earth she could be up to, John stared. Nothing moved anywhere. With a faint feeling of unease he turned away as he felt rather than saw someone bow before him.

"More champagne, Sir?"

It was a footman, a swarthy pock-marked fellow with a white wig which contrasted fiercely with his ravaged face. Even while not speaking his mouth moved constantly, giving the disconcerting impression that he was about to say more. John waited but nothing further came.

"Thank you," he took another glass and turned once more to the window. Yet again, there was no movement.

Michael O'Callaghan appeared, panting and out of breath. Despite the chill of the day there were beads of perspiration on his brow.

"Oh, there you are, Mr. Rawlings," he said without any preamble. "Your delightful wife told me of the coincidence. Me going into your shop and all. By the way, my hypochondrium is much improved thanks to your physicks."

"I'm glad to hear it. Will you be returning to Drury Lane?"

The actor flashed a great smile full of dazzling white teeth. "If they'll have me, yes. Of course. However, they were less than sympathetic about my injury."

Any further discussion was made impossible by the arrival of the children, who came in in a bunch, all six of them, chattering like monkeys.

John moved his head in their direction. "To whom do they belong?"

"The royal servants have the honour. They've been little pests during rehearsals."

The actor wiped his brow, still beaded with sweat, though his breathing was back to normal.

"In what way?"

"In a children's way. Making a noise and suchlike. I come from a family of eight and I can't honestly say that the experience endeared younger people to me."

"You don't like them?"

The actor spread his hands, looking comical. "I can take 'em or leave 'em, if you follow me."

There was a noise from the doorway and the Apothecary saw that Lady Georgiana, her face fresh, her lustrous ringlet still in place, had come in.

"A beautiful woman that," he said. "A pity she didn't have a larger part."

"Ah, she's a bit of a fool when it comes to acting. She's beautiful all right but not born for the stage. Priscilla was originally going to give her the character which your dear wife played. But Georgiana was not very good, so Emilia came in to help out."

"And thoroughly enjoyed herself," John added with a smile.

Lady Georgiana was looking round the room and gave a slight curtsey in the direction of the Apothecary and the actor. Then her face changed, becoming still and closed. Slowly, moving elegantly, she joined a tall, thin man, magnificently dressed and bewigged, who bowed before her then kissed her hand. John could not help but notice how stiffly she withdrew it from the embrace.

Princess Amelia and her ladies came back in, still moving in their regimented lines, John was amused to observe. However, they instantly broke ranks and went to join the various people with whom they were acquainted, the Princess hurrying to the side of the Prince of Mecklenburg. It occurred to the Apothecary that maybe there was something between them, this idea enhanced by the way the Prince kissed the lady's hand.

Then there was a buzz in the doorway as Priscilla herself came in. She looked attractive but for all that the poor thing seemed frozen with cold. A fact which made her features set and somewhat hard-looking. However, having gone to the Princess first and received a royal kiss, she made her way to where John stood with Michael.

"Oh, my dear Mr. Rawlings," she said. "I saw you in the audience. I was so glad you managed to get through. I thought this terrible weather might have made the ways too foul to be negotiable."

John took her hand. It was like ice. "No, my dear Madam, I managed in two stages. I thought the performance went very well incidentally."

"Then that is all that matters," she answered gaily. She turned to the Irishman. "You did well, Sir."

"Thank you, dear lady. I could say the same for you."

She took a glass of champagne from a passing tray. "Well, it's over and done, thank God." She turned to John. "Now we can get on with normal life again."

"Yes. Where is Emilia by the way?"

"I can't think what's keeping her. The last I saw of her she was in the room set aside for changing. She said she wouldn't be long."

Every protective instinct in the Apothecary rose. He thought of his wife, fourteen weeks pregnant, suddenly feeling faint, on her own and helpless.

"I think I'll go and look for her." he said. "If you could direct me to the changing room."

Priscilla turned on him a wonderful smile. "It's at the bottom of the grand stairs on the left. There are two rooms actually, one was occupied by the children."

"Thank you." John bowed to the other two. "Excuse me."

He hurried down the beautiful staircase and came to the room, full of abandoned costumes, obviously removed in a hurry as everybody hastened to the party.

"Emilia," he called.

There was no reply. Fearing she might have lost consciousness, the Apothecary searched the place, even going so far as to lift piles of clothes to look beneath. There was no sign of his wife. He hurried into the other room but, yet again, the search proved fruitless. Now the first signs of panic assailed him and he went back into the hall, uncertain as to what he should do next.

The great front door was closed but John knew that if Emilia had felt unwell she might well have stepped outside to get some air. With hands that shook very slightly, he pulled the door ajar.

Outside the sun had nearly set, turning the snow the colour of blood. In the distance the dark trees beckoned in a formidable group, their branches glistening white in the dusk. John's heart began to race and he called, "Emilia," once more. There was no reply and suddenly the Apothecary knew that something was wrong. He hurried down the steps, icy now in the gloaming, and towards the trees.

And then he saw it. There in the snow, her red cloak spread out round her, was Priscilla. Yet it couldn't be: he had just left Priscilla in the warmth and gaiety of the saloon.

"Oh God, no," he shouted and sprinted over the snow to where the figure lay on its back, so still and so pale in the blood-red setting.

He reached her side and scooped her up in his arms, pulling back the hood so that he could see the face. It was Emilia, covered in blood, bleeding into the snow, adding her own redness to that provided by nature, the knife that was ending her life still buried deep in her gut.

"Oh darling," he said. "Speak to me."

She opened her eyes and looked up at him, recognised him. Her lips tried to say something but he could not catch the words. Then she closed her eyes again and with a sigh her head fell to one side. Emilia had died in his arms as the Apothecary watched helplessly.

John knelt cradling her to his heart as round him darkness fell. He thought wildly, madly, that he had been a bad husband, that he had not come up to her expectations of him. He remembered everything with a terrible clarity, saw her again as she had first appeared to him, so beautiful and so fresh, close to Apothecaries' Hall. Recalled with shame the time when he had almost been unfaithful to her. Remembered how he had not been in the house when Rose had been born.

Eventually, tears came and he sobbed aloud, holding her close, letting her blood flow over him. And so he was sitting, in the dark, holding his dead wife, when he became conscious of a noise. A party had come from the house to look for them. Flaming torches were carried high and he recognised people advancing towards him.

He did not move, staying where he was, never wanting to shift again. Crouching over Emilia, his instinct was to protect all that was left of her, to save her from the stares and curiosity of unwanted bystanders. Yet nothing could be done; the crowd, carrying lit flares, was advancing ever closer.

They stopped three feet away from him, forming a semi-circle. John's wild thoughts turned to a pagan ritual, come to fetch the human sacrifice. Slowly, very slowly, he stood up, realising that the knife was in his hand, that he must have pulled it from Emilia's stomach without even realising he had done so.

Staring wildly into the depths of the crowd he picked out the face of Lady Theydon, her dark eyes fixed on him unblinkingly. He saw her tongue emerge like a snake and run over her moist lips. Then she let out a low shriek.

"Oh, murder, murder," she cried. "What have you done, Sir?"

John tried to speak but no sound came out. He stood where he was, opening and closing his mouth silently.

Then, suddenly he realised how bad he must look, soaked in Emilia's blood, the knife that killed her in his hand. He spoke at last.

"I found her like this, believe me."

Lady Theydon gave him an expressionless look. "Well I, for one, don't believe you. I believe you are a murderer."

There was a groundswell of muttering amongst the people. John heard Michael O'Callaghan say, "Oh no, 'tis not possible," then he saw two burly footmen advancing towards him.

Shouting, "No, I swear I am innocent," the Apothecary stood, petrified, where he was.

Then the swarthy face of the pock-marked man thrust itself within an inch of his nose. "I'll have to request you, Sir, to come with me," the footman said.

And a heavy hand clapped onto his shoulder.

Chapter Seven

He hadn't wanted to leave her body, had wanted to stay with it as the last vestige of her on earth, but he had had little choice. His arms had been seized, one on either side, and he had been frog-marched back to the house, quite roughly. Once inside he had gone straight to the closet and had vomited violently before they had locked him in a small room by himself. It had been empty of furniture other than for a chair and into this the Apothecary had sunk, his legs entirely devoid of strength.

How long he had sat there he couldn't tell but somewhere in the small hours there came a scrabbling at the door. They had provided him with half a candle and a pail for relief, that was all. Returning to full consciousness at the furtive noise, John saw that the candle was burning down and hastily blew it out to conserve it. Thus he sat in the darkness, listening. The scrabbling came again, followed by a faint voice saying, "John."

He went mad, thought he had been mistaken about Emilia's death and that she was outside, trying to communicate with him. He rushed to the door, leaning close to it.

"Emilia?" he managed to croak.

There was a pause, then came the answering whisper. "It's Priscilla. John, Emilia is dead."

"I know, I know," he whispered back, and suddenly he was in tears again, weeping as though his heart had broken, which it had.

There was the sound of a key in the lock and in the moonlight, which came through a high barred window, he saw the door open and a female enter the room. She crossed to his side and put her arms round him.

"There, there," she said.

But John was uncontrollable, crying like a little boy, quite unable to stop himself. Eventually, though, he quietened, though his body still quivered with sobs.

"I didn't kill her," he managed to murmur.

"I know you didn't," she answered him. "John, listen to me."

"What?"

"Emilia borrowed my red cloak. It was me the killer was after, don't you see?"

"My God," said John, collapsing back onto the chair. "Oh my God."

The thought that his wife had died because she had borrowed another woman's garment cut him to the quick, yet he could see the sense of it.

"Why did she borrow your cloak?" he asked.

"Heaven knows. She probably decided to take a turn in the grounds and couldn't find her own. I don't know the reason. All I know is that the killer's knife was meant for me."

Priscilla shivered violently, her face drawn and haggard.

"But who would want to kill you?"

"Oh, as to that I keep my own counsel. But be assured there are several people."

John stood up and took her by the shoulders. "What are they planning to do with me?"

"They will keep you here until they can hand you over to the Beak Runners. A rider is setting off for London tomorow morning to tell Sir John Fielding."

"Then at least I'll be fairly treated."

"But he is bound to arrest you."

"Why?"

"Because Princess Amelia believes you are guilty. Sir John would be flouting a royal command if he were to do otherwise."

"But you will speak up for me? Tell them about the cloak?"

"You know I will. But it is a question of proof. You must admit you looked mighty guilty."

John sighed. "You're right." His voice changed. "Where is Emilia?"

"They have brought her back to the house. She's in a room close by."

"May I see her?"

Prscilla hesitated, "I managed to find a key to fit the lock but should I let you out?"

John said angrily, "In the name of heaven, Priscilla, you know I'm not guilty."

She relented. "Yes, I do. Come."

The Apothecary struck a tinder and relit the candle, handing it to her. In silence they left the room and John found himself in a rough brick corridor. He had clearly been taken to the cellar – as had his wife.

She lay in another small brick room, this one entirely devoid of light. A hasty bier had been made from three large planks put together by a trestle beneath. They had covered her with a white sheet through which a small stain of blood had started to dry. With a hand that shook violently John pulled it back and gazed into her face.

Like this, with no visible sign of violence, she looked as if she were asleep. Yet the face had lost its colour and was a snowy white against which the darkness of her lashes showed starkly. The Apothecary turned to Priscilla.

"Leave us a minute, please. I beg you to do so."

She reluctantly set the candle down and headed for the door. "I'll be right outside," she said.

He never knew why he pulled the rest of the sheet back, but pull it he did. Emilia's wounded body lay exposed to his gaze. Fighting a terrible urge to shout aloud, the Apothecary examined her stabs.

The killer had grabbed her from behind and struck three savage blows to her abdomen, then left her to bleed to death. At least that was how John read the situation from the position of the cuts.

"My darling," he whispered to the corpse, "I'll find who did this to you and then I will kill him with my bare hands. I promise you that."

It seemed to him in the flickering light that she gave a little smile. John bent and kissed her hand, realising how stiff and cold it had become. Then he replaced the sheet, kissing Emilia on the mouth before he covered her face.

Priscilla was not outside the door. In fact, Priscilla was nowhere to be seen. Candle in hand, John walked along the rough corridor, searching for her. And then it came to him. Perhaps she had deliberately made herself scarce in order to give him an opportunity to escape.

He looked at his watch and saw that it was two in the morning. The entire household, with the exception of the night staff, would be asleep. Suddenly weak again, John sat on a rough stool and considered his options. If he remained in custody he would eventually be handed to the Runners who would escort him to Bow Street and into the custody of Sir John. If he escaped he could go to Sir Gabriel and explain what had happened, then give himself up to Sir John, hopefully in the company of Priscilla who could explain about the cloak and the mistaken identity. In short, there seemed little choice in the matter. It would be better by far to make his break for freedom while he had the chance.

John crept along the corridor, his heart thudding and there, as he had been certain there would be, he found a door. Locked and bolted it was indeed but the keys were on the inside. Feeling hardly in control of himself, he raised a hand and slid back the top bolt which creaked and groaned as he pulled it back. He paused, his breathing coming in little gasps, and listened. Nothing stirred. Certain now that Priscilla had given him this opportunity, the Apothecary bent to the lower bolt and slid it back. It, too, made a noise but opened. Now all that was left was the key. Grabbing it with both hands, John turned it and the door swung ajar.

The rush of cold air took his breath away, what was left of it.

So much so that he stood gasping in the entrance, his thoughts whirling in his head. To summon Irish Tom, no doubt asleep in the stable block, would be sheer folly. For how could he in his blood-stained suit present himself to anyone who might still be on duty. But then, as if in answer to his prayers, he saw in the distance that a coach was waiting near the gates of the house, a coach which he recognised as his own. John staggered forward and collapsed into the gigantic Irishman's arms.

"I knew you'd escape, Sorrh," a voice whispered in his ear.

"Did you hear about what happened?" John asked as Irish Tom carried him the rest of the way and deposited him inside the coach's freezing interior.

"I did, Mr. Rawlings. My deepest condolences to you."

"She was murdered by mistake, Tom. Poor Emilia borrowed a red cloak and that was her downfall."

He wept again, though he thought he had no more tears left in him. Very gently, Irish Tom wrapped him in a fur coverlet then climbed onto the coachman's box.

"Where to, Sorrh?" he asked.

"Sir Gabriel's," was John's answer as the motion of the coach finally lulled him into a deep sleep.

He woke in the cold light of dawning to see a friendless landscape. Tom had made what progress he could on the icy roads but the horses were tired and they were not much further forward than Turnham Green.

"I'm making for the inn, Sir..." Tom's Irish accent had become more subdued. "...We could both do with a substantial meal."

John put his head out of the window. He was hatless, had left his greatcoat behind, and his beautiful suit was covered in blood. "What shall I wear?"

Irish Tom called down, "There's a bag on the seat opposite you."

"Whose is it?"

"I don't know. I stole it from another coach just before I went to wait for you."

John shook his head but opened the bag and found a suit of clothes, made for someone far smaller than he was, within. Pulling it out, he stripped off, not easy in the carriage's swinging interior, and put the ensemble on. It was made of dark green worsted, a very sensible suit indeed. Furthermore the legs only came to just above his knees and the hose did not meet them, but it was clean and serviceable. With a sigh, John fastened on the cloak – there was no hat – and thought about Emilia.

A few minutes later they stopped at the inn they had patronised on the way down. Irish Tom pulled into the courtyard and jumping down himself, helped John descend. The Apothecary, weak as a child, was glad of an arm to help him into the smoky interior. Once inside, despite the earliness of the hour, Irish Tom ordered a large brandy for his master and a small beer for himself. Then he sat in silence and waited for John to speak.

He thought that he had never seen the Apothecary look so ill. He had lost his wig long ago and now his cinnamon hair hung lankly round his ears, while his face was so pale that his vivid eyes seemed twice the size. He seemed to have shrunk but, Tom thought, this was because he was walking slightly hunched, as if he could not stand upright and face the troubles of the world.

"She was killed by mistake," John repeated at last.

And with that thought came a poignant memory of himself looking out of the window and seeing Emilia hurrying through the grounds in the borrowed red cloak. At the time he had thought it was Priscilla but now he wondered what his wife had been doing, hastening through the grounds in the gathering gloom.

"Tell me about it, Sorrh," Irish Tom answered quietly, and John considered that he had never realised the hulking Irishman had this kind and gentle side to his nature.

"I saw her, Tom. I actually saw her. She was hurrying through the gardens in the red cloak. But I never realised it was Emilia – I thought it was Priscilla who had worn the cloak during the masque. I wonder where she was going, what important errand she was running, and for whom?"

"Perhaps she felt like a walk, Sir. Perhaps she was just taking a turn round the grounds."

John's pictorial memory flashed up a picture of Emilia as he had seen her. She had definitely been in a hurry, not carrying herself like a woman going for a stroll.

"No, Tom. She was about some business. But what in God's holy name could it have been?"

"Perhaps Miss Fleming will know."

John shook his head. "I don't think so." He sat silently. "Will the body be released soon?" he asked quietly.

"I don't have the answer, Sir. I expect it will though."

The Apothecary put his head in his hands. "Dear Lord, what a mess. I have to tell Rose that she will never see her mother again. Tell the world that my wife is dead and that I stand accused of her murder."

"The sooner you get to Sir Gabriel's the better, Sir. Now eat up, here comes a hearty breakfast. Once consumed, we can be on our way."

But John picked at his food, leaving nearly all of it on his plate.

The coachman looked at him in despair. "You must keep your strength up, Mr. Rawlings. How will you be able to face what lies ahead if you're weak?"

For once his master took no notice and it was left to the Irishman to do justice to the severe breakfast which had been brought to them.

John patted his pockets. "My money is in my suit, in the coach. Can you fetch it for me?"

"Certainly, Sir."

While Irish Tom was gone, John ordered himself another brandy and sat close to the fire, thinking. It was not only Emilia who had been murdered but his unborn child as well. But that his wife, that innocent woman, should have been struck down at all was almost too much even to contemplate. Yet it had come as no shock to Priscilla who, apparently, had several secrets in her past which could have led to her being killed.

She must bear witness for me, the Apothecary thought. Then, quite suddenly, realised how his case must look to others. He had been caught red-handed, actually holding the knife with which Emilia had been slain. Small wonder that Lady Theydon, that unpleasant woman, had accused him of murder. His hopes of clearing his name were pinned on the fact that Priscilla would vouch for him to Sir John Fielding.

The coachman came back in and paid the bill with John's money.

"We'd best be getting along, Sir. I won't rest easy until I deliver you to Sir Gabriel."

John went to stand up but once again his legs buckled and it was left to Irish Tom to ferry him to his coach. As they left the inn the Apothecary was more than aware of the curious stare of the maid who actually followed them to the front door to have a final look.

As luck would have it, Sir Gabriel Kent was just stepping forth from his house in Church Lane as John's equipage rolled up. This day, almost as if he had had a premonition, he was dressed all in black, only the white frills of his shirt relieving the gloom. His smile of welcome changed dramatically as he saw the state of John Rawlings, creeping out of the coach, pale-faced and puffy eyed.

"My dear child, whatever has befallen you?" he called out. Then he hurried forward to assist Irish Tom bring John indoors.

There, the sheer relief of being with his father caused the Apothecary to weep once more and it was left to the coachman to explain the circumstances of John's sudden reappearance. He had never seen Sir Gabriel grow pale before, John thought, but now he saw his father's skin become like parchment and his golden eyes fill with tears. It was a sobering sight, but after application of his handkerchief, Sir Gabriel became extremely business-like.

"Now, my lad," he said firmly, "the first thing you must do is go and have a rest. Then, tomorrow morning early, you must head for town and deliver yourself to Sir John Fielding. You will receive the best treatment possible at the great man's hands."

"But Father," John replied wearily, so exhausted with weeping that he could hardly concentrate, "I must get Priscilla to come with me."

"Then write her a short note which I will take with me when I go to see Princess Amelia."

"But why...?"

"My son, somebody must bring Emilia's body back for burial. No doubt the Coroner will have been informed this morning but I am sure he will release her as soon as possible. She must be buried here in Kensington where you and I can tend the grave."

"Oh God's life," John answered wearily, "to think of Rose without a mother."

"Rose must be brought here to live with me for the time being. Until this confusion has been sorted out."

"Father," said John seriously, "do you think Sir John will hold me in custody?"

"I think, my son," Sir Gabriel answered with equal severity, "he might have no choice but to do so."

"Then my future looks bleak."

"Until Miss Priscilla speaks up, yes. Now scrawl a note to her, do. I must leave within the hour if I am to make Gunnersbury House before nightfall."

A quarter of an hour later it was done and John was climbing the stairs to his bedroom. He found a shawl of Emilia's lying on the bed and when he picked it up to hold to his cheek he could smell her perfume still on it. Cradling it in his arms as if it were her, he lay down on the bed. But sleep would not come as over and over in his brain he ran the events of the previous evening. Eventually he got up and wandered downstairs where he found the house empty, Sir Gabriel and Tom having left for Gunnersbury. Going to his compounding room at the back of the house, John mixed himself half an ounce of the syrup obtained from the opium poppy. Then he sat in a chair and fell finally into a deep sleep.

He was awoken by a sound. Struggling back to consciousness he identified it as someone knocking insistently at the door. The house was in total darkness but at that moment Sir Gabriel's clock, removed from Nassau Street when he moved to Kensington, played The British Granadears for the half hour. Getting to his feet John felt his way to where he thought the candles were, found them by groping, and struck a tinder. Lighting a candle tree, he made his way to the front door.

A figure stood outlined against the moonlit sky, a figure made even darker by the frosty night beyond. John was just able to discern a man's cloak and hat but nothing further.

"Who is it?" he asked.

"Bless you, Sir, don't you know me?"

"No, I'm sorry. I've just woken up. Who is it?"

"It's me, Mr. Rawlings," and the man stepped forward into the light.

It was Joe Jago.

Chapter Eight

It was with an overwhelming sense of relief that John Rawlings stood back to allow Joe Jago to come into the house. Then while his companion made himself at home the Apothecary hurtled round lighting all the candles. Next Sir Gabriel's staff arrived, a footman and a cook, returned from shopping, and started to prepare dinner so that the pleasant smell of roasting meat filled the air. Half an hour later the Apothecary, having rapidly changed into a suit he had left behind in Kensington, and washed and shaved himself, came downstairs to greet his guest who was halfway through a bottle of claret.

"Well, Sir," said Joe comfortably, "would you like to tell me what happened?"

"You know that Emilia is dead?"

"Yes. An express rider came from Gunnersbury House today. He left at dawn apparently and made the journey by mid afternoon, though how he did it in view of the condition of the roads I'll never know. Anyway, Mr. Rawlings, let me tell you how sorry I am. Words cannot describe how I feel. Your wife was a wonderful woman – and beautiful into the bargain. You must be completely devastated."

"To be honest, Joe, it hasn't really sunk in. I'm still looking round for her. Expect her to come through the door at any moment."

"That will go on for a long time, Sir. You will turn to say something to her, then realise that she's no longer there."

Yet again John felt tears sting his eyes but this time he fought them off. "It is going to be very hard on Rose."

"My little friend," said Joe fondly. "But she's her father's daughter. She will cope."

"Joe," said John, cutting to the quick, "am I going to be arrested?"

"Well, Sir, we've already got sworn statements – though only written, so far – declaring that you were caught in the act. The most important of these is from Princess Amelia herself."

"But she wasn't there."

"Apparently she was, sheltering amongst her ladies of course, but for all that there."

John switched his pictorial memory to the moment when Lady Theydon had accused him and had to admit that there had been a large anonymous figure standing behind her. A figure that could well have been the Princess.

"So what is going to happen to me?"

"Now, Sir, that's the question."

"What do you mean?"

"Mr. Rawlings, it pains me to ask you but tell me straightly. Are you guilty of this crime?"

"No, Joe, I swear I didn't do it. In fact, Priscilla believes that the killer's knife was intended for her and that it was a case of mistaken identity."

And he proceeded to tell Sir John Fielding's clerk the entire story, leaving out not a single detail.

Joe listened in silence, sipping his claret and puffing on his pipe. Finally he said, "So it is her contention that Emilia slipped out, borrowed the nearest cloak, and thus met her death."

"Yes."

"And you say Priscilla let you escape?"

"It must have been deliberate, Joe. Unless she was called away somewhere. But I don't think that would have been possible in the middle of the night."

"And what is Miss Fleming's position in the royal household?"

"She attends Lady Theydon who attends, in turn, the Princess."

"I see. And she was at school with..." Joe cleared his throat. "... Mrs. Rawlings."

"Yes. But Joe, she believes that people wish her dead. She is the one you should be examining."

The clerk spoke through wreaths of smoke. "Mr. Rawlings, you and I go back a long way. And because of that I am going to do something that would cost me my job if it were ever discovered."

John drenched in sweat at the words, which had a terrible ring to them.

"When the rider arrived this afternoon," Joe contiued, "he said that you had escaped, had gone. But Sir John and I reckoned that you would be with Sir Gabriel. Because of that he sent me down in my own conveyance to bring you back to London. I'll tell you straight, my friend, that you will be remanded in custody in Newgate. Even the Beak cannot escape the word of a Princess. Therefore Mr. Rawlings..."

"Yes?"

"I am advising you to get out, now."

The sweat had actually started to run on John's back. "What do you mean?" he asked hoarsely.

"What I say, Sir. If I tell Sir John that I arrived in Kensington too late, that the bird had flown the nest so to speak, then there's no one but you and me to say otherwise."

The Apothecary raised the claret to his lips with a trembling hand. "But Joe, I can't let you take such a risk for me. It would be the end of you if you were ever found out."

"Yes," said the clerk matter-of-factly. "Now then, Sir, I've made you a fair offer. What do you say?"

"That I can't allow you to do so."

"You're a very old friend and I believe what you tell me. Sir, Newgate is a terrible place, even with garnish. It's not for the likes of you. Now, go for the love of God before I change my mind."

"But where?"

"As far away as possible. You've got friends in Devon, why not go there?"

John sat up straight. "But what about Emilia's funeral? What about bringing Rose to Kensington? Who will see to that?"

Joe waved the smoke away and looked John straight in the eye. "Mr. Rawlings, you have a straight choice. Either go or stay. Newgate or Devon? Which is it to be?"

"And who will hunt for Emilia's murderer in my absence?"

"I will, Sir. I will track him or her down, never you fear."

"But what can I do? Devon is like another world it's so far away."

"You can stay in touch with me by post. I will give you my private address in Seven Dials. Communicate with me there and there only. You are not to contact Bow Street."

The tears came again, tears of relief at the chance that had just been given to him. "Joe, how can I thank you. You are risking everything for me."

"What I am doing is against all I stand for. But what price that against our friendship?"

John wept bitterly.

"One day," answered Joe Jago seriously, "I might call in the favour."

They dined together, it being too late for Joe to travel back. John, realising that he had eaten nothing since early that morning, ate as well as he could. But again and again a vision of the sun setting over the snow, dyeing it the colour of blood, and that red figure lying so still and so helpless, came to haunt him and he returned the food uneaten to his plate.

Jago solemnly ate everything and helped himself to more. John, studying the rugged face, the bright blue eyes, the curling red hair – the clerk had long since removed his wig – thought of the risk the man was running for him and felt that he had never had a truer friend. Once, on catching the clerk's eye, the Apothecary mouthed the words, "Thank you," but Joe merely smiled and nodded by way of response.

Eventually, the meal done, John offered Joe a bed for the night which the clerk refused.

"No, Sir, I've already booked in at The Dun Cow, thank you all the same. If I arrived here to find you gone that is what I would have done. So that's what I shall do."

"You're certain?"

"Positive. Now, Mr. Rawlings, did you know that the London to Exeter Stage stops at Brentford tomorrow night?"

"No, I didn't."

"I suggest you get on it. How you proceed to Brentford I don't know. I'll give you a lift some of the way but I daren't add too much to my journey. Sir John is expecting me back with my report."

"Joe, are you sure you want to go through with this? Wouldn't it be easier if I just came with you?"

"It would be easier, my friend, of course. But life is full of challenges and this is the greatest I have faced so far. Go to Devon – fast. Leave me to solve the crime."

"It means I will miss Emilia's funeral."

"Her funeral will be in your heart, Mr. Rawlings," Joe answered simply.

Much struck by this remark, John lapsed into silence, wondering if anyone had felt as badly as he did at that particular moment.

Uppermost in his thoughts was his sad little daughter. The poor child was going to be devoid not only of her mother, but her father as well. Crazy ideas of going to fetch her, of taking her with him, raced through his mind. But he knew that to accompany a man wanted for murder would be a hazard he was not prepared to inflict on her. Much as he missed Rose, much as he longed for her company, he was certain that she would be better living under Sir Gabriel's calming influence. Yet the thought of her made his chest grow tight with emotion and tears filled his eyes once more.

Sleep would not come, much as he longed for it, and so he

roused himself at five o'clock and washed and shaved again. The ill-fitting suit he had abandoned. His best suit, ruined by blood, he had left on the seat of his carriage. Thus he travelled very lightly with only a small bag borrowed from Sir Gabriel. But his training was so instilled in him that John went to his compounding room and there packed a few bottles of physic together with some pills before he waited for Joe's arrival.

Punctually at five thirty, while it was still dark, Joe trotted up in the carriage belonging to Bow Street, with a pair of sturdy horses in front, himself driving.

"Ready, Sir?"

"Ready."

And John climbed aboard, wondering when he would see the Kensington house again. The previous night, before he had gone to bed, he had written a long note to Sir Gabriel asking him to do several things. First was to fetch Rose from Nassau Street, second was to see that Emilia was laid to rest befittingly, third was to close the shop in Kensington and ask Nicholas Dawkins to take over in Shug Lane.

"...my Beloved Father," the note had ended, "Joe Jago has given me the chance to Escape to Devon. I will Contact you as soon as I arrive. Your Loving Son, John Rawlings. Post Script: Destroy this Letter as soon as You have Read It."

Then he and Joe had gone out beneath the stars, realising as they set off in the freezing air that it was Christmas Eve.

"Happy Christmas, Joe," John said bitterly.

"Yours will be the unhappiest of your life, Sir. But this time next year all will be resolved."

"What do you mean?"

"That the criminal will be dead and that you will look forward to spending the time with your little girl and with Sir Gabriel."

"You know that Emilia was pregnant when she died?"

"Yes, I had heard from Sir John. What a tragedy."

"Yes," the Apothecary answered shortly, "it was."

Joe dropped him off at the far end of Kensington High Street and shortly after John hitched a lift with a labourer driving a cart, taking some sheep further into the country. This journey ended at a farm close to the river. John hung about for ten minutes and then the next carter turned up driving a covered wagon. In this way he reached The Three Pigeons in Brentford as a frosty night drew in.

The stagecoach, when it finally arrived almost an hour late, was packed with people desperate to get to Exeter for the Christmas festivities. Fortunately there was just room for John to squeeze into the luggage basket behind, where he almost went blue with cold. The first stop was at Thatcham, nearly six hours later, where they stopped for twenty minutes only before setting off for Marlborough, another three hours drive away.

It was the most appalling journey of John's life. The weather was terrible and at one point they got stuck in a snow drift with every passenger having to get off while the coachman and the guard heaved the horses through. Consequently the coach became more and more delayed and John and the other disgruntled people spent their Christmas Day grumbling pettishly about their troubles.

Afterwards, he never knew how he kept his patience that day. But he supposed that in a way the grumbling passengers helped him concentrate on something other than the death of his wife. Listening to their complaints, lists of various ailments, at the same time avoiding questions about himself, not only helped pass the time but kept him occupied. There were four others in the basket, all sitting on the luggage, all as uncomfortable as it was possible to be, and a strange camaraderie born of despair gripped the five of them, making them, when they finally disembarked at one in the morning of Boxing Day, arrange to meet again.

They were set down outside The Half Moon where John had spent part of his honeymoon. The sight of the building, all dark and shuttered, reminded him vividly of Emilia, so much so that he could have sworn she was standing beside him in the darkened street. He could almost smell her perfume. And then some drunken people staggered down the alleyway and the illusion was gone. Not knowing quite what to do, John set off for Sir Clovelly Lovell's house.

He had some money on him. Not a fortune but as much as he had gathered for his journey to Gunnersbury House. He could afford an inn for a week perhaps. But still John carried on, past the cathedral and into The Close, moved by some desire to talk, to tell Sir Clovelly what fate had befallen him. Yet when he got there he couldn't believe his eyes for the place still had candles burning and there was the noise of laughter coming from within. Emboldened by this, John rang the bell.

A footman answered, looking suspicious. "Yes, Sir?"

"Is Sir Clovelly Lovell within?"

"I am not certain, Sir. May I ask who is calling?"

"Could you tell him my name is Rawlings. He will remember me I feel sure."

"Very good, Sir. If you would wait where you are."

Not even allowed into the hall, the Apothecary thought, and felt wretched once more.

There was a commotion within and then waddling into view came Sir Clovelly himself looking mighty put out.

"What is it, Whistler?" he demanded.

Whistler made an apologetic face. "There's a person here who says he knows you, Sir."

"Knows me? Who..."

But at that moment John, ill-shaven and unkempt, stepped into the light of the hall. Sir Clovelly's many chins wobbled as he looked angry, then surprised and finally overjoyed.

"Rawlings!" he exclaimed. "My very dear chap. What brings you to Devon again? How delightful to see you. Come in, come in."

John took a step inside and the warmth and the general ambience hit him hard. He staggered very slightly, leaning heavily against the footman.

"Are you all right, old fellow?" Sir Clovelly's anxious moon face peered into his.

"I've just had a difficult journey," the Apothecary answered, smiling wanly.

He sat down rather hard on the hall seat and put his head in his hands. Instantly Sir Clovelly, who had, if anything, gained weight since John had last seen him, ordered some wine to be brought into the hall.

"My boy, I do believe you're exhausted. Where are you staying? Or have you just arrived?"

"I've just come, Sir. I journeyed by stagecoach and travelled in the basket. As you can imagine it was extremely chilly."

"What's happened to your coach?"

"I loaned it to my father."

"Dear Sir Gabriel," said Sir Clovelly warmly. "How is he?"

"As active as ever. Age has been no hindrance to him."

The wine arrived and was handed to John who drained the glass. The he turned to Sir Clovelly. "Sir, I'm going to ask the most enormous favour. As it is so late – the stage was very delayed because of the snow – I wonder if I might beg a bed for tonight. In the morning I'll look for somewhere to stay but meanwhile I'm fit to drop."

"My dear fellow, of course. You can tell me all about your news in the morning. I've got some friends sitting down to whist but they won't be staying much longer. However, as it's Boxing Night one must make an effort. By the way, just in case Sir Gabriel forgot to tell you, I lost the wife recently. Happy release really."

John nodded. "Emilia died too. A few days ago. It was the unhappiest thing that has ever happened to me. You see, I miss her."

Chapter Nine

He had not been sure how much he should tell Sir Clovelly Lovell, but some warmth, some element of sympathy in the little fat man, made him recount his story in full, down to the detail of Joe Jago's offer to him and the way he had caught the Exeter stage on Christmas Eve and endured the most agonising Christmas Day of his life.

"Of course that particular service to Exeter is advertised for its speed," Sir Clovelly had said, sighing over his sausages.

"Does it not bother you, my friend, that you are breakfasting with a man on the run?" asked John, ignoring the last remark.

"Hardly that, dear boy." Sir Clovelly looked thoughtful. "I wonder what Sir John Fielding will do?"

"He has little option but to put up Wanted posters. After all Princess Amelia herself swears that I am the guilty party. There's bound to be a hue and cry."

"Yes, but how loud, that is the question." Sir Clovelly's jolly water rat eyes looked earnest. "Listen, old chap, you can stay here with me as long as you like. Don't bother with an inn. They'll all be full of Christmas visitors. Feel free to come and go as you please and treat this as your second home."

John laid down his knife and fork. "No, Sir, I couldn't do so. I will be more anonymous in an hostelry. Besides, should there be recriminations I don't want to involve you. I thank you kindly for your offer but it is one I must refuse."

"Oh. Oh, I was rather hoping for some company."

"I will call frequently."

"Then I will have to make do with that." Sir Clovelly looked worried, which meant that his chins and his eyes practically vanished in folds of flesh. "The thing is, dear fellow, with what will you occupy yourself all day? Staying with me, now, would be one social whirl." He looked contrite and his jolly eyes appeared once more. "Mark you, with yourself in mourning, you might not feel up to cards and such like."

John smiled. "To be honest with you, dear friend, I would rather take things quietly for the time being. My circumstances are so odd as to make me anti-social." He looked at the fat man fondly, grateful that Sir Gabriel and he had become acquainted.

He felt refreshed for the Apothecary had slept deeply on the previous night, and for many hours at that. As soon as his head had touched the pillow he had lost consciousness, and thus he had remained, with no dreams to bother him, until eleven o'clock this morning. Now he sat, toying with breakfast, still unable to eat properly, still having mental pictures of blood red snow with a solitary figure lying so still on it.

"Terrible business," said Sir Clovelly, helping himself to toast and marmalade.

John toyed with a grape. "Do you think I did the right thing to run away?"

"Seems you had little choice. Being clapped up in Newgate would be no laughing matter."

"Joe said that even with garnish it would be hard."

"What's garnish?" asked Sir Clovelly, cutting a hunk of pie, presumably having some odd corner to fill somewhere.

"A fee for the gaoler. The greater the garnish the better the treatment. But I still don't think it would have been an easy time."

"It would have been bloody hard and there's an end to it."

"Still I believe I'll have to go back."

Sir Clovelly looked astonished. "Why? What for?"

"To find Emilia's killer. I know Joe Jago is on the trail but it's not going to be easy for him. I have this notion that perhaps I could work undercover."

"How would that transpire?"

"I could remain in hiding, perhaps don a disguise. I could hide out at a friend's house, then go in search of the bastard who murdered her."

Sir Clovelly chortled, a merry sound. "And how would you disguise yourself, pray? You've a very recognisable face, young man."

"I don't know how. Maybe dress as a curate or something."

At that Sir Clovelly laughed all the more and John sat, feeling infinitely depressed, while his friend guffawed away cheerfully.

Eventually the noise died down and the little fat man wiped his eyes with his napkin. "Sorry, dear boy," he said. "It was just the thought of you posing as a curate." He gave another subdued giggle. "But I really shouldn't laugh in the circumstances. Proper respect and all that."

John nodded. "No need, Sir Clovelly. I know you mourn Emilia. The thing is you haven't seen her for four years. But I..."

His voice died away as, yet again, he saw that figure, dying as the sun died also.

Sir Clovelly's deep eyes glistened.

"...I found her. I saw her recognise me before she...she..."

John drained his cup of tea deeply, unable to continue.

Sir Clovelly rose from the table and went to John's side where he laid a hand on the Apothecary's shoulder. "There, my boy. Be easy. Why don't you cry it out?"

But as John gave in to tears he felt a strong current inside him which said that this must be the last time, that he must not indulge this torrent of weeping again, that it was not fair on those left alive for him to do so. With this idea uppermost in his mind he brought himself under control and looked up to see the big jolly face looking anxiously at him.

"I'm sorry, Sir. I promise you I won't do it again."

"I could do with a brandy," said his host. "And I think you should certainly have one."

John nodded. "Thank you for being so patient."

Sir Clovelly crossed to the sideboard, a fine piece in polished walnut, and poured from the decanter. John was amazed by the size of his portion but sipped it none the less.

"That'll do you good," said the older man, deeply imbibing. "Drink it down like a fine fellow."

The Apothecary decided to be reckless and swallowed a great gulp and, strangely, did feel his spirits lift slightly. Sir Clovelly brought the decanter to the table and refilled John's glass.

"Saw a friend of yours t'other day," he remarked conversationally.

"Oh? Who was that?"

"The Marchesa di Lorenzi. Elizabeth."

Even at the mention of her name the Apothecary felt himself grow hot. How could you, he chastised himself. Yet even with Emilia so newly dead, with the fact that four years had passed since he had last seen the Marchesa, he had suffered that reaction and was ashamed of it. Sir Clovelly, however, clearly noticed nothing because he continued to speak.

"She still lives by herself in that great place of hers overlooking the Exe. Sir Randolph Howarth came courting her and we all thought it would end in marriage but she refused him apparently. He was mighty upset and took himself off abroad."

Why, the Apothecary thought wretchedly, should I be glad that she is still single? What difference does it make to me? I am a married man... Then he stopped short, gasping with shock, realising that Emilia had gone and that he was on his own once more.

"...of course," Sir Clovelly was saying, "she wears well, I'll give her that. She's forty-six or thereabouts now but could be ten years less. I suppose that's what comes of being thin."

He patted his own stomach and chortled happily.

John's voice sounded strained. "Do give her my best wishes if you should see her again."

"Better idea," said the little fat man. "We'll call on her. After all, it is still the festive season, Christmas time and all that. I'll order the coach to be prepared." And before John could say another word he had rung the bell.

"But I have nothing to wear," the Apothecary protested. "I only possess the suit I stand up in."

"That'll do," said Sir Clovelly. "After all, it's not as if you're trying to impress her."

But for all his words of reassurance John felt uneasy in his grey worsted as they drove out of Exeter, following the line of the Exe for a way until the carriage began to climb upwards, the horses straining, to the high ground that lay above. It was bone-chillingly cold but here in Devon the snow had started to melt and lay gathered like lumps of wool in the corners of the fields. Then the house came into view, not changed in the four years since John had seen it last.

They passed by the lodge house, the coachman saluting the keeper with his whip, and continued to climb up the drive. Then they heard the beat of distant hooves and a rider atop a great black horse came into view, clearly visible from the carriage windows. He was going at a hell of a lick, John thought. Then his heart pounded as he realised that he was looking at her. That she was out exercising her mount, dressed in men's clothes, as lithe and as exciting as when he had last seen her.

His stomach knotted painfully and yet again he felt ashamed of himself. He had loved Emilia with all his heart, no question about it, but Elizabeth di Lorenzi had once excited him – and her power had not weakened. With a feeling that his guts were made of iron, John proceeded inexorably on to the house.

She saw that she had visitors because she wheeled her horse round and cantered for home, waving as she did so.

"Ah, there's Elizabeth," said Sir Clovelly. He leant out of the window and waved in return. Recognising him, the Marchesa gestured for him to enter and vanished into the stable block. A few minutes later they were being shown into the huge reception hall, still painted pink, still with Britannia waving her spear above their heads. John gazed around him, remembering every detail, his stomach wretched within, his determination to appear calm paramount.

There was a noise behind them and, turning, they saw that Elizabeth di Lorenzi was coming in through a side entrance. Both men bowed, John deeply, Sir Clovelly as low as he could over his portly stomach. The Apothecary heard her sharp intake of breath, followed by a low laugh. Hoping that the flush in his face could be ascribed to the depth of his bow, he straightened.

She was, if anything, even more attractive than when he had last seen her. She had been riding and her colour was up, and this, together with the lustrous black hair, combined to give a stunning effect. He was aware that her dark eyes were sweeping over him and hated his sensible suit bitterly. He cleared his throat but it was Sir Clovelly Lovell who spoke.

"Forgive our intrusion, Ma'am, but I thought as 'twas Christmas time I would call on my neighbours. Truth to tell, Mr. Rawlings has had a terrible experience recently and I thought it would do him good to see you."

Her scar, running from beneath her eye to her cheekbone and until that moment not noticeable, stood out as she lost colour. John met her gaze and knew that she had guessed something of what had befallen him already.

"Pray come in," she said. "It is always a pleasure to see you, Sir Clovelly. Mr. Rawlings, I am sorry to hear you are in troubled times. You can tell me as much or as little as you like over refreshments."

He bowed again formally. "Thank you, Madam."

She led the way, the two men following at a respectful distance, into the Blue Drawing Room where she sat down on a small sofa. Sir Clovelly occupied another, while John sat in a chair opposite her seat.

Servants entered bringing wine and food, consisting of beef, ham, chicken, cheese and fruit.

"A cold collation," she explained. "But do say you'll dine with me. I would like that very much. I have some other guests but I think you will enjoy their company."

Sir Clovelly caught John's eye and silently asked a question. The Apothecary gave a slight nod.

"We'd be delighted, Ma'am. A great pleasure," the fat man answered.

Elizabeth dismissed the servants, then rose and went to the claret jug. She poured out three glasses, passing one to Sir Clovelly, the other to John. Then she sat down again.

"Tell me your story, Mr. Rawlings."

"My wife was contacted recently by an old school friend of hers, Priscilla Fleming. Priscilla invited Emilia to be in a theatrical production, *The Masque of Christmas*, which Miss Fleming had written. I should just explain that Priscilla is connected with the court of Princess Amelia in a minor capacity and it was for that court that the production was to be put on. Anyway, the Princess decided to spend her Christmas at Gunnersbury House outside London and Emilia duly made her way there."

John paused, realising that the Marchesa was studying him intently. Then she said in that direct way of hers, "You look somewhat older than when I last saw you."

He gave her a small smile. "That is because I am older. I'm thirty-two now."

"And I am forty-seven."

They were speaking as if Sir Clovelly was not present and John, realising this, hastily continued with his story.

"The performance took place on the twenty-second. During it Priscilla wore a bright red cloak. Later on I saw a woman I took to be Miss Fleming darting amongst the trees opposite the house. Anyway, the show was over but there was no sign of Emilia."

He became conscious of the Marchesa's breathing which had become somewhat shallow.

"So I went to look for her."

"And you found her?"

"I found her, dressed in the red cloak. She was dying in the snow, alone and unaided. She had been stabbed in the stomach several times, then left."

"How terrible!" gasped Elizabeth and one hand flew to her throat.

"She died in my arms, and I just sat with her; I don't know for how long. Anyway a gang of people came from Gunnersbury House and accused me of killing her. They locked me up overnight but Priscilla let me escape. I went to Kensington where Joe Jago came to take me back to London. But he, too, told me to get out of town so I set off for the only place where I knew I had friends. That is how I come to be here."

He had spoken calmly, even his voice under control, telling the story as clearly and coolly as was possible in the circumstances. Yet all the time he was aware of Elizabeth's dark gaze on him, absorbing every detail of what he said, giving him every ounce of her attention.

There was a silence, into which she finally spoke quietly. "John, accept my sincere condolences. No man should have such a terrible thing happen to him. I never met Emilia but from all you said she was an honest and good person. I am so sorry."

He looked directly at her, something he had been avoiding. "Thank you," was all he said.

Sir Clovelly Lovell cleared his throat. "Well now, perhaps we should speak of jollier things."

"That might be difficult," said Elizabeth, getting to her feet. "When we have finished our cold collation why don't John and I go for a ride? You, my dear Sir Clovelly, may stay here and rest until the evening's activities." She turned to the Apothecary. "Please say yes."

Suddenly the thought of being on a fast horse, racing over the sweeping hills, seemed the most desirable thing in the world.

"I would love to," he answered. "Would you mind, Sir?"

"Not at all, dear boy. It would do you good. I shall sleep

awhile. I enjoy that after a good repast." He folded his hands comfortably over his stomach and closed his eyes.

"Are you sure that you would like nothing further to eat, Sir Clovelly?"

He opened them again. "Perhaps one more of those delicious patties." Having secured one, he munched cheerfully.

Elizabeth caught John's eye and winked very slightly. Normally he would have winked back but today he was beyond such frivolities and merely smiled, then realised that this was the first time he had done so since finding Emilia dying.

She poured herself another glass of wine. "John, would you like some more?"

Suddenly he felt like getting drunk, like losing memory in the warm embrace of the bottle. He nodded. "Yes. Yes I would." Realising how abrupt this sounded he added the word, "Please."

He drained the glass and held it out for a refill but Elizabeth shook her head. "Wait till we come back. I want you in full control of the horse this afternoon."

He nodded, put the glass down and stood up. "Then let's go while it's still daylight."

"Yes."

They both looked toward Sir Clovelly but he had fallen asleep, still chewing, so they left the room silently and after giving orders for the servants, headed for the stables. Once there, a groom lead out two horses, one sable black, almost identical to the one Elizabeth had ridden earlier, the other a rich chestnut.

"I thought Jet for you," she said, and allowed herself to be helped into the saddle, which she rode like a man, still dressed in men's clothes and blissfully unaware of how attractive she looked in them.

John gazed at the mount appreciatively. "Is he mettlesome?"

"As much as you are," she answered, and was off.

John gazed at her departing back, then swung into the saddle and clattered out over the cobbles, feeling that first exhilarating rush of air as his mount gathered speed and sprinted off into the afternoon.

Chapter Ten

It was one of the most exciting rides of John's life. He crashed through the bracken in hot pursuit of the Marchesa who led him by a quarter of a mile, never once turning to see whether he was catching her up. She seemed to be part of her mount, clearly as at ease in the saddle as she was walking around her home. Yet though the Apothecary urged his horse to go faster, always she led by that tantalising, never changing, gap.

Just for a moment he forgot the terrible circumstances that had brought him to Devon and relished the vast expanse of sky and moorland. He had forgotten the drama of Devon skies. Today's was clear blue, that brightness that indicates deep winter, with a golden sphere of sun just starting to descend the heavens. A picture of deep red on snow came into his mind which with a mighty effort of will he forced away. Ahead of him Elizabeth cantered on, regardless – or so it seemed – of his presence behind her.

"Marchesa," he called and, at last, she glanced over her shoulder, gave a bewitching smile, then continued her reckless press forward.

Around him the world looked huge, the Exe a small snake far below, the green downs, undulating and curvaceous as a woman, a few houses – tiny at this distance – scattered about. He wanted to shout, then; shout at the cruelty of Emilia's death when there was such a lot of life yet to be lived, such a lot of wonderful country to explore. Yet again tears stung his eyes but he forced them away. He had done with crying. He would not cry again until the ruthless murderer, the destroyer of all he had held close to his heart, was dead. Briefly the thought made him breathless and he reined in his horse just to take in some air.

It was four years since he had travelled this path but he could have sworn that they were coming to that scrubbish terrain in which Wildtor Grange was situated. How well he remembered his visits there. Emilia had been with him on every occasion – except one visit, by night, when he and Elizabeth had been alone together.

Below him he could see her as she swooped out of the trees, still not looking backward. He careered down the hill after her, anxious to catch her up, afraid of losing his way now that he was deep in a wood. But he emerged on the other side quite safely, his mount seeming to know its pathway through. There beneath him, diminished by the distance, lay the crumbling remains of the Grange, its spines bleak and raw against the fading winter sunshine. Of Elizabeth there was no sign.

How strange it was, almost like a slip in time, to tether his horse to a nearby tree and make his way on foot to that stark and crumbling ruin. Weather and time had undone it even further since his last visit, and he gazed upward to a mouldering east wing where, so legend had it, Lady Thorne had once been held prisoner. Stepping through a glassless window at ground level, John entered that dim house of memories.

Yet time had blurred his recollection of that huge entrance hall with its ghostly suites of rooms leading off it. Looking straight ahead John ran his eyes over that bleak, overpowering staircase rising like some monster to the upper floors. Keeping his eyes firmly fixed on it he steadfastly made his way forward and put his foot on the bottom step.

Memories came of happier times. Of Emilia walking beside him, clinging to him in fright, of hiding in the clothes cupboard in Elizabeth's private apartments, of him being forced into the role of voyeur, watching the Marchesa undress and despite all the outside influences, admiring her muscular body. Now, his footsteps faltering despite himself, John made his way, in the listening silence, towards the place where she dwelt.

As he went he marshalled his thoughts about her. Despite the fact that she had attracted him to the point where he had almost betrayed Emilia, that had been then. Now he wanted none of it.

Yet, despite this, he still found her utterly charming, needed her friendship desperately. In fact, he considered Elizabeth di Lorenzi was very special to him in an utterly inexplicable way.

His feet echoed along the bare boards of the East Wing, past the dreary suites of rooms with their white-draped furniture. The atmosphere was stifling, horrid, almost tangible in its oppressiveness. Yet again he asked himself how anyone could bear to live here until, reaching the door at the end, he threw it open and stepped into opulent comfort, warmth and splendour, and knew that the Marchesa had been right to choose this extraordinary ruin for her secret habitat.

A fire had been started and Elizabeth had opened a bottle of wine and lit the candles, placed in wild profusion throughout the place. She looked up as he entered, turning from holding a taper to a seven pronged candle tree.

"You were very slow," she said with a smile.

"Yes, I probably was," he answered, suddenly weary. "May I sit down?"

"Of course. Have a glass of wine."

She had already poured it out and the Apothecary sank into the comfort of a fireside chair and picked up the glass. He raised it.

"To you, Elizabeth. Thank you for your friendship."

She flung herself into the chair opposite his. "So you have a child. What is she like?"

"Beautiful, intelligent, pleasant. In fact she's every parent's dream. Do you know I had to run from Kensington. I had to leave my father to cope with fetching Rose, leave him to tell her that she would never see her mother again. I couldn't even say goodbye to her."

Elizabeth looked at him levelly. "You can explain all that to her when you see her again, no doubt."

"But when will that be?"

"That rather depends on you."

John drained his wine and held his glass out for a refill. "What do you mean?"

"What I say. You are welcome to stay in Devon, you know that, but I think you should return to town."

"And get arrested?"

"Not necessarily."

The amount of wine he had had during the day was beginning to affect the Apothecary, who leant back in his chair. Staring at Elizabeth, noticing the way a strand of dark hair had come loose from the bun she wore for riding, he said, "You're still very beautiful, you know."

She gave him a cynical smile. "I'm glad you think so. But let us talk of more important things. If you were to return and take lodgings somewhere near Gunnersbury House surely you could find out more about Emilia's murder."

"But I couldn't go into the place. I would be recognised instantly."

Elizabeth was silent, staring into the flames of the fire which had caught well and was now starting to throw out warmth. "What you need is someone working with you," she said eventually.

The Apothecary became rigid, wondering whether he was interpreting what she was saying correctly. "Do you mean yourself?" he asked.

Her wonderful eyes, a deep topaz in colour, flashed in his direction. "Of course," she said. "Who else would I be referring to?"

He sat in wonderment, amazed by her offer. "You mean that you would return with me – a wanted man – and ask the questions I need to know the answers to?"

"Yes," she replied simply.

"But why?"

She stood up, a certain impatience in her manner, and walked round the room, examining the candles. "Because we are friends."

"But that exceeds the bounds of friendship by far."

She stopped her pacing and turned to look at him. "Does it? I think not. I told you that I killed the man who stalked me. That was how I got this –" Her fingers traced the outline of her disfiguring scar. "A woman capable of doing that is capable of asking a few questions to help a friend, surely."

"Yes, but..."

She raised a hand and John fell silent. "Take it as done. Now, Mr. Rawlings, I would suggest that you stay here in Devon and regain your strength until Epiphany. Then, the day after, we will travel by my private coach to Brentford which, I believe, is near to Gunnersbury. Then I will go off in search of work near to or, indeed, in Gunnersbury House. After that we can confer again."

He stared at her blankly, overwhelmingly glad that someone else was temporarily in control of his life. For once he had no wish to make plans or do anything other than obey orders.

"If you think that would be best."

"I do." She laughed softly to herself. "How strange to see you so compliant."

"I don't have the energy for anything else."

Elizabeth came and stood in front of him, leaning forward and brushing his hair lightly with her hand. "Time heals all things," she said, then she abruptly turned on her heel and went to the window. "It's starting to snow," she remarked over her shoulder. "Time we were off."

"Yes," the Apothecary answered, getting to his feet.

He put the fireguard in front of the fire and turned to her where she was snuffing out the candles.

"Can we take one of those down the stairs?"

"Why? Are you afraid of the dark?"

"In this house," said John, "I am frankly terrified."

They arrived back to find Sir Clovelly Lovell awake and moodily staring through the window.

"I thought you'd got lost," he said and gave a laugh in the depths of which was a decidedly testy tone.

Elizabeth di Lorenzi handled him superbly. "Oh, my dear Sir, I do apologise for our late arrival. Truth to tell the horses went further than we had reckoned on. Please forgive my rudeness in not being here to offer you refreshment. But it won't take a second to rectify that. A little sherry perhaps to revive you before the evening onslaught."

He perked up. "Yes, that would be very nice. Mr. Rawlings, will you join me?"

"When I've washed myself, yes indeed. But at the moment I feel a little the worse for wear."

"John, make full use of our closet and other facilities, do. May I offer you the suite in the West wing?"

"I'm afraid I only have the clothes I stand up in. I left my entire wardrobe behind in London."

"You look splendid as you are. However, should you wish to change for dinner I can arrange for a suit to be brought to you."

"Really?" said John, astonished.

"Really," the Marchesa answered firmly, closing off any questions as to the suit's original owner.

He bowed to her superior force, said, "I would be pleased to change, Marchesa. If you'll forgive my further absence, Sir Clovelly," and left the room to make his way upstairs.

Strangely, it was a part of the house he had never visited and now he revelled in its peacefulness, the gracious way in which it was decorated. The footman who was accompanying him bowed before one of the doors

"This is the suite, Sir. If you would like to enter."

Inside it had been fashioned in shades of green, all soft and soothing to the eye. John gazed round him at the plush wallpaper, so subtly made that it was difficult to tell whether the interior design was grey or merely a darker shade of green. The bed was a jubilation with a gilded headboard ornately carved, and two posts supporting the end. The Apothecary hazarded a guess that it had been designed by Chippendale. Wherever he looked there was understated luxury and his realisation that Elizabeth was a woman of wealth was reinstated at every turn.

John crossed to the washstand and stared at himself in the mirror above it. He had come without a wig and his hair was growing long, springing liberally in all directions. But it was to the face beneath that his eye was drawn. He looked slightly crazed, he thought. Haggard and wild-eyed, his mouth compressed tightly into an almost straight line. He also looked thin and pinched, as if finding Emilia dying had halved him in size. Half-heartedly he picked up the razor and brush, thoughtfully provided by his host, and soaped his chin.

There was a knock at the door which opened to reveal a servant carrying a suit. It, too, was dark green; velvet breeches and a satin skirted coat. It was not the latest fashion admittedly but the main thing was that it fitted. Gratefully, John put it on and went out into the corridor.

And then he saw Elizabeth, wearing a crimson open robe, proceeding towards the staircase in front of him. Hearing him, she turned and smiled.

"Ah, the suit becomes you."

"Thank you."

"It belonged to my son. He was more or less your build."

Reminded then that she, too, had known the pain of loss, indeed twice in her life, the Apothecary made her a small bow, then offered her his arm.

"Madam, may I escort you downstairs?"

"Yes Sir, indeed you may."

And with that they proceeded to dinner together.

Chapter Eleven

With a clatter of wheels over the cobbled yard the coach of Lady Elizabeth di Lorenzi drew to a halt outside The Three Pigeons coaching inn in Brentford. The coachman pulled the two horse team which had brought them from Devon, to a panting stop, then climbed down from the box.

"Will this do, my Lady?"

She put her head out, the feathers on her hat swishing as she did so. "It will be perfectly adequate, thank you."

"Right, Madam," and with that Ruckley pulled down the step for Elizabeth to alight.

She was followed immediately by John Rawlings, looking slightly less haggard than when he had arrived in Devon but for all that quite thin and gaunt of feature. Together the two of them made their way into the dark and somewhat noisome interior of the coaching inn while the coachman led the animals round to the stables.

It had taken eight days to arrive, with the horses accomplishing twenty-two miles a day. Every night they had stayed at a coaching inn, while the creatures rested and fed. Then in the morning they had been harnessed up and gone again. It had been close to a nightmare but John, realising with every step that he was getting nearer to finding Emilia's murderer, had made the best of it. However, he was running very short of money and now he turned to the Marchesa with an apologetic face.

"I'm sorry to ask but could you lend me enough to pay the bill?"

"Of course. Tomorrow we will get work. You can repay me when you're in funds again."

He loved her openess, her frank approach, but he merely answered, "Thank you."

They had become rather formal with one another, partly to

survive being together in a swaying coach for all those hours, partly for some other inexplicable reason which John couldn't begin to explain. But the fact remained. In many ways he knew the Marchesa better than ever before; in others she was a complete stranger to him.

The landlord, a ruddy-faced country man if ever there was one, came hurrying to greet them.

"Good afternoon, Sir and Madam. How may I help you?"

Elizabeth rustled her magnificent hat. "We would like two rooms and a third place for my coachman. Will that be possible?"

"Certainly, Madam. If you would like to follow me."

She turned to John. "I personally am panting for a drink." Then back to the landlord. "If you could take our luggage up to our rooms we can follow later. My coachman will head for the kitchens I dare swear. Please look after him well."

And with that she swept into The Unicorn, one of the private rooms put aside for travellers. Once inside she pulled her hat from her head and her mass of dark hair tumbled round her shoulders.

"What a journey," she said, fanning herself with its brim, "I thought we would never get here."

John chuckled. "It was you insisting on keeping the same horses that caused the problem."

"That and the fact that it gets dark so early. As it was we set off before dawn each day. Anyway, those beasts of mine are too fine to leave behind. They're not old country nags, I'll have you know."

"Everything you possess is admirable," John answered.

She gave him an unfathomable look and changed the subject. "Did you write to your father? And to Joe Jago?"

"I certainly did. I told them that I was returning to London and would shortly give them an address at which they could find me."

"Good."

A waiter came in and took their order at this point so nothing further was said until they were alone once more. Then the Apothecary sighed.

"I suppose Emilia's funeral will have taken place by now. I wonder where she is laid to rest."

"In St. Mary's, Kensington, I feel certain. You will be able to go and visit her, John."

He smiled without humour. "Tell me about your husband's death. How did you feel?"

She put the hat down. "I've told you before. Luciano died in the street, a drawn sword in his hand. I was not with him. No one was with him except for his murderer, the man who for months had been following me. But my case was not like yours. I knew who had done the deed. So I sought my stalker out and killed him. Then I went on the run and came back to England."

"I shall kill whoever murdered Emilia when I finally track them down."

"Yes, and you will be justified in doing so. But be careful. First get them to confess in front of a reliable witness or you'll find yourself swinging at Tyburn."

She put her hand to her throat and stuck her tongue out, a sight so funny that John gave one of his rare laughs.

"I'm sorry but you looked rather amusing."

"It's good to hear you laugh again," Elizabeth answered. "You don't do it very often these days."

"I'm sorry. I expect I've turned into a dour companion."

"No, you could never be that. With all your troubles, with all your sorrow, you still possess that liveliness of spirit which is a vital part of your personality."

"I'm glad."

There was a short knock followed by the waiter coming in with their bottle of canary. John poured two glasses, then raised his.

"To you, Elizabeth. Thank you for everything you are doing."

She looked at him levelly. "Don't be too previous, my friend. You can toast me fully when we have achieved our objective."

The Apothecary felt chastened. "Very well. To our success."

"I'll drink to that." The Marchesa drained her glass. "Now, John, you mentioned a disguise. What are you thinking of?"

"I don't know. I suppose I could don some sort of garb. I've no idea really."

"Um." Elizabeth considered. "What work are you hoping to get?"

"Again, I don't know. Perhaps as a labourer. As I told you, I won't be able to get into the house so something nearby would suit."

"There are farms scattered around. Perhaps in one of those. Red hair!" she exclaimed suddenly.

"What do you mean?"

"If I can get hold of some henna dye I could lighten your hair colour. That should do the trick."

"Yes, I'm game. You think that would disguise me sufficiently?"

"Yes, if it's bright enough. You would be thought of as a redhead. Now where could I purchase some?"

John smiled. "You could try the local apothecary."

Elizabeth looked thoughtful. "I'll send the coachman. I don't want to be seen around the place, it being the shopping area and market that would serve the big house. You see my plan is to infiltrate Gunnersbury House itself. I shall get a job as a servant."

John looked shocked. "You couldn't possibly. It would kill you."

The Marchesa shook her head. "How wrong you are. I have been as poor as a mouse during my life and have worked accordingly. I'm not afraid of scrubbing floors."

The Apothecary couldn't answer, lost in admiration for this most remarkable of women.

"So let's finish the bottle and then I'll see Ruckley and arrange for him to go to the apothecary's shop. I'm sending him home tomorrow, by the way."

"But what will you do without your coach?"

"Walk," said Elizabeth shortly, and smiled at him over the rim of her glass.

That night they dyed his hair, leaving the henna paste on a long time. When John eventually washed it off, his locks – normally the shade of cinammon – had lightened several tones and were now the colour of copper. He looked at himself wryly in the mirror.

"I don't think anyone would know me."

"That was the general idea," Elizabeth answered, her own dark hair falling about the place.

They were in her chamber, crouching over the washstand, where the rinsing water had turned the colour of blood. Seeing it, John was once again reminded vividly of Emilia's stab wounds but thrust the thought away. Yet something in his manner must have revealed what he was thinking because Elizabeth said quickly, "I'll empty this into the slop pail and take it downstairs. We don't want to give the maid nightmares."

And before he could argue she had emptied out the water, scrubbed round the basin and, tucking up her skirts, gone away with the bucket.

Waiting for his hair to dry, John sat before the mirror and tried to formulate a plan. There were several farms surrounding the Gunnersbury House estate, two of which he had noticed on his fateful drive there, though what their names were he didn't know. A job at either of those would suit him well. Yet this was the time of year when farmers were laying men off rather than taking them on. Casual work, like haymaking and apple-picking, were strictly seasonal. Still, he might be lucky and find something. Hoping that both he and Elizabeth would have good fortune, he sat and watched his hair dry.

It was even brighter than he had originally thought. In fact, in a shaft of the fading January sun it looked as if his head had caught fire. Brushing it forward over his brow the Apothecary stared at himself in the mirror. With his eyes shaded by curls only his nose and mouth were clearly visible and these would hardly give him away. Satisfied that it would take someone peering at him closely to recognise him, John waited for Elizabeth to return.

They set off early the next morning, bidding farewell to Ruckley, who headed his team off on the route taken by the Exeter stage. Then having breakfasted – a meal during which the serving girl stared fixedly at John's hair – they paid the bill and left The Three Pigeons, starting the walk to Gunnersbury House.

Elizabeth was unrecognisable. She had darkened her skintone and brushed her long black hair loose, so that she looked a regular working woman. She wore a dark skirt, darned here and there, a white blouse and a red shawl. On her feet she had a pair of old red shoes.

"Tell my fortune," John said impulsively.

"Is that how I appear? A gypsy woman?"

"You could be."

"I'd better whiten my skin, else I'll never get employment."

"You can wash it in a pond somewhere. There are plenty of springs on the way."

They were approaching The Butts, a shady square of redbrick houses, in the centre of which was a market. Booths had been erected sellings goods as varied as gloves and firkins of wine, with every conceivable kind of item – wool, cradles, clothes – inbetween. Added to this, the local farmers had brought produce – hens, ducks, even sheep – together with winter vegetables and eggs for sale.

John could not help but notice, with a certain wry amusement, that Elizabeth had adopted the gait of the woman she was supposed to be and was walking with a definite swing to her hips.

They passed by stalls and trestles on which were laid country clothes, woven by the women while their men worked the fields. Elizabeth paused, picking up a sheepskin and leather jerkin.

"I think you should have this..." she started to say, then stopped as a beefy young man, also thumbing his way through the goods, was suddenly seized from behind and lifted bodily into the air.

" 'Ere," he remonstrated.

"I know you," came the reply. "You're Tom Thatcher – and you're a thief."

"I ain't," the other answered, but got no further as a fist flew through the air and landed on his lip, dislodging a rotting tooth which he spat onto the ground.

Almost instantly there was a ruckus as people took sides, some quite violently. Pushing Elizabeth behind him, John attempted to move away but without a chance. On every hand men were fighting and he saw that he was going to have to defend himself, like it or not. As a young giant with a mop of blond hair took a swing at him, the Apothecary ducked and landed his aggressor a blow in the guts which doubled him over. Hastily chopping him on the back of the neck, John Rawlings turned to see who he should fight next.

A man of about fifty, weatherbeaten as a birdscarer and somewhat resembling a haystack, caught his eye. But before either could exchange blows the newcomer was beaten over the head with a mallet and fell, twisting his leg agonisingly beneath him. Lying right in the path of the mêlée as he was, John grabbed him under the arms and succeeded in lugging the man between two stalls, out of harm's way.

Elizabeth, meanwhile, had climbed onto a vacant stool and was watching the fracas with an interested eye.

"There's a gang at work," she called to John. "See them stealing from the stalls."

And sure enough men and women were shifting goods into

their pockets at the speed of lightning. Thinking that the entire fight had been deliberately started with theft as its main objective, the Apothecary bent over his patient who had recovered consciousness and was starting to sweat with pain.

"My leg," he groaned. "I think it's broken. Get me to a physician."

John almost said 'I'm an apothecary' but thought better of it. "I know a little," he ventured, and amidst the man's screams of agony, straightened the leg. It was fractured in two places, below the hip and above the ankle, that much was obvious. He looked up at Elizabeth.

"Fetch me a long stick, as quickly as you can."

She got down from the stool and disappeared amongst the stalls, returning eventually with a shepherd's crook which she had obtained by some means or other.

"Will this do?"

"Fine. We can cut the crook off later. Now, my dear, can you sacrifice a petticoat?"

But he had no need to ask. Elizabeth had already stripped one off and was busy tearing it into strips. Working as best he could in the cramped conditions, John bound the fractured leg to the crook.

The fight, meanwhile, was petering out, the gang of thieves presumably having filched as much as they could manage to carry. Further, someone had had the good sense to blow a whistle, the noise of which had people coming from their houses. Order was being restored and the hurling of punches was practically at an end. Cautiously, John put his head out to survey a scene of superficial damage. Several human casualties were sitting down, however, nursing their heads. He turned to the man he had rescued.

"I've done my best for you, Sir. Now how to get you home? That's the question."

The man, whose lids had been firmly closed, opened them.

Eyes, bright as sunbeams, blue as forget-me-nots, gazed into John's.

"Thank you, my friend," he gasped painfully. "I came here by cart. It's the brown one over there with the dappled horse. Tethered to the trees."

"I'll fetch it," said John, but Elizabeth was already on her way, untying the animal and leading it over to where the man lay.

"I'd better drive you," said John. "Which direction are you going in?"

"I'm Hugh Bellow from Bellow's Farm. It lies the far side of Gunnersbury House, the nearest dwelling. Do you know it?"

"No, but I'll find it. Now, let's heave you up."

With the help of the glover, whose stall had seen the start of the fracas, they managed to get Hugh, giving the occasional shout of agony but for the most part biting his lip, into the cart where he sat, his bad leg sticking out in front of him.

"Just a minute, I'll get the luggage," said John.

He jumped down and picked up two bags, both small. Yet in his he had placed his medicines, finding it completely impossible to travel without the most basic things to hand. Now he opened it and produced a bottle of white physick, the juice of the opium poppy already prepared. Carefully he measured out a dose.

"Here, drink this."

Hugh eyed it suspiciously. "What be it?"

"It will relieve your pain, Sir. Trust me."

The farmer downed the dose. "You're a funny sort of labourer," he said.

Elizabeth came in. "He studied with an apothecary for a time, Sir. He knows the basic things to do in situations."

Hugh eyed her. "Are you his wife, young lady?"

Her gorgeous smile lit her eyes. "Thank you for that."

"For what?" asked Hugh, puzzled.

"For calling me young lady," she answered, and suddenly burst into laughter, which turned into a song. It was a deep, clear voice that stayed in tune. The Apothecary thought of Emilia's singing; so sweet and gentle, totally at odds with Elizabeth's. His wife's clarity, quite high and juvenile, had always tugged at his heart-strings. But this was the sensual sound of a siren.

It felt good to be leaving the village of Brentford and heading into the open countryside. John, the reins held loosely in his hands, felt himself relax and wished that he could capture the moment; Elizabeth's unashamed singing and Hugh Bellow nodding off as the opium wore on.

Making his way up Brentford Road, the horse plodding peacefully at its own pace, John turned left up Gunnersbury Lane. To his left lay Gunnersbury House, the dark woods where tragedy had changed hid life forever, clearly visible. He glanced over his shoulder and saw that Hugh had gone to sleep, while Elizabeth realising that they were close, had abruptly ceased to sing.

"There," he whispered, "amongst those trees. That's where I found her dying."

His voice sounded harsh, even to his own ears. Elizabeth followed the line of his pointing finger.

"It would be possible for any assassin to hide himself in that dense foliage."

"Yes." There was a catch in his breath but he conquered it. "If you stand up you'll just be able to see the outline of the house."

"Um. So that is where I'll be working."

"Elizabeth, how do you know? The court has probably gone back to London and the place closed down. How can you be so certain?"

"Because I am determined," she answered. "They always want people to do the dirty work. And what about you?"

"I shall ask Hugh Bellow to refer me somewhere. That is, when he wakes up."

"I wonder where his farm is?"

"If I'm not mistaken it's there on the left."

And John gazed over the fields to where, beside a fast-flowing brook, a farm with sheep and cows grazing could be seen.

"I think you're right. Drop me at the top of the road and I'll go to the house directly. I'll meet you at this spot at seven o'clock tonight. No arguments now."

Much as John hated to leave her he had little choice. He stopped the cart and watched her swing down, lithe and graceful.

"Don't forget to wash your face," he called.

"I won't, don't worry."

She was gone, hurrying off in the direction of the mansion, waving until she disappeared from view.

John turned right, away from Gunersbury House, and proceeded down Brentford Lane. A rough bridge crossed the river beneath, over which he passed, then he turned right once more down to the track leading to the farm. A woman appeared in the doorway, staring fiercely at the stranger driving the cart. Then she saw Hugh Bellow lying in the back and started to run towards them.

"Hugh," she called frantically. "Are you all right my love?"

"Mr. Bellow has broken his leg, Ma'am," said John politely. "I'm bringing him back from the market."

But she had already turned away and was shouting, "Jake, come here and help your father."

Slowly, John got down from the cart and, turning back, looked through the trees. The rooftop of Gunnersbury House was distantly visible. This place, he thought, would be ideally situated for observation. He turned back to the little woman who was bustling about giving orders rather ineffectually.

"Madam," said John, giving his best bow, "allow me to introduce myself. I am John Rawlings."

Chapter Twelve

It was evening, the quiet time of day. Jacob Bellow, who seemed to be the general factotum round the farm, had finished for the night and now sat before the inglenook, feet outstretched, taking down a goodly measure of ale. So far he had addressed John hardly at all and the Apothecary had come to the conclusion that he must feel threatened by his presence. Not that John had had a great deal of time to worry on that account, his entire afternoon being taken up with attending to Hugh Bellow.

He had restrapped the leg to a plank, once one of suitable length and width had been found. He had also used proper bandages to bind the damaged limb securely, though not so tightly that it would prevent the blood flowing. Meanwhile Hester Bellow had watched wide-eyed, eventually saying, "Sir, are you a doctor fellow?"

Realising that he must tread carefully, John had sighed and said, "No, Ma'am, I spent a year assisting an apothecary, that's all."

"Well, you should have taken it up is all I can say. You've such a way with you. So gentle and yet so firm."

John had stood up. "Thank you, Ma'am. I do my best."

"No physician could have done more. Now then, Mr. Rawlings, where are you staying? In Brentford?"

"No, truth to tell I'm looking for somewhere – and also for employment. I've recently been in Devon but came south in order to be closer to my father."

"And where does he live?"

"In Kensington, Ma'am."

Mrs. Bellow looked thoughtful. "Well, we could do with an extra pair of hands round this place while Hugh is laid up."

The Apothecary's heart rose though he kept his features casual.

"I'd appreciate that, Ma'am. Give me time to find my feet while I look round for something more permanent."

"Well, that's agreed then. Provided Hugh doesn't object. But there's little chance of that I feel."

"I'll await confirmation till tomorrow then."

For while restrapping the leg the Apothecary had given Hugh another mild dose of opium for the relief of his pain.

Now, though, he had been invited to stay the night and sat before the fire, on the opposite side from Jacob Bellow, drinking a deep tot of home-made elderberry wine and contemplating the man who, unlike his parents, clearly resented the Apothecary being in his home.

"Been a fine day," John ventured.

"Ah," said Jake.

"Thank goodness the snow has gone."

"Yes."

"I was over this way last Christmas. The weather was particularly bad."

"Oh ah."

John decided to take a risk. "Mr. Bellow, would you rather I remained silent because I can easily do so. It's just that I thought we ought to become more friendly."

Jake regarded him for the first time. "Why?"

"Because we might be working together – temporarily."

"Oh might we."

There was a silence during which John, who had returned his gaze to the fire, felt himself being thoroughly examined. He cast a fleeting glance in Jacob's direction.

He was short, squat young man with fair hair like his father and mean grey eyes. Just for a second John was reminded of Priscilla Fleming, though there was no actual resemblance other than that both possessed a way of staring at one. But where she was pale, Jacob's skin was highly coloured, with two bright spots of red on either cheek, brought about no doubt from always working outdoors. In short he was fairly unattractive and had a nature to match.

Catching his eye, John smiled sweetly, a gesture that was not returned. Thinking that the best way of getting on with such a taciturn individual would probably be by ignoring him, the Apothecary finished his glass and stood up.

"I think I'll go for a little air. Time I gave my lungs a shock."

"Please yourself," said Jacob, and lit a long-stemmed pipe which he proceeded to puff ferociously.

Aware that he had been dismissed John hurried outside and consulted his watch. It was pitch dark but the light from the door showed him that it was half past six. He should easily be in time for his meeting with Elizabeth if he set off now. Waiting for a few moments until his eyes adjusted to the darkness, the Apothecary pulled on an old coat that he found hanging on a nail, and set off.

It took him ten minutes to get to the top of the drive but he was guided all the way by the lap and ripple of the energetic brook, which seemed to be racing to keep him company. He turned left and crossed the rough little bridge, making his way down Brentford Lane to the big house. Then he flattened himself into the hedge for he could distinctly hear the sound of hooves and wheels approaching.

A carriage, going slowly over the rutted way, passed him and John peered within to be rewarded with a glimpse of three women, Lady Kemp and Lady Featherstonehaugh – still looking unbelievably alike – together with the egregious Lady Theydon. So the court had not removed to London but was still assembled at Gunnersbury. Praying that Elizabeth had achieved her objective and was now employed at the mansion, John proceeded on cautiously.

She came out of the darkness like a shadow, whispering his name.

"John?"

"Yes, it's me."

She went directly to the point, one of the characteristics he so admired about her.

"Did you get a job at Bellow's?"

"Yes. I thought I might be offered something in view of his injury. There's a surly son who resents me, though."

She smiled in the dimness. "There's always somebody."

"But what about you? How did you fare?"

"I told you I would be alright. I am to clean out the grates and empty the chamber pots. But at least I am to live in."

He squeezed her arm. "Are you sure you can cope with that?" She nodded and he changed the subject. "I take it the court is still there?"

"Yes. Apparently the Princess was far too shocked by the murder to face the upheaval of moving. Then the poor creature went down with influenza and is now slowly recovering. Naturally everyone is hanging on for her to get better before the whole place packs up and goes back to London."

"I see, yet..."

But John did not complete the sentence. The sound of another carriage approaching was audible. Without a word he dived into the hedge, pulling Elizabeth after him.

It was another member of the company of players, though one who had been relegated to a smaller part. Exquisite as a spring cloud, yet a cloud that was about to play a capricious trick on the world, for Lady Georgiana was frowning deeply, turning her head to look out, avoiding the gaze of the other occupant. Even without seeing him properly, John knew who it was. The tall, thin, somewhat elderly man who had kissed her hand.

He squeezed back into the hedge as Lady Georgiana's gaze met his, lit by a sudden shaft of moonshine as he was. She stared but a second later the coach had passed on its way, leaving him with the impression that he had been seen.

"She saw us," confirmed Elizabeth, emerging. "Who is she, do you know?"

"Lady Georgiana Hope. She had a minor role in the masque in which Emilia appeared."

"And the man with her?"

"I don't know. But judging by the look of him he is someone who lusts after her."

"Is he attached to the court?"

John shook his head. "Again, I can't answer."

"I'll find out," Elizabeth answered in that determined way which once, in another life, had so appealed to John.

He turned to look at her, studying her intently in the moonlight. She had washed her face and was now devoid of any kind of paint. She was ugly, with her great scar being caught by the lunar beams, and yet in another way she was totally beautiful. In any other circumstances John's heart would have quickened, yet now he was drained of any feeling, lacking all emotion. And Elizabeth, regarding him with a half-smile, seemed somehow to understand this and turned to leave.

"You're going," said John, and it was a statement not a question.

"Yes, there's nothing further to report. I shall meet you tomorrow evening at the same time."

"But not in the same place. Let's meet just below the bridge. It might be more private there."

She smiled. "Away from people in carriages with sharp eyes."

"Precisely." He took one of her hands. "Elizabeth, thank you for everything you're doing. It far exceeds the bounds of friendship."

"Nonsense. I was growing damnably bored. It's given me something to do that has a purpose."

"Even emptying chamber pots and lighting fires?"

A smile transformed her features. "And scrubbing out the kitchens, don't forget."

"I never will," he answered.

"Good night," came the reply, and with that she was gone.

John walked back through the darkness of the night, thinking to himself that less than a mile away his wife had breathed her last. A longing to see Rose suddenly possessed him, the child that she had brought into the world. Determined to write to Sir Gabriel the very next day, John entered the farmhouse and went straight to his room.

He rose an hour before dawn the next morning, shivering in the cold and the darkness. Directed into the fields by a surly Jacob Bellow, he fed the cattle and the sheep, puting food into their troughs and checking the water supply, then he turned back in the direction of the farm for breakfast just as dawn broke over the pasture land.

It was a dawn like no other he had ever seen. The sky turned pink for a few moments before the sun appeared, so that everywhere reflected that glorious roseate plumage, suffusing the clouds with an insidious, demanding shade. The Apothecary stood transfixed, letting his eyes enrich themselves with the colour, wishing for the thousandth time that Emilia was standing beside him, enjoying such a wonderful sight. Then he stared, startled by what he was looking at. For there, in the far field, etched black against the brilliant ball of the sun, she stood, gazing towards Gunnersbury House.

"Emilia," he called, though his voice came out as a harsh rasp.

She half turned towards him, as if the sound had reached her ears. Then she turned back again and began slowly walking in the direction of the house.

"Emilia, wait," he called again, and for a moment closed his eyes. When he opened them again she had gone; vanished completely. Shivering violently and only partially from the cold, John Rawlings made his way to the farmhouse.

"Hugh has agreed that you may stay until he is up again," announced Hester Bellow, as she cut thick slices of bread and heaped them on the Apothecary's plate.

"How very kind," he muttered through a piece of cheese.

"Perhaps you'll go and check on his welfare later," she continued, cutting at ham and adding it to the collection on John's trencher.

"Of course. Gladly."

Jacob gave him a sour look. "We need to cut the reeds by the river bed today. So as soon as you've seen to Father you can go and get on with it."

John tugged his forelock. "Yes, Sir."

Hester remonstrated. "Jake, let the poor man eat his breakfast. He's been out in the fields since five."

"Five!" Jacob said with a loud snort. "I'm up at three when t'is lambing time."

"Well that ain't yet," she retorted, and in her anxiety put two more slices of meat on the Apothecary's already overflowing plate.

"Please, Mrs. Bellow, I have more than enough. No more, I insist."

For since Emilia's death his appetite had decreased enormously. True he was eating more normally than he had at first, but for all that great mountains of food now made him feel quite ill, therefore he left a great deal of his breakfast uneaten, much to Jacob's disgust. In fact it was a relief to go upstairs and see his employer.

Hugh was lying comfortably enough, his strapped leg outside the bedclothes.

"Well, Sir, how are you this morning?" the Apothecary asked cheerfully.

"Much better, thanks to your good self. You've done a grand job. I don't think it will be necessary to call the physician after all."

"I think you should, Sir. He will be able to prescribe for you. The medicines I carry are very limited."

Hugh looked thoughtful. "Indeed. Not quite what I had gathered. Tell me, lad, did you only do a year with an apothecary?

How come you were able to break your indentures?"

John hesitated, thinking that to lie now would be dangerous. Eventually he took a breath and said, "Sir, I told you a falsehood. I actually am an apothecary but for personal reasons which I cannot discuss with you I am temporarily away from my shop."

Hugh looked even more pensive, then said eventually, "Tell me, are you connected in any way with the recent affair at the big house?"

John sat down rather heavily on the edge of the bed but made no comment.

"We heard tell that a young apothecary's wife was murdered up there and that he was guilty."

"Then you heard wrong, Sir. I did not do it. I loved my wife with all my heart. I found her dying and sat with her. A gang came from the house and accused me but I managed to escape and now I have returned to find my wife's murderer and hand him or her to the authorities."

He thought it wise to keep to himself his intention of killing the guilty party when he finally discovered them.

Hugh sat silently, listening. Eventually he spoke. "I believe you and trust you. So it suits us both for you to work here for the time being."

"Indeed it does, Mr. Bellow."

"Well, you can go to the big house straight away, if you like. We deliver eggs, bread and milk there daily. Tell Jacob that I said I'd hand the task over to you."

"But supposing I am recognised?"

"Take a big hat and pull it well down. Nobody will connect you with the respectable young man you must have been. Now go and get the cart loaded up."

It seemed odd, thought John, trotting along Brentford Lane having crossed Bellow Bridge, to be going towards Gunnersbury House once more. His mind went back to his escape, at which

Priscilla had so obviously connived, to say nothing of Irish Tom. What a pitiable creature he had been then, what a sobbing wreck. But he was determined that he would not shed another tear until the sad, sorry business had been brought to its conclusion. For somewhere inside the big house he felt certain that Emilia's killer lurked, unseen, smiling at his – or her – apparent triumph.

"You wait," said John, and realised he had spoken aloud.

To his left, across the lane, lay the kitchen gardens, orchards planted beyond. Everything looked very black and bleak at this time of year. In fact, other than for a rather sorry display of winter cabbages, there was no colour at all. On his right, however, rose the grand columns of Gunnersbury House. Feeling that even from this distance he might be noticed, John pulled the hat down and walked the cart round to the kitchens, where he dismounted.

A kitchen lad came strolling out. "Hello, have you brought the order from the farm?"

"Yes. Sorry I'm a bit late but Mr. Bellow has met with an accident and I've taken over some of his duties."

The boy called over his shoulder. "Sir, come here, if you please. Mr. Bellow has had an accident."

An older man appeared, wiping his hands on a cloth. "What's all this?"

"Mr. Bellow has broken his leg," John answered, handing the man a basket containing four dozen eggs.

"Oh dear. How's that?"

"He was involved in an affray at Brentford yesterday. I'm the new farm hand, by the way. Name of Will. Where would you like your loaves put?"

"On the kitchen table, away from the eyes of the cook. He hates the fact that Princess Amelia prefers Mrs. Bellow's bread to his. A very jealous man, he is."

For the first time since Emilia's murder John entered Gunnersbury House, carrying a big basket, this one containing freshly-baked loaves, wrapped in cloths and still warm. He was

just placing them on the table when he heard a commotion outside the door leading into the house and stopped what he was
doing to look.

A woman flung herself into the opening and started to
harangue the occupants of the kitchen.

"You lazy good-for-nothings. The Princess is upstairs demanding her breakfast and you tell me the bread has not yet arrived."

"It's here, Mam," John muttered, pulling his hat well down.

"And about time too. You know that she likes a couple of fresh
slices with her tea." The woman paused. "Oh, you're not Bellow."

"No, Mam. The master is indisposed. I'm the new help."

The woman drew nearer. "I see. And how long do you expect
Bellow to be laid up?"

"A good month. Fact is, he's broke his leg."

John was putting on a rural drawl, hoping that his voice would
be disguised. From under the brim of his hat, which good manners should have decreed he removed, he studied the woman,
realising with a shock that he knew her. Plain as anything, the little porcine eyes gave it away. He was conversing with Priscilla herself.

"I do hope this doesn't mean we can expect late deliveries?"

"On the contrary, Mam. I shall endeavour to be even earlier
than he was in future."

He was aware of her eyeing him up and down. "Has no one
ever told you that it is polite to remove your hat when entering a
house?"

"No, Mam."

"Well, it is. Pray do so."

Oh God, thought John, she'll recognise me sure as fate. He did
the only thing possible and turned away.

"Would someone give me a hand with the churns? I wouldn't
like to keep the Princess waiting."

And he was out of the door and back at the cart before anybody had time to draw breath. Behind him he heard the woman

say, "Impudent fellow. I shall ask for someone else to come in future," but he was already heaving a churn from the back of the cart and being helped in with it by the kitchen lad.

The woman swept from the kitchen in a flounce of crackling skirts. But not before she had shot John one last searching look over her shoulder. Hoping against hope that Priscilla had not recognised him, the Apothecary busied himself with the churns.

Chapter Thirteen

It was late by the time John Rawlings managed to slip away from the farmhouse, leaving Jacob and his mother snoozing before the fire. Drawing his watch out from a pocket he saw that it was already half-past seven, and he started to run through the silvered night. There was a hard frost, the stars glittering fiercely over his head, the fields covered with white. He spared a thought for the poor cattle, herded together for warmth, and hoped that they would all be alive in the morning. But his principal worry was that Elizabeth would already be by Bellow Bridge and shivering in the icy conditions.

But there was nobody there when he arrived. In fact the lady had obviously not been able to get out as planned. He called her name and walked round the bridge on both sides but there was no answering call and he was just about to head back for the farmhouse when he heard the sound of light footsteps. Imagining it to be the Marchesa he called out softly, "Elizabeth," and heard the feet come to an abrupt halt. Instantly suspicious, John flattened himself behind a tree and only just in time. The moon came out from behind a small cloud and bathed the surroundings in its radiance. And he saw in the moonshine, wrapped in a long fur-trimmed cloak, the hood of which was up but her face showing quite clearly, Lady Georgiana Hope.

"Michael?" she said tentatively.

John made no answer, not certain what to do next.

But he only had a second to wait before he heard another set of running footsteps and a man came into view.

"Sweetheart," the newcomer called, and swept the girl into his arms, kissing her ardently on the mouth.

'Zounds, the Apothecary thought, it can't be Michael O'Callaghan! But it was, quite definitely.

The lovers paused for breath and he heard the Irishman say,

"Oh, darlin', how I've missed you."

"And I you," she answered, and John could not help but smile at the contrast in their accents, Michael's straight from the bogs of Ireland, hers frightfully upper-class English.

"Can we be together soon?" he asked. "You gave me your word, remember."

"Of course I remember. But there is the matter of Conrad to be considered. I must plan my escape to the last detail."

So that would explain her reluctance to be with the tall, dark, sinister man. But who was he? A father, husband perhaps? Her next words gave the answer.

"I hate him, I really do. If only I'd had the power to refuse him. But my father wanted it so much."

"An impoverished peer can be very dangerous," Michael answered as if he had known dozens.

"And when they have marriageable daughters..." Georgiana's voice trailed away.

Michael's delivery assumed the husky timbre that John thought very attractive. "You're going to be short of money with me, my sweet. I'll have nothing to offer you until I become a proper player. There might be a year or two of hardship."

"Oh, my love, I won't want for anything as long as I can be with you. You know that."

How many times have girls thought likewise, the Apothecary considered cynically. Then he thought of the old saying, When hardship comes through the window, love flies out the door, and gave a silent bitter smile.

There was another silence while they exchanged more rapturous kisses. Then, eventually, she said, "Darling, I must go. Conrad is gaming with the Princess but I daren't be absent much longer."

"Oh, sweetheart. Leaving you is like a physical pain."

"Yes."

"I'll walk back as far as the gates with you."

"No, don't. You might be seen."

"Till tomorrow then?"

Georgiana wept a little. "I don't know. It all depends on what Conrad is doing."

"Blast Conrad to a million pieces. Anyway, I'm lodging in Brentford till the end of the week. Then I must return to London. But I'll be here every night until Friday. Whether you come or not."

He spun on his heel, clearly put out, and began to cross the bridge. As John could have predicted Georgiana ran to catch him up.

"Michael, darling, I love you. It's just that I must humour Conrad until we get back to town and put our plan into action. Do you forgive me?"

The beautiful voice took on a thrilling edge. "There's nothing to forgive, my angel. Just try to be here every night."

"I will, oh I will," she responded, and there were more kisses.

Eventually, though, they went their separate ways and John emerged from his hiding place. So he was not the only person keeping himself hidden round the Gunnersbury Park estate. The Irish actor, possibly Emilia's murderer, though he would have had to be quick about it, was also playing a covert game. The Apothecary waited another five minutes in case Elizabeth had been delayed then decided it was too cold and hurried back to Bellow Farm.

Hester was waiting up for him, rather flushed in the cheeks.

"Dr. Rice has been. He would have called sooner but was delayed by an accident. Anyway he said that whoever bound up Hugh's leg was a professional and we should think ourselves lucky to have him on the premises."

"Good." The Apothecary sat down on the chair opposite hers and held out his frozen hands to the blaze.

"Would you like a glass of mulled wine? It's a bitter cold night for going on a walk."

"One of my little foibles, I fear. Yes, I'd love one. Mrs. Bellow...?"

"Yes?"

"Do you think the sheep and cattle will survive this frost? Oughn't they to be in sheds?"

"Yes, they ought. But who's to do it? Jake has gone to bed."

"I will muster them. You can be mulling the wine while I'm gone."

And before she could argue he had stood up, placed a hat on his head, and gone out. Beyond the farm the night was like an ice-filled furnace, millions of stars scintillating over his head, the moon almost full, glittering in the sky like some enormous beacon, momentarily blotted out by a wisp of black lace clouds. John made his way to the field where the sheep and cows stood in a huddle, their stertorous breathing frosting in the freezing air. First he rounded up the sheep – two dozen at the most – and herded them into the big barn. Then he went back for the cows.

Back in the field he felt his eyes drawn to the spot where earlier that day he believed he had seen Emilia walk. Now there was nothing but plunging white, the trees like black skeletons outlined against the pallidity. What had been there? he wondered. Had it really been a phantom or was there some more earthly explanation? Still deliberating, the Apothecary rounded up the small milking herd and led them towards the barn.

The next few days were solid work and John found himself aching in every part of his body. Muscles never used before were being called into play and he was so tired at night that he fell into bed and slept without dreaming, ready to rise in the darkness and milk the cows.

He had not been back to the bridge since that night, nor had he been allowed the privilege of going to the big house with the produce. But today Jacob was going to market in Brentford so John, in company with the farmer's boy, Ben, loaded the second

cart – Jacob having taken the big one – and the Apothecary set off
for the kitchens of Gunnersbury House.

As soon as he entered the gates he slowed his pace, hoping that
he might see something, anything indeed. And today he was
rewarded. For Princess Amelia, in company with her four ladies,
namely Kemp, Featherstonehaugh, Theydon and Hampshire,
were out taking the air. Today the Princess was walking with a
cane and indeed looked pale. John hoped fervently that she
would linger in the country another week before returning to
Curzon Street.

Keeping his eyes fixed firmly on them he did not see the
obstruction in his path and the first warning he had that anything
was wrong was when he heard the wheel splinter. Cursing to
himself he brought the pony to a stop and jumped down.

A large piece of masonry had fallen from the roof and landed
in the drive, ready to catch the first person who rode over it.
Furious, John took the pony by the reins and led it round to the
kitchen. The usual lad appeared.

"Morning, Will." This was the name John had adopted in
order to be safe. "Nice to see you."

"Thank you. Listen, when we've unloaded the produce can
anyone help me mend my wheel? A damnable piece of masonry
has fallen in the driveway and splintered two of the spokes."

"Take it round to the stables. Someone will give you a hand
there."

"Right. By the way, have you seen anything of the new maid?"

The Apothecary put on a knowing look and slowly winked his
eye. The kitchen lad appeared thrilled to be the recipient of such
juicy gossip.

"Do you mean Lizzie? The new rum strum?"

"Aye, that's the one. I tell you straight, I fancy her."

"You're not alone there. Though how she does it with that
great scar on her I'll never know."

"Does what?" asked John, genuinely interested.

"Has all the coves panting after her."

"Oh." The Apothecary felt very slightly annoyed. "I see."

"Anyway, she'll come down to the kitchens soon. She's lit the fires and emptied the slops so it's time she had a break. So meanwhile let's move your produce."

John was bent double beneath a churn when he spied Elizabeth's feet coming towards him. With a gasp he straightened up, placing his burden on the floor beside him.

"Morning, Master Will," she said, giving him a smile that could only be described as impudent.

"Morning, Mistress Lizzie," he answered, scowling.

Elizabeth lowered her voice. "I'm sorry I didn't get to the bridge the other night. I was here gathering information. I did go last night but you weren't there."

John moved into the doorway, indicating that she should do likewise. Looking round to check that nobody could overhear them, he said, "Can you tell me what it is you've observed?"

"Briefly this. Lady Theydon is always murmuring in corners with her companion, Miss Priscilla."

"What do they murmur?"

"That I don't know. But something about their manner makes me suspicious."

"Of what?"

Elizabeth shook her head. "Again, I don't know. All I'm aware of is that they seem unusually close."

"What else?" John asked.

"There's a certain footman here – you may have remarked him – he has a swarthy pock-marked skin..."

"I know who you mean. He arrested me after Emilia's murder."

"Did he by God! Well, his name is Benedict and I swear that he is the paid lackey of someone important."

"Meaning?"

"That he is everywhere at the same time as I am; listening at doors, looking around in chambers when their owners are elsewhere. In short, he does everything that I am trying to do for you."

Suddenly aware that they were being observed, John took one of Elizabeth's hands in his and was shocked by how rough it had become.

At exactly that moment she said, "Your hand is calloused."

"Quiet," he murmured. "We're under scrutiny from the cook. Look loving."

She turned on him a delightful smile and moved a step nearer. "Tonight at the bridge," she whispered.

"Till tonight, darling," John answered loudly, and kissed her hand.

There was a collective 'Ooh' from the kitchen staff during which Elizabeth strutted out with a sway to her hips.

"Looks like she'll pray with knees upwards soon," said somebody.

John ignored them and hefted in the other churn.

With the delivery of goods done there was no further excuse to hang round so he slowly made his way, together with pony and cart, to the stable block, recalling as he did so the night he had escaped. In fact he was miles away when it suddenly became clear from sounds behind him that he was being followed. Glancing over his shoulder John saw that Benedict was strolling along in his wake. Pulling his hat down, praying that the red hair would disguise him sufficiently, John continued on his path.

"Hey fellow," he heard the footman shout.

Turning slowly, John said, "Be you addressing me, good sir?"

"Yes, I am."

"What be you wanting?"

"I wondered why you were going to the stables. What business do you have there?"

"Well, Sir, if you'll bend down you'll see that two spokes of my wheel be broke. It was suggested to me that someone in the stables might be able to help."

Benedict flashed his large and powerful eyes in the wheel's direction. "I think you'd be better off going to the smithy," he answered.

John briefly removed his hat, scratched his bright red curls till they stood on end, replaced the garment, then said, "I don't know that I'd get that far, Sir, without some temporary repair."

Benedict was clearly irritated. "Oh very well, if you insist." He fell into step beside John, something that the Apothecary found uncomfortable. "Are you new to the farm?" he asked. "I don't seem to know your face?"

"Oh yes, Sir. I come to assist Mr. Bellow who has had a fall and broke his leg. He's put me under Mr. Jacob, that's what."

All the time while this conversation had been going on John had kept his face towards the pony's flank. Now, however, he turned and gave Benedict a full stare. There was a flutter, as if the footman thought he knew him. Then John saw it pass.

"And why be you going to the stables, Sir?" the Apothecary asked.

"Mind your own business, my good fellow," retorted the other, and striding past John headed off down the path.

"Bastard," said John under his breath.

From the back the stable block was built to the left of the building, a large block for the carriages, a longer series of loose boxes for the horses. Entering the coach house, John paused and looked round him. There was a smell of hay in the air, coming from the building next door. The Apothecary inhaled its grassy fumes, then looked behind him through the arched doorway. As always on a winter's day the sky was a cloudless blue, a hyacinth shade. Just for a moment he forgot why he was there and exulted in the feel of the sun on his back. Then he remembered and called out, "Hello. Is there anybody here?"

There was no reply and he began to wander to the back of the building, examining the exquisite workmanship of the coaches; the brightness of the bodywork, the doors painted by an artist of the foremost kind. Then he heard a noise in the doorway and turned to see who it was.

A figure stood there, a figure wiping its hands on a cloth and peering into the depths of the building to see who else was present. The sun was directly behind the figure which made it hard to recognise. Yet there was something familiar about the way it stood, about the movement of the head, as bright a red as the Apothecary's own dyed mop.

"Hello," said a voice.

John stood riveted to the spot, then took a step or two forward. Then he started to run.

"Joe," he shouted. "Joe, my friend, is it really you?"

Chapter Fourteen

He continued to shout as he ran towards Joe Jago but was silenced by the clerk clapping a strong and sensible hand over his mouth.

"For Heaven's sake, Sir, keep quiet. Do you want everyone to know who I am?"

John shook his head violently, mouthed, "No," and the hand was eventually removed.

"Joe," he said in a gasping whisper, "is it really you? What are you doing here?"

The clerk looked round cautiously, then motioned John to go to the back of the coach house, meanwhile raising his finger to his lips to indicate utter silence. It dawned on the Apothecary that Sir John's right-hand man was putting himself in the gravest danger for the sake of their long association and he shot him a look of great gratitude.

It was all there, just as he remembered; the rugged profile, the abundant red hair, the light blue eyes with a riverbed of wrinkles round each one. Yet for all that Joe still had an air of youthful determination about him, a fact which his strong lean body bore out.

Having reached the far wall Joe silently indicated that the Apothecary should sit down and, after another few seconds during which he looked round once more, joined him.

"Now keep your voice down, Sir. Walls have ears, especially round this place."

"But Joe, why are you here?"

"I've been employed in the role of hostler, Sir, and you can take that surprised look off your face immediately. Or have you forgotten I've a special way with horses?"

The memory of Joe's handling of equines during the time that the two of them had been in Surrey during the affair of the Valley of Shadows, returned graphically to John's mind.

"No, you are wonderful with them but..."

"Let me tell you the story, Sir. Just you sit quiet and comfortable. All right?"

John nodded.

"When I got back to London I went straight to the Blind Beak and told him that you had fled and that I had missed you."

"Did he believe you?"

Joe laughed gently. "Who's to say, Sir? Maybe he did and, there again, maybe he didn't. It was Christmas, see, and too late for him to act. Anyhow, when the festivities ended he called me into his study and there we had a long chat. The fact is that you are still wanted for arrest."

"Have posters gone up?"

"Yes, indeed they have. Meantime, I asks the Beak straight out if he believed you guilty. He flew up in a mighty palaver, I can tell you. Indeed not, Jago, he said very firmly. That young fellow is incapable of taking a life. If it were not for the fact that Princess Amelia virtually ordered his arrest I would be looking elsewhere for the killer. It was then, Mr. Rawlings, that we came up with the plan."

"Which was?"

"Well, Sir, you know that the Runners sometimes adopt ordinary guise when they attend Ridottos and so on."

"Yes."

"Well it came to me in a flash that I should go undercover, as it were. We had connections with the stables here and persuaded one of the hostlers to leave, temporary like, to give me the opportunity to apply for the post. So during the time when I would have been on holiday – a time that the Beak detests I need hardly add – I was duly given the job and here I am. But what of you, Sir? Did you get to Devon?"

John nodded. "I did indeed. But how could I rest easy knowing that Emilia's murderer was still at large? I came back and have been fortunate enough to get work at Bellow's Farm."

"And what of Lady Elizabeth, Sir?"

With those brilliant blue eyes fixed so firmly on him, John, for no good reason, felt slightly uncomfortable.

"She came with me and has got a job as a servant's servant, if you understand me. In other words, she does the most menial tasks."

"But surely someone of her breeding must find that abhorrent."

"I expect she does but she does not grumble. The Marchesa is a very strong woman, Joe."

"I'm sure she must be." Joe's eyes suddenly became alert. "Someone's coming," he murmured. "Remember, you don't know me nor I you. Let's take a look at that wheel of yours, young man," he added in full voice.

"Yes, it was unfortunate the way those spokes split. But someone ought to be looking at the roof. It must be in a bad state for masonry to fall like that."

"Yes, indeed, Mr... What did you say your name was?"

"I'm Will Miller," and John held out his hand.

Joe shook it enthusiastically. "Pleased to meet you."

All the time they had been conversing they had been making their way to the door of the coach house and now they saw Benedict, standing motionless and watching them.

"And how may I help you?" Joe asked pleasantly.

"By getting on with your work, that's how. You're not paid to stand here gossiping with every farm hand who comes asking."

"And what might you be doing here, Mr. Benedict, if I might enquire?"

"I've come with a message from Lord Hope. You can saddle up the mare for Lady Georgiana. She feels like riding."

Joe's blue eyes took on a hard aspect. "I'll just take a look at this person's wheel then I'll prepare a suitable mount for her ladyship."

"This person doesn't really matter in the scheme of things. I suggest he makes his way back to Bellow's as best he can. They can repair it there."

"I doubt he'd get that far," Joe replied, still in the same pleasant tone. And with that he marched out of the coach house and up to John's cart.

Ten minutes later it was done. The two broken spokes had been bound round with wire, strong enough at least to get him back to the farm without mishap. Thanking Joe and bidding him a cheery farewell, the Apothecary jumped into the cart and picked up the reins. But he had plodded no more than two hundred yards up the drive when a very familiar figure stepped into his path and imperiously waved him down. Unwillingly, the Apothecary brought the pony to a halt.

"Have you made your delivery?" Priscilla Fleming asked.

"Yes, Mam," John answered, pulling his hat as low as it would go.

She peered at him. "I've seen you before somewhere. What did you say your name was?"

"Will Miller, Mam. Will that be all?"

"No, it won't. There's a stone in my shoe. Pray assist me to get it out."

John gaped at her, affronted by her peremptory manner yet powerless to resist. Then slowly, unwillingly, he clambered out of the cart.

She leant back against the wheel and held her right foot aloft, gazing down at the Apothecary who crouched before her.

"Go on, remove my shoe."

He did so and saw that there was indeed a small pebble inside. Turning the shoe upside down, he shook the obstruction out. He raised his head to look at Priscilla and at that moment she snatched off his hat, then gazed at him, wonderment surfacing in her eyes.

"John," she breathed. "John Rawlings. So you've come back. I thought you would."

"Priscilla," he answered in an undertone, "for the love of God keep your voice down. I am here under false pretences, as you know. It is imperative that nobody is aware of my true identity."

Her cheeks flushed rosily and her eyes grew wide, making her look suddenly rather pretty.

"I thought I recognised you the other day in the kitchens," she whispered, "but you played your part so well that I wasn't sure. Oh my dear, tell me everything."

"This is too public a place. Where can we be private?"

"Meet me tonight in The Temple."

John shook his head. "Where is that?"

"To the west of the house. It lies beside the Round Pond. Come at nine o'clock. Enter from Brentford Lane and turn right. I'll be waiting for you." She raised her voice and said theatrically, "Thank you my good man." And with that set off down the drive with her nose in the air.

John's thoughts rushed. If she had seen through his disguise then might not somebody else? Perhaps he should alter himself further. But eventually he gave up the idea. Dyed red hair and a slouch hat would have to suffice. He must be as discreet as possible, that was as much as he could manage.

For the rest of that day he was frantically busy. Jacob returned from market in an inexplicably bad mood and gave him a million tasks with which to occupy himself. The Apothecary set about them with a will, knowing that it would make the time pass quickly. And, sure enough, when he next looked up it was dark and time to go in to dine.

He clomped into the kitchen, and, having washed, made his way upstairs to see Hugh Bellow. He found the invalid sitting comfortably in bed, reading a newspaper. He looked at John over the rim of his spectacles.

"There's appeal for anyone with any information regarding the recent murder at Gunnersbury Park to contact Sir John Fielding at his house in Bow Street."

John sat down on the edge of the bed. "Is there now."

"Yes. Tell me, young man, do you have any suspects yet?"

"I suspect everyone and no one, if you follow me. But, Sir, I beg you not to reveal my secret to anyone." John paused, then said directly, "Not even your son."

Hugh shot him a look. "I take it you two don't get along?"

"Shall we just say that I find him fractionally forbidding."

The farmer chuckled. "He's not the easiest of people, I admit. But under all his gruffness he has a heart of gold. Once you're his friend, that is."

"Well, he and I seem to have got off on the wrong foot. But I promise to try harder."

Hugh nodded fiercely. "It's time I was back in control. How long before I can walk again?"

"As soon as I can fashion some kind of crutch for you, you can try. I'll find time tomorow."

"You most certainly will. I'm still the gaffer here and I'll tell Jacob that's what you'll be doing."

John stood up. "Very good, Mr. Bellow. But don't get me into any trouble, will you."

"I'll do my best to soothe the miserable young brute."

Not feeling too confident John went down the stairs, the smell of Hester's cooking wafting in his nostrils.

Jacob did not say a word throughout the meal, gulping his food as quickly as possible. He also consumed several pints of home-brewed ale, wiping his mouth with the back of his hand and belching loudly at the finish. Then he stood up.

"I'm going to Brentford," he announced.

The other two looked at him in surprise.

"But you were there this morning," Hester said.

"Well, I'm going again. I've some business to conclude."

"Wrap up well," John remarked, "it's going to be another freezing night."

"When I want your advice I'll ask for it," Jacob answered nastily, and slammed out of the kitchen.

Hester looked at John with a sad smile. "And I suppose you'll be off on your nightly perambulation, Will."

"I haven't been for the last two so I really must go tonight."

"Do you meet anybody?" Hester asked with a flash of perception.

"Sometimes I do and sometimes I don't," John answered truthfully.

As he left the house he saw Jacob mounting the smaller cart. He ran forward to tell him that the wheel spokes were only tied with wire and that it would be dangerous to take out. But as he saw John approach, Jacob cracked the whip over the pony's flanks and was off too fast for the Apothecary to catch him up.

"Serve you right, you silly sockhead," John shouted after him, but his voice echoed emptily in the frosty night.

This time Elizabeth arrived at the same time as he did, wearing only a shawl to protect her against the cold.

"My dear girl, you'll freeze." And the Apothecary took off his greatcoat and wrapped it round her.

She gave him a look of gratitude mixed with another emotion which he found it hard to interpret. But when he glanced again the underlying look had gone and he thought it must be his imagination.

"Elizabeth," he said, drawing her beneath the little bridge so that they might talk privately. "How are you? Is the work proving too much for you?"

"I detest it," she answered forthrightly, "but I'll continue as long as I'm useful."

"Apparently you have caused a stir amongst the men, that is according to the kitchen boy."

"I need everyone as an ally if I am going to find things out," she answered, a fraction sharply.

"Of course," John said soothingly.

There was a silence, then he said, "Well, I personally am no further forward but at least we now have a friend at court, literally."

"What do you mean?"

"Joe Jago is here." And very quietly he told her of the development that today had brought.

"And what of Miss Fleming?" Elizabeth asked. "I saw you talking to her in the driveway."

John hesitated momentarily, then said, "Alas, she recognised me, red hair or no."

Elizabeth gave a slightly sardonic laugh. "Well, she knew you better than the others, did she not?"

The Apothecary felt strangely comforted by this remark. Indeed, the more he thought about it the more likely it seemed that this was why Priscilla had known him so readily.

"You're quite right, of course. Miss Fleming had met me several times before."

Elizabeth twisted round to look at him, her skirt slithering a little on the icy grass. "Did you not tell me that she used to come to your shop to fetch some of the Princess's medicines."

"Yes, she did."

"Well, there you are then." She gave him a very direct glance. "John, do you think I am helping you? Am I finding out any information at all?"

"Of course you are. It may seem as if nothing is happening but everything you discover adds up to form a picture."

"But there is no picture," Elizabeth said firmly. "You have no more idea of who killed Emilia than when you first came here."

John was silent, considering this statement. But what the Marchesa said was true enough. He was no further forward. Indeed had it not been for the advent of Joe Jago he would have given the situation up as hopeless.

"You're right," he said, with a catch in his voice. "I have no idea who murdered my wife and quite honestly I don't see how I am going to find out."

"If only you could consult with Sir John Fielding."

"That is out of the question. I should be arrested at once. But Elizabeth –"

"Yes?"

"You must act with Joe Jago on my behalf. Make an excuse to visit him daily, in secret if necessary. Then report back to me everything that he has to say."

"You know I will."

"Good girl."

He took hold of her arms and just for a moment she was very close to him and they stood clasped together. Cruel memories of Emilia came, so cruel that he drew in breath audibly. Elizabeth stared at him without speaking then slowly withdrew from his grasp and started to walk back to Gunnersbury House. John, without speaking, fell into step beside her.

"You're going the wrong way," she whispered.

"No, I forgot to tell you that I am meeting Priscilla in The Temple at nine o'clock."

"You're going to be early."

"I'll use the time looking around."

"Don't get caught. Be careful."

"I will."

They parted at the gates, she going off to the left of the house, John slinking through the shrubbery and woodlands that lay to the right.

It was pitch dark, the moon obscured by passing clouds. The Apothecary, walking through the trees, felt a frisson of fear. Somewhere, lurking round this house and grounds, was a maniac killer handy with a knife. And pointless as Emilia's murder had been, so this killer obviously struck at random. Unless, of course, he had been aiming for Priscilla all along.

John recalled an earlier conversation he had had with her. A conversation during which she had as good as told him that there were people determined to cause her death. Now he was determined to get at the truth. Make her elaborate on that theme and name them. Then he suddenly stopped short, struck to the heart by the sight before him.

The moon had just come out and was lighting a sheet of blue water that sparkled beneath her beams. In this strange half-light the landscape was transformed and he gazed at The Temple almost with longing, as perfect and beautiful a building as he had ever seen. Standing beside the Round Pond, it threw a deep shadow of mauve onto the artificial lake, which rippled deep and mysterious beneath its shade. Slowly, moving silently, John made his way towards the folly.

The building was rectangular, built on classical lines with four Doric columns topped by a white wooden pediment decorated with ox skulls and garlands. In the middle of these columns stood a front door, open.

"Priscilla," John called in a whisper.

There was no reply.

Despite himself, he heard his breathing speed up and grow laboured. Desperately trying to keep calm, the Apothecary crept towards the door.

A pit of darkness lay within and John stood in the entrance motionless, waiting for his eyes to adjust. Then the moon, which had vanished again, re-emerged and threw a silvery beam inside.

A grinning faun playing a pipe leered at him and John, startled, took a step back. Then he saw orange trees, a model swan serene and calm, and realised that these were merely decorations, things which would look quite normal to the gaze in daylight. But of Priscilla Fleming there was no sign.

He called her name softly once more and then a hand wrapped itself round his ankle. Fighting like a lunatic to get free, the Apothecary looked down at his feet and there, lying utterly still, was the girl he had arranged to meet. It would appear that she was quite, quite dead.

Chapter Fifteen

The Apothecary froze, momentarily unable to grasp what he was looking at. Then the moon came out in full and he was able to see that Priscilla lay motionless on the floor, apparently devoid of life. Yet there was no visible sign of blood, nor, indeed, of a struggle. Released from his catalepsy, John squatted down, feeling for a pulse, and to his enormous relief found one. Fishing deep in the pocket of his greatcoat he retrieved his bottle of salts and held it beneath her nose. Priscilla gave a gulp and her eyelids flickered, then opened.

She stared at John blankly, then he saw fear come into her eyes. She moved as if to crawl away from him.

"Let me go, you blackguard," she shouted.

"Priscilla, be calm. It's John Rawlings. We arranged to meet here, do you remember?"

The moon went in at this moment and all he could see was a wriggling dark shape which suddenly grew still.

"Oh John, is it really you?" she asked huskily. "I thought it was my attacker."

"Yes, it's me. But Priscilla, what happened?"

In the darkness he saw that she was trying to rise to her feet and went to help her, holding her under her arms and steadying her as she clambered up. A faint smell filled his nostrils, rather sickly and cloying.

"Oh John, John," she sobbed, "It was terrible. I was waiting here for you, standing alone in the darkness. Then a man came through the door. I thought it was you and rushed to meet you – him. Then he put his hands round my throat and squeezed hard until I lost consciousness. You must have disturbed him. For where is here now?"

"Nobody rushed past me. Oh God's life, perhaps he's still here."

For answer Priscilla screamed loudly, a sound which made John jump out of his skin.

"I'll have a look," he said, motioning her to be quiet.

"I'll come with you. I'd feel safer than left here on my own."

Beside the front door John had noticed a spiral staircase. Now, treading carefully, he and Priscilla made their way to the attic above. Because of the darkness, probably because of being afraid, she clutched his hand in hers, holding it tightly.

"Who's there?" he whispered, peering into the attic's gloomy depths.

There was no reply and nothing moved in the blackness. Then the fitful moon came out once more and he could see that other than for one or two pieces of old furniture covered in white cloths, the attic was empty.

"What about the cellar?" he said.

"We'd best go and see," Priscilla answered fearfully.

They crept back down the spiral which linked the three parts of the building, descending into the dankly dark basement. But yet again there was no one there. Whoever had attacked Priscilla had either made his escape before the Apothecary arrived at The Temple, or had crept out while they were searching the attic.

"He isn't here," said John, as they returned to the front door.

"Perhaps he thought I was dead and his task was done."

"Probably. Anyway, let me have a look at your throat."

They had left the folly and were standing outside by the magic blue of the Round Pond. The clouds which had been teasing the moon had finally scudded away and Priscilla was clearly visible in its brightness.

"Please do," she answered, and loosened her cloak at the neck.

Maybe it was the uncertain light and maybe his eyes weren't as sharp as they used to be but the Apothecary could only see scant bruising. It looked as if whoever had attacked her had been disturbed and had fled from the place before the Apothecary had even appeared. The girl, however, was still weakened by her tribulation and clung to John as they walked back to the house together.

"You've just saved my life," she whispered.

"Hardly that," he answered truthfully.

"No, but you did. Listen, I've got an idea as to where we could meet regularly."

"Yes."

"In the grounds there are some ruins. Nobody ever goes there after dark. I'm sure it would be excellent for a rendezvous."

"But Priscilla, I really want access to the house. But how the devil can I get in without being recognised. I truly need to see people, talk to them even. But the minute they set eyes on me they will know who I am."

"I doubt it. The last time they saw you you were dressed very fine, talked well, wore a wig. Now you've got your own hair, dyed red, wear rough clothes and speak with a rural voice. They might think you were similar to the man they met once but I do not think any of them will connect the two."

"Then can you smuggle me in?"

Priscilla leant close to him and again that overpowering smell filled the air. "Yes, why not? Come on, let's start now. I'll tell how I was attacked, and introduce you to Lady Theydon as a man who rushed in and saved me as he was passing by The Temple."

"Doing what?"

"Heaven knows. Checking for poachers."

"Poachers?"

"We could say you're some sort of gardener. Will that fit the bill?"

"It will have to. Come on. Let's do it."

They had drawn near to the house while they spoke and now Priscilla entered through a door in the side of the building. This led into a small hall with a curving staircase directly ahead. Following her beckoning hand the Apothecary climbed this and found himself on a landing off which led several doors. Going to one, Priscilla knocked quietly.

"Come in," said a plummy voice.

Following Miss Fleming, John stepped inside and stood, head bowed, waiting to see what would happen next.

"My dear," continued the voice, obviously coming from someone resting supine, "you look distraught. What troubles you?"

"Oh Lady Theydon, I have been attacked."

"Attacked? How can this be? It wouldn't happen in a truly great house I can tell you. What would my husband say, I tremble to think indeed. Where did it take place?"

"In The Temple."

"No, you foolish child, I meant on what part of your anatomy."

"My throat. The villain strangled me and I think I would have been dead were it not for being rescued by..." She hesitated. "Will, the gardener."

There was a swishing sound as Lady Theydon sat up straight. "'Zounds, child, let me see."

John allowed himself a glance upwards and saw that Milady had thrust Priscilla into a chair and was busily examining her neck, her great mournful dark eyes rolling in her head as she did so.

"Oh my God, t'is enough to drive one to an early grave. Tell me exactly what happened."

"I thought I would take a turn round the gardens before I retired. I was walking round the Round Pond and sheltered momentarily in The Temple. The next thing I knew was that a man came through the door and throttled me. I lost consciousness and was revived by Will, who heard my cries and came to my aid."

This last was a gross distortion of the truth but was as good a version of events as any.

"Heaven be praised." Lady Theydon turned her gaze in his direction, raising her quizzer, which hung around her neck on a chain. "Step forward, my good man," she said in a voice reserved for addressing the lower orders.

Reluctantly John did so, standing in what he hoped was a gardener pose, shuffling his feet and desperately trying to look out of place.

"Did you see anyone, fellow?" Lady Theydon's glutinous voice continued.

"No, Mam," he answered, his accent richly bucolic, "I just heard Miss Priscilla crying out and ran to her aid, like. Nobody come past me."

"Do you think that lunatic man – the one that Sir John Fielding has dismally failed to catch – can be on the loose again?"

"I don't know, my Lady," Priscilla answered nervously. "Why should it be him?"

"Why shouldn't it be?" Lady Theydon said with heat. "I think I had better report this matter to the Princess."

"Oh no, Ma'am, I beg you not. She has been so ill and news of this might make her worse. It was probably totally unrelated to that other most unfortunate incident."

"Incident?" exclaimed Lady Theydon in high dudgeon. "You call that foul murder an incident? I tell you I can't sleep easy in my bed with that madman still at large."

Priscilla giggled nervously and John cleared his throat.

"But I do take your point about the poor Princess. Let us say nothing at present." She turned her full attention on John, who, at that moment, wished that the floor would open up and deposit him by the side door through which he had entered.

"You say you saw no one?"

"No, Mam," he mumbled.

"Well, you're to keep a look out, d'ye hear. Note any suspicious characters hanging round the place. You are to particularly look out for a well set-up young fellow who dresses above his station. Says he's an apothecary and therefore will have medical knowledge. Keep your eyes open. Do you understand?"

"Yes, Mam."

"Very well, you may go. Priscilla, you are to go straight to bed."

"Yes, Lady Theydon."

She curtseyed and John gave an oafish bow. Then they left the room, he heading for the stairs, she to a door along the passage-way.

"This is my bedroom if you want me," she whispered.

John looked at her, wondering if she realised what she had just said. But Priscilla did no more than give him a blown kiss before she vanished into the room.

The Apothecary stood hesitating, debating whether to snoop round and see who else might be about. But the decision was taken from him by the side door opening once more and Lady Hampshire appearing with a young man in tow. She looked round surreptitiously and put her finger to her lips, motioning him to be quiet. Their very attitude told John that they were up to no good and he flattened himself behind a pillar.

"Come on, lovely boy," said the woman. "Come along."

"You can be assured I will," answered the youth, who was twenty-five at the most and clearly hoping for the best.

"My chamber lies in the west wing but this entrance is the one used for little secrets," Lady Hampshire said gushingly.

"Madam, I can scarce control myself," answered her lover, and planted a kiss on her rather unpleasant little mouth.

In his place of hiding John winced.

"No, indeed I cannot," the young man continued, and plunged a hand straight down the bosom of her gown.

"How forward," she said, tapping him with her fan and clearly adoring every minute.

"Shall I take you here, on the stairs?"

"No, indeed not, Sir. Let us be private at all costs. Now hurry along, do." And removing his hand – quite slowly, John noticed – she scuttled along a bend in the corridor, her gallant in hot pursuit, and vanished from view. The Apothecary, sighing, went down the stairs and out into the chilly night.

* * *

It was as he reached the little wooden structure that bore the name Bellow Bridge that John saw the cart lying on its side, half-immersed in the fast-flowing stream. So it had presumably got as far as Brentford and collapsed on the return journey, judging by its position, which was facing towards the farm rather than away.

"Jacob?" he called tentatively.

A loud groan was the only reply.

Cursing his luck, the Apothecary strode into the icy water and peered into the depths of the vehicle. Jacob, clearly the worse for drink, had hit his head, which was bleeding profusely, and was lying in a heap on the cart's tipped up floor.

"I tried to warn you," John said, but got no reply other than for the vague swinging of a feeble fist in his direction.

"I've a bloody good mind to leave you to it," he continued, but his training was too strong and he clambered into the cart and attempted to lift the drunken man free. But Jacob, at dead weight, was heavier than he looked. Try as he might the Apothecary could not shift him. He had to satisfy himself with cleaning the head wound and binding it with a bit of cloth torn from Jacob's shirt. Then he left him, sleeping in an upright position and covered with an old blanket. The pony, frightened and shivering with cold, standing in the stream as it was, John unhitched and led back to the farm where it was put in its stable and given some hay.

The clock struck eleven as he entered the door and tiptoed up to his room. Undressing quickly, the Apothecary got into bed but for some reason did not sleep as soon as his head hit the pillow. Instead he was vaguely aware that something was worrying him but had no tangible idea what it was. Eventually he did sleep, only to have dreams and to wake again, feeling uneasy and sad, in the terrible blackness of the hour before dawn.

* * *

As soon as it was light, he rose and crept from the house. Going back to the scene of the accident he saw that Jacob still slept, though not as deeply as he had on the previous night. Filling the bucket he had brought with him with icy water from the brook, John, with a great deal of satisfaction, emptied it over Jacob's head.

"What? Bastard! God amighty..."

"You can stop that," said John forcefully. "I ran after you yesterday to tell you the cart had a damaged wheel but off you sped to Brentford. You've no one to blame but yourself."

"You miserable little..." Jake began, attempting to get to his feet but falling over as he hadn't taken into account the cart's list.

"Mind your head, for God's sake," the Apothecary continued. "You've a hell of a bump on it. Now do you want me to help you or not?"

"Not," Jake retorted. "I can manage on my own."

And he did, scrabbling to his feet, balancing precariously on the vehicle's tipping floor, eventually heaving himself out and landing waist deep in the brook's icy waters. John stood on the bank, arms folded, as Jake, cursing and swearing like a seaman, heaved himself out and up the side.

The farmer's son reached the top and stood glaring at him ferociously. "I saw something interesting in Brentford last night," he said.

With a sinking of his heart John knew what it was. The Wanted posters had reached the towns beyond the capital.

"Oh? And what was that?" he asked, keeping his voice casual.

"It was a Wanted poster. It had on it a description of a man who sounded just like you. I copied it down." He drew a soggy piece of paper from his pocket.

"Go on."

Laboriously, Jake started to read. "Wanted, John Rawlings.

One yard, two feet and seven inches high. An apothecary by trade. Wanted for the murder of his wife at Gunnersbury House last Christmas. A reward of One Guinea is offered for information leading to his arrest." He laughed raucously. "That's you, isn't it, William Miller?"

"Yes," said John evenly. "What are you going to do about it."

Jacob looked decidedly crafty. "Well now, that depends."

"If you're thinking of blackmailing me you can forget it. I'd rather give myself up. If you're thinking of telling your father, I have already done so. Don't forget, my dear Sir, that you are going to be horribly short-handed without my services."

"Farm labourers are easy to hire," Jacob retorted.

"That's as may be. But where are you going to find one who will tend Mr. Bellow so closely as I do? Besides, what do you stand to gain by betraying me?"

"A guinea, that's what."

"Come back to the farm and we'll discuss it," John replied calmly, and set off down the track.

Behind him he could hear the farmer's son groaning as he walked and guessed that he had a head like a bear in a pit. He turned and grinned.

"I pity you, Jacob, I truly do."

"I'll give you pity, you little turd."

They reached the farmhouse and there John went straight up the stairs to where Hugh Bellow lay in bed. Swiftly the Apothecary made the room decent, removing the chamber pot and finding Hugh a crisp pillow before the sound of Jacob making his way upwards could be heard.

John turned to the farmer. "Sir, your son has seen a Wanted poster offering one guinea for information leading to my arrest. I offer now to leave this house and not bother you again but I beg you to restrain him for a day."

Hugh's jaw dropped. "What's all this, Jake?"

"Nothing that need concern you," he mumbled.

The farmer sat up in bed. "Right from the start Mr. Rawlings dealt straight with me. Admittedly it was him who was found with his wife's body but he told me he didn't kill her and that he's come back to find who did. Stands to reason; why else would he return to be so dangerously close? If he was the killer he'd be at the other end of the country by now."

The truth of this obviously struck some kind of chord and Jacob nodded his damaged head slowly.

"So if you betrays him you'll get the rough end of my belt, by God you will."

Jake looked ugly but said nothing and John thought he ought to try and lighten the atmosphere.

"Look, I'll leave. But give me a few hours start."

"You're not leaving," Hugh stated ferociously. "Even with a crutch – which you promised to rig for me today – I'm going to be useless round the farm for some time to come. You can't walk out on me now, John."

Jacob looked at his father meaningfully. "If he's going to make you a crutch he'll be no good to help me rescue the cart." And with that he slung out of the room.

Hugh looked at the Apothecary. "He won't betray you. I'll flay his hide."

"Thank you, Sir. I hope you're right."

But as John followed Jake down the stairs he had the definite feeling that all was not well.

Chapter Sixteen

Later that day, an answer came to the letter he had written to Sir Gabriel Kent. Fortunately John, who was searching for a suitable bit of wood from which make the crutch, saw the postboy turn down the track leading from the bridge and intercepted him. So he was able to creep round the back of the woodshed and read the correspondence in peace.

My Dear Son,

How Pleased I am that You have found Employment so near Gunnersbury House. I also Note that Others of Your Acquaintance are Near to You. I will not Put Their Names for fear this could Fall into the Wrong Hands. Your Daughter blooms like the Rose after which She is Named and seems Happy with Her Grandfather, though She often asks After both Her Parents. I Have said Nothing of the Truth to Her. I Leave this to You when You Return.

I remain, My Dear John,

Yr. Loving Father,

G. Kent

Post Script. I hear Tell that Jocasta and S. Swann have been Safely Delivered of a Son.

John read the letter several times, then he hid it in a pocket of his coat and continued to fashion the crutch. An hour later it was done and he spent the rest of that day teaching Hugh how to use it, concluding eventually that the farmer would be better off with a second one to aid his sense of balance.

By the time he had made this it was growing dark and John realised that today he had seen no one at Gunnersbury House, Jacob deciding that the farmer's boy should take the deliveries that morning. John, therefore, planned to make his way there after he had eaten and try to track down Joe Jago. So as soon as he had dined, he put on his greatcoat and went out.

He had found time to rebandage Jake's head, despite the voluble protests of the farmer's son.

"I don't need no help. Go away."

"As you put it so nicely, I will. But I'll send a note to the physician that he's needed at Bellow's Farm urgently. Take your choice."

He had started to walk away but Jacob had called him back.

"Will, you may as well have a look. I don't want no old doctor fiddling about with me."

The cut was deep, a horrible gash that should really have been stitched. The Apothecary bathed it clean, rubbed in an infusion of the boiled leaves of Adder's Tongue which he had carried in his medical bag, and rebound it with clean bandage.

"I'll have to examine you daily for a week or so?"

"All right," Jacob had said. And John thought that that was the nearest he had ever come to being pleasant.

He wondered, now, as he set off up the track towards the bridge, whether Jake was going to the Brentford constable about him. Perhaps he would in secret, John thought. Whatever, there was no point in worrying about it. He had far greater matters on his mind, the first and foremost of which was to find Emilia's killer.

He ran through the possibilities in his head. It could have been almost anyone in the cast of the masque or in the audience, with the exception of Princess Amelia. But why except her? Just because she had royal blood in her veins did not exempt her from wrongdoing. He thought back. Where had the others been? But try as he might he could not remember. Everyone had been present during the performance, of course, but afterwards it had been a mêlée, a great rainbow of people moving from place to place.

Much as it hurt him, John forced himself to think of the last time he had seen Emilia alive. He had looked out of the window and seen a figure in a red cloak moving swiftly amongst the dark trees. At the time he had thought it was Priscilla but that notion was soon to be shattered. The only person who had remained in the room while he had watched her was the unpleasant pock-marked footman, Benedict. He, at least, could be cleared.

It was as he was walking over the bridge and starting towards the house, that he heard footsteps and automatically froze behind a tree. To his amazement he saw that it was Lady Theydon and Michael O'Callaghan, a couple he would not have placed together if he had been asked for an opinion.

"...but Michael, I have already loaned you five pounds," the woman was saying.

"But fairest lady, I have spent that on living in Brentford. And now I must return to London with empty pockets."

"The answer is no."

"But, dear sweet..."

"Enough of your silvered tongue. I have listened to it too well and too often. You must make your own way in future."

The voice took on the husky timbre that John so admired. "I swear to you by all that's holy that I will pay you back every last penny piece, so help me God."

"You have lived like a lordling. How else could you have squandered so much. I know what you're up to, Michael. You want to win the heart of Georgiana and you are showering her with frills and furbelows. Well, she's a married woman, my dear. And a married woman she will stay."

"Not while there's breath in my body. I swear I'll have her."

"And what of Lord Hope. Do you think he is conveniently going to vanish in the night?"

"No, but Georgiana and I have plans."

"Which are?"

The beautiful Irish voice dropped an octave. "Now that would be telling, my lady. Suffice it to say that our future is mapped out."

She became excessively glutinous. "Well, I think you both very foolish. I want to have nothing further to do with the matter. And you can't have any more money. Good evening to you, Sir."

She had hardly got out of earshot when Michael started to curse volubly. "Oh, be Jasus, t'is a miserable old bitch, so t'is."

John stepped out of his hiding place. "Good evening to you, Sir."

The actor jumped. "Oh, I didn't see you there. Good evening. Do I know you?"

John took a chance and said, "No, Sir, though I've seen you around."

"Have you? That's odd, for it's staying in Brentford I am."

"Ah," John answered, sounding as rural as possible, "I've seen you of a night with a beauteous lady, here by the bridge."

Michael turned a glittering stare on him. "Oh, a peeping Tom are you?"

John bowed, tugging at his forelock. "Oh no, Sir, not I. I just be about farm business, checking on the stock and so on. I couldn't help but notice her because she's so extremely fair."

The Irishman relaxed. "Aye, she's that and more. Have you ever been in love, my man?"

"Yes, I have. Very much so," the Apothecary answered quietly.

"What happened?"

"She died," John answered bitterly.

For answer his arms were pinioned behind his back and the hat was knocked from his head with one deft blow.

"I thought it was you, so I did. Though I'll admit you had me guessing for a moment. By God, I've got the wanted man. Why the devil did you come back?"

"To find Emilia's murderer and to kill him," John answered baldly.

"So you're maintaining your innocence?"

"Of course I'm innocent. Why the hell should I kill the woman I was in love with? She was a good wife and a good mother, further she was expecting our second child. Logic alone should prove me free of guilt."

Michael gave him a knowing stare. "As a matter of fact, dear boy, I never thought you had done it. Oh, I know it looked bad, you covered in blood and holding the knife and all. But judging by our past relationship I had always thought you blameless."

"Well you were right."

"The Irish instinct." The actor looked round. "It's cold. Would it be safe, do you reckon, for you to step out to Brentford and have a drink with me?"

"I should imagine so. But how will I get there?"

"I've a conveyance waiting for me at the other side of the bridge. If you'd be kind enough to share it I've a mind to hear your side of the story."

They crossed the wooden footbridge and there, sure enough, was a man with a cart.

"Not exactly a hackney but the best that the village had to offer," said the Irishman with a grin.

They sat opposite one another, saying little, until the cart rolled into The Butts and finally came to a halt outside The Red Lion. John looked round for a Wanted poster but failed to see one.

"I'm staying here," Michael O'Callaghan announced grandly, and led the way in.

It was obvious from the greeting he received that he had already talked his way into the good books of most of the regulars. So much so that having exchanged greetings he and John were given a fairly private place at a table.

"Now," said the Irishman, downing a glass of wine in a swallow, "tell me everything."

This John proceeded to do, leaving out no detail, even relating the story of Hugh Bellow's accident at the fair.

"You were lucky to get that job."

"Yes, I was. Though I must admit that I've never worked so hard in all my life. But what worries me, Michael, is the fact that I can't get into the house – well, hardly at all. For how in heaven's name am I going to catch the killer, stranded, as I am, at a distance?"

The actor sat silently, withdrawing a pipe from his pocket, lighting it and puffing. "Have you thought of a disguise?" he asked eventually.

"Well, I've dyed my hair."

"Yes, but that alone is not enough. It's your eyes that give you away. If you could hide those somehow."

"Perhaps I should wear a black bandage like the Blind Beak."

Michael removed the pipe and pointed the stem at John. "Wait, that's given me an idea. How about an eye-patch and a limp? Could you not be a veteran of the recent war? Then all you need is for someone to introduce you into the Princess's court and, by Jasus, you're away."

Priscilla, John thought. She'd be willing to present him as a friend.

"Would I have to increase my age at all?" he asked.

"No, you could have been wounded young as old."

The Apothecary sat silently for a few minutes, toying with his wine glass. The he said, "I'll do it, by God."

"And what about the Bellows, father and son?"

"I'll ask them for a few days leave."

"And if they refuse?"

"Then I'll have to rethink. I really can't leave them in the lurch at a time like this. Just pray they'll see fit to release me."

The Irishman shuffled in his seat then leant forward confidentially. "As a matter of fact I grew up on a farm."

"Oh yes?" said John, feeling he knew where this was leading.

"Yes, till it failed. Anyway, I wouldn't mind a week's work. Fact of the matter is I've enough to pay my bill here then I'm clean out of money. I could do with a few shillings in my purse. What do you say? Will you ask them if I can have your job?"

"You would rather do that than return to London and acting?"

Michael O'Callaghan sighed. "Until my sweet girl goes back to town, I'd rather be here; however menial the task."

He said this with full theatrical weight and the Apothecary laughed aloud. "Right. Come to the farm tomorrow morning. I'll put it to Hugh Bellow."

"You're a gentleman, Sir."

"Quite so," John answered, and laughed again.

At first light the Apothecary rose and went to milk the cows. Then he let them out into the field. As ever his eyes were drawn to the spot where he had seen Emilia – or someone very like her – walk across his line of vision. But there was no one there and though he stood staring for several minutes, nothing happened, and he turned back towards the farm. It was at that moment John saw a familiar figure carrying a bag of luggage come striding down the track, and he waved with enthusiasm. Michael O'Callaghan had kept his part of the bargain and was arriving at Bellow's Farm bright and early.

Seating the actor in the kitchen John hurried up the stairs to sort out Hugh, and was astonished to find him hobbling round the room on his crutches.

"Well, Sir, this is a surprise."

"I thought the worse that could happen would be that I fell over."

"Indeed. Sir, I want to ask you a favour."

And John explained, only leaving out the manner of his disguise and the fact that Michael O'Callaghan was an actor, a profession much mistrusted by country folk.

"And you really think this week will be sufficent for you to discover who committed the crime."

"It has to be, Sir. After that I believe the Princess will recover fully and pack up and return to London for the rest of the season."

"You're probably right. It is very rare for her to be here at this time of year."

An hour later it was done and Hugh had shaken hands with Michael O'Callaghan. John had stowed his few belongings and in company with the farmer's boy was off to the big house with the day's produce. But instead of going to the kitchens he was dropped off in the drive, close to the stables, and went in search of Joe Jago. He found his old friend grooming a big chestnut stallion.

"Good morning, Joe," John said in a whisper.

"Good morning, Sir," Joe answered cheerfully.

"That's a fine horse you're tending."

"Aye, Sir, this is Eclipse. The Princess's own mount."

John lowered his voice even further. "Joe, I've got to speak to you."

"Go to where we talked before. Take your bag. Wait for me. I'll be about another ten minutes."

Walking nonchalantly and looking round to make sure that he was not being observed, John went to the rendezvous and sat down on the stone floor, closing his eyes. Immediately, unpleasant visions flashed before him; visions of Emilia lying dead, of crimson blood and white snow, of terrible gashes in her gut, of her recognising him before she died. He opened his lids, feeling near to tears. But yet again he controlled them. He had sworn to himself that he would not cry until this sorry affair was ended and this was something he meant to stick to.

He heard approaching footsteps and looking up saw Joe, a piece of straw between his teeth, smiling at him beatifically.

"Well, Sir, what's afoot?"

"Plenty," John answered, and told him of his plot to enter the house and, hopefully, to stay there.

"If they won't put you up you can share my room over the stables," the clerk said practically.

"Thanks, Joe. Now, what have you discovered?"

"Quite a lot, Sir. First – and I'm sure you'll be amused by this – Benedict the footman has fallen madly in love with Lady Elizabeth."

For no reason John felt thoroughly irritated though he joined in Joe's uproarious laughter.

"And does she respond?" he asked when they had quietened down.

"Not she. But she's leading him on because she thinks she might get facts out of him."

"Oh good," said John, not meaning it.

"Further, Lady Georgiana and Michael O'Callaghan are planning to run away together."

"Yes, he told me something of that."

"Lady Theydon plays an interesting role in all of it. She appears almost like a disapproving mama."

"And what of Priscilla? Has there been any sign of her attacker?"

"Not a breath of him anywhere. That was a very odd business."

"It must have been Emilia's assailant, which proves Priscilla right. The original attack was intended for her all along."

"Yes." Joe looked thoughtful. "Unless..."

"What?"

"Nothing, Sir. I was just musing aloud."

"Please tell me."

"No, Sir, I can't. I was following an idea which came to naught."

With that the Apothecary had to be satisfied. He turned to Joe. "Is there anyone you suspect? Anyone at all?"

Joe looked thoughtful. "They're all up to something, as people from the higher walks of society always are. Consequently I suspect them all, yet I have nothing truly tangible to lay against any of them. The difficulty is, Sir, that much as I pick up gossip here in the stables, I can't get into the house and talk to the folks concerned."

"Exactly what I've been feeling. But now, thanks to Michael O'Callaghan's cunning conceit, I've a chance of doing just that."

"It will certainly do good, Sir, as long as you can get away with it."

"The next thing will be to get the right clothes and to track down Priscilla. Everything depends on her."

"No, not everything, Sir. It will be up to you to use your initiative and powers of deduction. Miss Fleming will merely be the source."

"You're right. It will be my actions that will decide the outcome."

They parted company, Joe returning to his duties, John to reconnoitre the park land. Tracing a long semi-circle from the stables, he stood as far away from the house as was possible, trying to see it as Emilia must have done that last time. His eyes took in the horseshoe shape of the lakes, the formal gardens, the steps that rose to the house itself.

From this angle the Round Pond and The Temple were to the left of the building, though some distance removed. On the right, however, was a building which John took to be a grotto. This was more or less facing the spot where Emilia had been done to death. Gritting his teeth and praying that he would not be discovered and challenged, John made his way through the trees to try and locate the actual spot.

And then he found it. There was still some blood on the ground, though this had dried to a mere reddish stain. But the fern had broken where she had fallen and John, leaning over, just as he had done on that fateful night, could picture her lying there quite clearly. Then his eye was caught by a tiny piece of material snagged on one of the branches. He picked it off, very gently, and saw that it was bright red. It was a piece of the cloak she had worn. Yet it was in an odd position. Quite high up as if she had been standing silently amongst the trees.

For the millionth time the Apothecary wondered why she had gone into the gardens at all, what errand she could have been running and for whom. That she had gone about affairs of her own had not even occured to him, though now he gave it some consideration, sitting down on the ground to ponder the idea.

Then he suddenly flattened as he heard the unmistakable sound of footsteps approaching. Lying almost where Emilia had breathed her last, John waited.

Chapter Seventeen

The footsteps drew nearer, paused for a moment, then proceeded on their way. John, from his prone position, peered through the trees and was fascinated to see the tall, saturnine figure of Lord Hope stride out of the wood and make his way towards the Grotto. Then, peering round to check that he was unobserved, his lordship entered the folly and disappeared from view.

John stood up, dusting the dried leaves from his clothing. Checking that the fragment of red material was safely in his pocket, he made his way cautiously out of the spinney and across the lawns. Realising that he was in full view of anyone who should be standing at a window, he pulled his hat as low as it would go and sauntered across.

To his right lay the Grotto, interesting because he had never seen it. Yet to go inside would be highly dangerous. Lord Hope had not reappeared and was presumably about some private business of his own. John imagined that he must be meeting somebody, obviously to discuss personal matters. Longing though he was to look, John resisted and made his way round to the side entrance of Gunnersbury House.

Now he really was on dangerous ground. Up to that moment he could have bluffed his way as being a gardener but once inside there were no excuses. Praying that he would not be discovered John crept through the door up the stairs. From Lady Theydon's room he could hear the sounds of conversation.

"My dear ladies," her self-important voice was saying, "have some more tea, do."

"Thank you, Madam. I will." John thought he recognised Lady Kemp.

"And I too." That was definitely Lady Featherstonehaugh.

So she was giving her companions morning tea, the Apothecary realised. And at that second a devastating thought came to him, that his life would never be normal again, that never more would the humdrum round of everyday things be his lot. For a moment he stood, feeling dizzy with the sheer horror of it, wishing yet again that Emilia was waiting for him in Priscilla's room, that everything could be restored to what it once had been. Then he rallied, mentally braced up, and continued on his way.

Gently knocking on the door, he waited for Priscilla to call out. But there was total silence. The Apothecary knocked once more, fractionally louder, but still there was no reply. Gently he put his hand on the knob and turned it. The door swung open and John peered inside. Of the owner there was no sign. Drawing his courage to him, he went inside.

He instantly noticed a door in the wall leading to Lady Theydon's apartment and hurriedly turned away from it, hiding himself in the bed draperies. The ridiculousness of his position struck him, yet he had to see Priscilla and set his plan in motion. Or else, he realised, his case was hopeless. He would never discover who had truly stabbed Emilia and would spend the rest of his days on the run, cut off from all that he cherished and loved.

From his hiding place he could hear the sounds of the tea party continuing and he also heard a pair of feet running up the stairs. A minute later the door was flung open and Priscilla herself appeared, hurrying breathlessly, her clothing somewhat disarrayed. Once inside the door, she leant against it, fanning herself with her hand.

"Priscilla," said John from the midst of the bed draperies.

She screamed, quite loudly, turning towards the bed, white-faced.

"It's me," he said, disentangling himself. "Please don't be frightened. The Irish actor and I have formulated a plan."

"Oh, my dear, how strange to see you," she said, sitting down suddenly. "You gave me the most tremendous fright."

John rolled his eyes in the direction of the door that led to

Lady Theydon's apartment. "I hid because of that. I was afraid she might come through."

For answer Priscilla tiptoed forward and silently turned a key. "I do that sometimes when I want to be private," she said, and giggled.

She looked quite attractive with a becoming pink in her cheeks caused by her recent exertion. In fact, she was looking the best that John remembered for some while.

"Is it too early for a glass of sherry?" she asked, dimpling at him.

"Never," he answered gallantly, coming out of the bed hangings and making her a small bow.

She poured from a crystal decanter and handed him a glass. "Now, tell me the latest."

John took a sip, then outlined his idea, adding, "So everything depends on you introducing me into the court."

"We'll have to be quick. Princess Amelia has announced that she is closing this place down next week."

"Then time is of the essence. Shall I go to Brentford and arrive here by hired cart tonight?"

"Oh, surely that would lower the tone. A horse would be better. But what are you going to do about clothes?"

"I was hoping you would be able to help me."

Priscilla looked thoughtful, pursing her lips. "I suppose we could borrow something from the Prince of Mecklenburg who leaves clothes here rather than carry them abroad."

"But he is stouter than I."

"No matter. I am handy with my needle. Now then, you must be Colonel Richard Melville, invalided out of the army, veteran of the recent conflict."

"And why am I here?"

"You have come with a message for me. Now as I said, I suggest you hire a horse. It will not look as good as a coach but there is a livery stable in Brentford with some reasonable nags, which should create the right impression."

John raised his glass to her. "Thank you, Priscilla. Emilia told me how good a friend you were to her. Now I can see that it is absolutely true."

She blushed. "Thank you. Now, where shall I leave the clothes when I have altered them?"

"In the stables at Gunnersbury House, put them in a bag under the hay trough. I'll creep in there after dark and change. Then I'll come to the house. The rest is up to you."

"You can rely on me, John. You know that I won't let you down." She leant across from where she was sitting opposite him. "Also please know that I will be as good a friend to you as I once was to Emilia." She stretched out a hand and touched his, which automatically he put forward in response.

Again, he acted without thinking, raising her fingers to his lips. A very slight movement on her part made him suddenly glance at her. She had turned away, only her arm extended, and he saw that she had a strange expression on her face, an unreadable look. Then she turned back and just for a second he saw an aspect of total joy upon her features before it vanished as quickly as it had come. In fact he wasn't sure that he had seen it at all in retrospect.

She refilled both their glasses. "Let us drink to your speedy success," she said.

"Yes," John answered heavily. "With the Princess leaving shortly I really do have to find the murderer fast."

On the dot of seven-thirty a somewhat aged black horse, the best that Brentford could boast, trotted up to the front door of Gunnersbury House, facing Brentford Lane, and the rider dismounted. An hostler came smartly to the summons and opened his eyes very wide when he saw the equestrian, who was a dashing fellow, supremely well-dressed and handsome, his looks marred, however, by a black patch over one eye.

"Good evening, Sir," said Joe Jago.

"Good evening, my good man," answered John Rawlings.

"Will you be requiring the beast again this night, Sir?"

"I sincerely hope not," John replied in an undertone.

A footman responded to the ringing of the bell and, having shown John into the reception room, took a card on a tray to Miss Fleming, who was currently attending the Princess in the drawing room. Shortly afterwards she arrived, looking somewhat flustered.

"Oh, my dear Colonel," she said. "What a surprise. I had no idea you were in the area."

"Madam, I had quite a journey of it," responded her visitor. "I have been in Bath, don't you know, but received a letter from my aged mama in which was contained a message for you. I therefore set forth by post-chaise, caught another, and ending up hiring an horse in Brentford. Anyway, here I am at last, and somewhat famished I might add."

"My dear Sir, all shall be attended to shortly. But I must confess we are currently in something of a panic here. A member of our household has gone missing and we are shortly to organise a search for him."

"Missing?" said John, genuinely startled. "Who is that then?"

"Lord Hope. He did not return to dine and that is when the alarm was raised. The Princess is hardly fit to receive a visitor, I fear."

At that moment there was a piercing scream and Georgiana appeared in the entrance hall, visibly shaking.

"We must search for him," she announced to the world in general. "We must find Conrad." She turned her eyes on the new arrival. "Oh, please help us, Sir," she asked beseechingly.

Recalling her performance at the bridge with Michael O'Callaghan, John thought her one of the best actresses he had ever come across, despite the Irishman's somewhat scathing review of her abilities.

He bowed deeply. "Madam, whatever you wish. I am entirely at your disposal."

She fluttered, despite herself. "Priscilla, pray introduce me to this gentleman."

"Lady Georgiana, may I present Colonel Richard Melville, my cousin." She curtseyed. "Colonel Melville, this is Lady Georgiana Hope."

John bowed and kissed her hand. "Honoured, Madam," he said.

He rather liked the role of military man, which gave him the opportunity to display bluff good manners. He also decided that Colonel Melville cut something of a dash with the ladies and resolved to play that part of the character for all he was worth.

"Colonel Melville has brought me a message from his mother," Priscilla said by way of explanation.

Lady Georgiana gave him a melting glance. "And what a time to arrive, Sir, with the whole place in an uproar. You see, my husband often goes off for the day, shooting and such-like, but today he has failed to return. I am so desperately worried about him."

Like the devil you are, thought John, though he continued to smile.

"I will do all I can to help, Madam. But first, out of courtesy, I feel I should be presented to the Princess. That is if she will receive me of course."

"Allow me to present you, Sir. It is true she is currently flustered but I am sure she will be delighted."

John gave his second best bow. "I would be greatly honoured, Madam. Thank you so much."

"Think nothing of it, Sir. I will go to her directly."

And with that Lady Georgiana, who had most rapidly regained her composure, turned on her heel and swept into some inner sanctum.

In the silence that followed John and Priscilla exchanged a glance. "Thank you for the clothes," he whispered.

"It's a miracle they fit. He is much more fleshy than you are. I'll alter some others tonight and bring them to your room."

"That is if the Princess invites me to stay."

But there was no time for further conversation. Lady Georgiana, pale but determined, came back in.

"If you would be so good as to follow me, Colonel Melville, Her Royal Highness will receive you now."

John, suddenly nervous, went out of the room in her wake, limping slightly to give a touch of authenticity to the wounded Colonel.

This night the Princess gleamed in silver with a necklace of large diamonds, but clearly her mood did not match her clothes. She looked up listlessly as Georgiana, John and Priscilla processed into the room, which had been set up for card play, several small tables having been erected and placed round.

She glared at John moodily and, just for a second, he saw a spark in her eye and thought he had been recognised. But then the look passed away and she stared at him blankly.

"Ma'am, may I present Colonel Richard Melville, a cousin of Priscilla Fleming."

John let rip with the most extravagant bow in his repertoire. "Your Royal Highness," he said, his tone sufficiently awestruck.

"And what brings you to Gunnersbury, Colonel Melville?" the Princess asked, her accent slightly Germanic.

"I had a message for Miss Fleming, Ma'am. It was from my mama and was sufficently urgent to ensure that I travel forth-with."

"Do you play cards?" she asked unexpectedly.

"A little, Ma'am."

"That is good. Tell me, have you seen recent service?"

"I was wounded at the Battle of Torgau, Ma'am," the Apothecary replied slickly, "after that I came home and spent the rest of the war in administration."

It was good a story as any and Princess Amelia obviously

approved because she nodded her head several times.

"Excellent. I like to meet fighting men. Where are you staying?"

"Probably in Brentford, Ma'am. I have booked nowhere as yet."

"Then allow me to put you up for tonight. On condition that you aid the search for Lord Hope. He went out shooting today and has not returned. But perhaps Lady Georgiana has told you of it?"

"She has, Highness, and I was about to volunteer my services."

"Then do set forth at once. Then when you have found him you may return and tell me more of the recent war. I am particularly interested in it."

"I am yours to command, Ma'am," and John bowed fulsomely once more.

Priscilla caught his arm on the way out. "Well done," she mouthed.

"At least I'm staying tonight," John murmured back.

"This way, gentlemen," called a man the Apothecary did not know. "Let us organise ourselves into little groups."

A bevy of males, mostly servants armed with flaming torches, were waiting outside plus one or two house guests. John, vividly reminded of the posse who had come searching for him, gritted his teeth at the memory and thought hard about how Colonel Melville would react.

"Where do you intend to look?" he asked, lowering his voice slightly.

"That's just the point, Sir," said the mystery man, whom John thought was more than likely the Princess's steward. "Where indeed? Lord Hope spent hours in the saddle. He could have fallen and be lying anywhere."

"Then why don't I take some men and search the grounds while you and the others ride out and look for him?"

There was a murmur of agreement and another house guest

stepped forward. "Good idea. I'll take a party of horsemen and ride east. You others can go in the opposite direction."

There was a general shift towards the stables and John found himself left with half a dozen men, one of whom, he was alarmed to see, was the unpleasant Benedict.

"Right. We'll divide into groups of two and search the grounds thoroughly. You two take the woods, you can do the area which includes The Temple and Round Pond. You and I –" He grabbed a rather elderly footman by the arm, "– will search the east of the estate."

They set off, the servant carrying a flaming torch, John, still limping a little, following in his wake. Searching painstakingly they covered every inch of the gardens, rural and ornamental, till at last they had reached the south wall of the man-made terrace. Here lay the folly known as the Grotto. With nothing to light it the place assumed a dark and foreboding aspect and John was suddenly reminded that he had seen Lord Hope enter it that very morning.

"We'll look in here," he commanded.

"I'm a bit shaky on me pins, Sir," the elderly footman confided. "Here's the torch, Sir. Will you forgive me if I don't accompany you?"

"Of course, my good man," answered John in a colonel's voice, and stepped into the blackened interior.

The torch threw amazing shadows on the walls which danced and grew to enormous size as John raised it higher over his head to see more distinctly.

At his feet was a slate-lined basin in which one could bathe, water for this being provided by a lion's head spout which gurgled and gushed even as the Apothecary looked at it. Drainage from the basin was presumably provided by a hidden culvert for he could distantly hear the flow of water from beneath the surface. Yet it was to none of those things that John's eye was drawn, but instead to something far more sinister. For sprawled in the basin, lying face down, his cloak spread round him like a grotesque pair of wings, was the man he sought. He had found Lord Hope, and he had found him absolutely dead.

Chapter Eighteen

Leaving Lord Hope exactly where he was, John stepped outside the Grotto and said quietly, "I've found Milord and he is dead. I'm afraid I will need you to hold the torch while I examine him."

"Examine him, Sir? But surely..."

"We military men are used to such things," the Apothecary answered firmly. "Now come along, my good fellow, be of stout heart."

He re-entered the Grotto, the footman standing well back, holding the flambeau in trembling fingers. Kneeling down by the basin, John attempted to heave the body out but had not considered the weight of water.

"Can you give me a hand?" he said over his shoulder.

"Oh, Sir, it's my pins. I'm getting on in years. I only do light duties round the house," the poor old fellow quavered.

"Very well. You stay here and guard the body. I'll go and get help."

"But Sir..."

"No arguments. I order you not to leave your post," John answered militarily, and stepped outside.

Once there he ran as fast as he could to the house, just in time to see Benedict going in.

"I've found him," he gasped. "You're to come with me and give me assistance."

Benedict paused and looked him fully in the face. "Don't I know you, Sir?"

"We may have met somewhere," John answered vaguely, "but that's not the issue. Lord Hope is in the Grotto, lying face down in the water. Are you coming to help me or aren't you."

The footman gave a sarcastic smile and said, "Of course, Sir," then followed John, who limped magnificently back to the folly.

The sight that awaited them would have been hilarious in other circumstances. The old footman, obviously having ventured a step or two forward to take a closer look, had lost his footing and toppled into the basin on top of Lord Hope. Here he thrashed violently, uttering shrill cries, and getting himself into difficulties. Fortunately Benedict carried a torch which he now placed in a wall-ring, presumably put there for the benefit of those who wished to bathe at night. Then he knelt down, John doing likewise, and they heaved at the old man – the Apothecary seizing him unceremoniously by the seat of his trousers – and pulled him from the water, gasping for air.

"Back to the house with you," Benedict said sternly. "Get some dry things on before you catch your death."

The old man's teeth – which John suspected were not his own – chattered violently in his head but he nodded and hastened from the folly without a backward glance.

"Right," said John, "now for this poor soul."

Together they pulled at the dead man's cloak which rose like a billow beneath their grasp. Feeling beneath it, the Apothecary located the man's coat and gave a tremendous tug which succeeded in half-turning him in the water. John gazed into features pale and grinning, the lips drawn back from the teeth in a terrible snarl.

"Come on, Benedict. Heave hard."

They did and succeeded in lifting him out of the water. John looked down at the saturnine Lord Hope and saw that he was whiter than a shroud, his lips a shade of vivid purplish blue.

Crouching down beside the body, John pulled the cloak and coat to one side and realised at once what had caused the man's death. He had been stabbed in the stomach then pushed into the pool to drown. And, differing from Emilia's case, the knife was no longer there. Other than that, it was an identical killing. It seemed Emilia's murderer had struck again.

He straightened up and stared into Benedict's dark eyes.

"I'm leaving you to guard the body. You can remain outside if you like. I'll go back to the house and inform them. A physician had better be called."

"Very good," the footman replied, then added, "Sir."

A few minutes later John walked into a scene of conrolled chaos. The return of the old footman, dripping wet, bleating out his hysterical story, had been enough. Georgiana had gone into a spectacular faint, while the four ladies who attended Princess Amelia were busy administering to their charge, who was taking brandy for medicinal purposes only.

Without thinking John approached the royal presence and took her pulse, then remembered himself.

"Forgive me, Ma'am. Force of habit. We army men are used to acting so. It's how we're trained."

She revived. "Oh really? Do tell me about it." Then she frowned. "But this would hardly be the time, would it? With poor Lord Hope drowned."

John cleared his throat. "I'm afraid it's slightly worse than that, Ma'am. Lord Hope was stabbed before he fell into the basin. To put it bluntly, there is a murderer lurking somewhere here."

The Princess's hand flew to her neck. "Oh, mein Gott! How terrible. So whoever killed poor Mrs. Rawlings is back."

Lady Theydon weighed in. "I knew it," she said. "I knew that lunatic fellow would return and take another victim. We are none of us safe in our beds. None of us." She rolled her large brown eyes in her doughy face and sighed dramatically.

"I shall leave for London tomorrow," the Princess put in. "Johnson, make the necessary arrangements."

"Very good, Ma'am," said the fellow whom John had thought to be the steward, and bowing left the room.

The Apothecary's heart sank. With the entire court removed he could make no progress whatsoever. He tried a last ditch stand.

"Do you think that wise, Highness?" he asked.

"Vise?" In her confusion Amelia's Germanic accent had become more noticeable. "Vise? Of course it is. Vy not?"

"It's just that I feel we ought to have a little longer to consider the evidence and to make the necessary arrangements. Surely another twenty-four hours could make little difference?"

"It will make all the difference in the world," she retorted with feeling.

Georgiana recovered from her faint. "Oh, Madam," she said pleadingly, "please allow me to stay. I must remain with poor Conrad until he is laid to rest."

"And someone," said John "should ride to Sir John Fielding's house in Bow Street."

Lady Kemp and Lady Featherstonehaugh made a simultaneous sound of contempt. "Huh! A great deal of good that wretch has been. Put up a few Wanted posters and that's that. Why, if he had acted more efficiently Lord Hope might well be still alive."

Georgiana rolled her eyes upward. "Oh, I'm going again."

John couldn't help himself. Pulling his salts from the pocket of the much taken-in trousers of the Prince of Mecklenburg, he duly adminstered them.

Georgiana opened an eye and looked at him suspiciously. "What are you doing?"

"Salts to cure swoons, Madam. They never fail."

She peered into his face which at that moment was quite close to hers. "Do I know you, Sir?"

"We may have met in London, Lady Georgiana. It is possible, indeed probable."

"Yes, that must be it." She sat up and turned towards Princess Amelia. "Oh, dearest Highness. I beg you to let us stay here a day more. A day in which to collect ourselves."

"Meanwhile," said John, "I suggest that a physician is sent for forthwith. Lord Hope really should be examined before he is moved."

The Countess of Hampshire, who had left the room briefly,

returned with, of all things, a bowl of grapes which she handed to the Princess. John, taking a long hard look at her, decided that she had definitely been an actress in the early stages of her career. He tried to remember whether her husband was still alive and presumed as she was not called Dowager that he must be.

Priscilla spoke. "I think the rest of the party are returning. I wonder what the other gentlemen will think."

It appeared that the Princess had two other male house guests. One, a handsome man of advanced years with bright wise eyes; the other a fellow for whom John did not altogether care, being young and loud and somewhat full of himself. After being informed of the news that Lord Hope had been found, John was invited to describe the scene, which he proceeded to do as precisely as possible.

The younger man, who turned out to be the Honourable Gerald Naill, third son of the Earl of Grimsdale, immediately put in, "I must go and have a look. Damn, what a turn up. Old Hope dead, eh? Hare and hounds, whatever next?"

"I wouldn't advise you to go, Sir," John answered. "You might move things around. Which reminds me, Benedict is there on his own." He turned back to the Princess. "Ma'am, may I suggest that the footmen stand watch in pairs until the physician has been. It is rather eerie down there."

The Honourable Gerald, who had been lolling in his chair, sat up. "Excuse me, Sir, but what right do you have to give orders?"

"My right, Sir, is my rank. Colonel Melville, late of His Majesty's Guards." As John said the words he was praying that nobody would question him.

"Oh." The young fellow looked slightly chagrined. "I see. Well I volunteer to go on watch at once."

There was no challenging that and John saw him depart with a certain amount of relief. He turned back to the Princess.

"And now, Ma'am, we really must send for a physician."

The older man made a very deep bow and said, "Highness, I

am actually a doctor, though retired for some years. Would it be in order for me to examine the body?"

"Of course you are a doctor," the Princess exclaimed, clasping her hands. "It had quite slipped my mind in all the excitement. Dr. Peter Phipps. Oh please do go and look, my dear Sir. It will save such a lot of effort. Then if you say poor Lord Hope may be moved, we can place him in a cool cellar."

At this remark Lady Georgiana burst into copious tears, sobbing, "Oh my poor husband. Oh cruel fate. What shall I do now?"

John, who was growing thoroughly tired of such high drama was very tempted to say, "Send for Michael O'Callaghan, that's what," but bit back the words. Instead he turned to Dr. Phipps. "Sir, if I might accompany you?"

"Certainly, my dear chap. Let us proceed."

Yet again the night had turned bitter and the Apothecary and the doctor both shivered as they left the house by the doors leading to the garden.

"Can you think of anyone who would want to murder Lord Hope?" Dr. Phipps asked as they walked towards the Grotto.

John, recalling the relationship between Georgiana and Michael, chose his words carefully.

"I don't know that he was popular in all quarters, Sir."

"Meaning?"

"I'm not quite sure what I mean. But it was a vicious attack as you will see for yourself."

The interior of the Grotto was filled with pools of shadow which assumed terrifying shapes in the darkness. John was amused to see that the Earl's son had come outside and was gulping fresh air as if it were water.

"Did you touch anything?" he asked in a commanding voice.

"No, Sir. But I could have sworn that he moved. It frightened me totally."

Dr. Phipps gave a half-smile and went inside, John following him closely.

The body was where he had left it, the head to one side, the terrible lips drawn back from the teeth in an evil grin, clearly visible in the torch's flickering light. Very carefully John knelt by the corpse and turned it over. The physician squatted down beside him.

"Stabbed in the guts, and viciously at that."

"Then pushed into the basin to finish him off."

"A cruel murder."

"They're all cruel," John answered with a humourless smile.

"You sound as if you've experienced quite a few."

"Army life," the Apothecary stated.

"Quite so. Well, shall we take a look round before we go?"

"By all means. I'll hold the torch."

As best they could in that uncertain light they examined the walls surrounding the basin and, sure enough, there was a blood stain on one wall.

"So that was where he was stabbed," said Dr. Phipps. He delicately felt the corpse, then looked at John. "He's stiff now, though of course the extreme cold would certainly help."

"Yes," John exclaimed thoughtlessly. "At least twelve hours for rigor mortis. That would make his death earlier today."

Dr. Phipps gave him a strange look but said nothing.

"Tell me about this other murder that took place here. Round about Christmas, wasn't it?"

"Yes, Sir. I think the two are related."

"Oh? Why is that?"

The Apothecary answered. "Because I feel they are, that is all."

"Then there is a dangerous killer at large," the physician stated soberly.

They walked back to the house in silence, leaving the Honourable Gerald Naill hovering in the entrance to the Grotto, too frightened to go in yet determined to appear brave.

A half hour later and it was over. Lord Hope had been carried back to the house on a makeshift stretcher and was presently lying in the very cellar in which John had last seen Emilia. The ladies, meanwhile, had stayed up with the exception of Lady Georgiana who had retired to her room to weep crocodile tears. Presently they were sitting at a simple supper table at which the three men joined them. Princess Amelia sat at the head and was, John noticed, very slightly inebriated.

"Oh my poor guests," she said brightly. "What you have had to endure. But we couldn't have managed without the help of the gallant gentlemen. I thank you, all three, most warmly."

Gerald, who had completely recovered his equilibrium and was now tending to be boastful, raised his glass.

"Ma'am, thank you for your kind hospitality. Tonight has been strange indeed but momentarily putting aside the horror and revulsion that we all feel at this terrible circumstance, I would like to raise my glass to the principal Princess of England. Princess Amelia."

Everyone murmured her name and drank, though in far more restrained a manner than usual, John thought.

"Have you come to any conclusion about leaving tomorrow, Ma'am?" he asked.

"The day after, I have decided. Tomorrow I and my ladies must rest. The whole affair has been a terrible strain on our nerves."

"Have you informed Sir John Fielding of the sad occurrence?"

"A rider has been despatched. I expect the Runners to appear some time tomorrow. That is partly why I have decided to stay."

The Apothecary's heart sank. It had been inevitable that the Beak Runners would be informed but the thought of them appearing some time during the day meant that he must vanish before they came. He decided that tonight he would not go to bed but would spend the hours searching for clues and talking to as many people as possible. Which, he thought, would not be many judging by the number already suppressing yawns.

"What will happen to Lord Hope's remains?" he asked, realising even as he spoke that he had mentioned a subject not fit for the dining table.

Lady Theydon fixed him with a glassy stare. "They will stay here until Lady Georgiana has them removed."

"Or until the Runners put them in the care of the Coroner." There was a stony silence and John continued, "Has anyone thought to communicate with her family?"

Princess Amelia gave a small sigh. "Kemp, will you see to it please."

"Certainly, Highness. They are based in Ireland, are they not?"

"They are. Lady Georgiana's father was that impoverished Irish peer, the Earl of Galloway. Her brother now has the title, I believe."

Ireland, thought John. Was it possible that Georgiana and Michael had known each other a long time? That he had courted her before she had been married to the man now lying in the cellar? Whatever, the way ahead was clear for them now.

The clock on the mantelpiece chimed ten and the Princess stood up, at which signal everyone else got to their feet.

"I am retiring," she announced. "Ladies, attend me. Gentlemen, farewell. We shall meet in the morning."

The four women dutifully followed her from the door and yet again the Apothecary was reminded of the four Marys who had attended Mary, Queen of Scots. Priscilla, after smiling round the room, went out behind the others. John turned to the other two men.

"Gentlemen, if you will forgive me. I have travelled a fair distance today and am feeling exhausted."

"Of course," answered Dr. Phipps. "I shall turn in myself when I have finished my port."

The Honourable Gerald, quite red in the cheeks by now, said, "Well, I'm going to sit up a bit. I feel too damnably excited to go to bed yet. Might take a turn round the grounds before I do."

"It's bitterly cold," warned the doctor.

"I'll be splendid, thank you."

John left them arguing mildly and escorted by a footman with a candle tree, went up to the room on the first floor which had been designated as his. Once there, however, he took a glass of water to clear his head and as soon as all was quiet, went silently back down the stairs. His first task was to find Elizabeth and warn her of his presence.

The staircase on which he found himself was not the private one used by Priscilla. In fact the Apothecary cursed as he followed the curve and found himself back in the main hall. A footman standing at the bottom, looked up.

"Can I help you, Sir?"

John put on his bluff hail-fellow-well-met face. "I'm a stranger to this house and thought I'd aquaint myself with its layout before I sleep. Can you tell me where the kitchens are?"

"There's no one in 'em now, Sir. Can I fetch you something?"

"No, that's perfectly all right. Goodnight to you."

"Goodnight, Sir."

Horribly aware of the man's curious gaze, John turned to the right, making his way through a dozen elegant rooms, now somewhat mysterious in the shadows thrown by his candles, until he found what he was looking for at last. At the back of the house, hidden behind a door, was the entrance to a steep spiral staircase. The tread of the stairs was so narrow that he wondered at the servants labouring up and down with food and cleaning equipment. Nevertheless, he started to climb as best he could, staying on the outside of each stair, circling round and round as he sought the top of the house. For this, surely, must be where the Marchesa slept. And it was imperative that he get word to her tonight that they were under the same roof once more.

As he climbed ever upward the Apothecary considered the fact that she might share the bedroom with other serving women. Then he would just have to creep in and wake her, he decided.

Though it was all very impractical it was the best he could come up with.

Eventually, panting and somewhat out of breath, he reached the third floor. Here there was a long landing with doors leading off on either side. Cautiously, John opened one. The sound of stertorous breathing from within told him that this was one of the men's rooms. Quietly closing it, he took to gently opening several and found that women slept to the left, men to the right.

He stopped to think. If he went into one and Elizabeth was not there he would wake the entire population of the servants' floor. Somehow he must identify which room she would be in. He remembered standing outside the house and looking up. At the end of the row on the top floor there had been a tiny window with obviously a tiny room behind it. Surely she as the most lowly member of staff might be incarcerated in such a place. Quietly, he opened the door at the far end of the corridor.

He knew at once by the light, high breathing that a boy lay within, and without a sound closed it again. Tiptoeing down the corridor he tried the door at the far end and this time was rewarded. A shaft of frosty moon was coming through the uncurtained window and he could see in its light that Elizabeth lay there, her black hair spread like lace upon the pillow, her features pale as death in that unearthly light. Crossing to the bed – a mere footstep for him – he put his hand over her mouth and gently shook her shoulder.

She woke at once and gazed at him, not terrified but calmly. Beneath his fingers he felt her mouth smile. "John," she said in a muffled voice.

He took his hand away and she sat up, curtained by black locks. "My dear, how are you?" she continued, then putting her arms round his neck, she kissed him.

Just for a moment John forgot everything and returned the kiss, deeply, his tongue seeking hers. Then he remembered Emilia's face as she died and he gently disentangled himself.

"I'm well but I've a great deal to tell you."

And there, in the cold moonlight, he recounted the story, even down to the Honourable Gerald being too frightened to enter the Grotto.

"I've yet to meet him. But your disguise as Colonel Melville? Is it working?"

John raised his eye-patch. "It seems that this is helping enormously. Some people seem to think they've met me before somewhere but are not at all certain."

"But you say the Princess is leaving the day after tomorrow?"

"Yes, that's her intention. I've got to move fast."

"Yes, you certainly have. Is there anything I can do to help?"

"Just stay close and run if you have to."

She leant her head back on the pillow. "Don't worry, I'll be near by." She smiled her enigmatic smile. "You know that Benedict has a passion for me."

"Yes, Joe Jago told me."

"It is purely one-sided."

"So I should hope, you witch."

She gave him a look from her dark eyes. "Who do you think is resposible for the latest murder?"

"Whoever it was who killed Emilia. The wound was almost identical."

"Then we must find out who visited the Grotto today."

"That," answered John Rawlings with determination, "is exactly what I intend to do."

Chapter Nineteen

He left her within the next five minutes, filled with the knowledge that the strange deep attraction she held for him was returning, in fact had probably never gone away, merely been dulled by the pain of losing Emilia so savagely. All the way down the creaking spiral, John thought of Elizabeth's hauntingly ugly beauty and wished that he had spent longer with her, even the night itself. Then he took himself to task. There was much to do and very little time in which to do it. Every minute counted. Yet as he reached the bottom step he sighed deeply for the things that might have been which had not taken place.

Leaving the house by a back door John headed for the stable block, thinking that he would have to wake Joe Jago up. But there was a dim light in the building and much to his surprise he found the clerk dozing, sitting up by a bale of hay, his eyes closed but obviously conscious for he said, "Is that you, Mr. Rawlings?"

"It is. How did you know?"

"By the way you walk, Sir." Joe opened one eye which gleamed at the Apothecary brightly.

Amused by his reaction, John sat down beside him. "I saw you go off with the mounted search party."

"Yes, and by the time we'd got back you'd found him in the Grotto."

"I want to talk to you about that."

Joe opened his other eye and sat upright. "I rather imagined you might. Tell me, Sir, was it the same killer?"

"Without a doubt. He was knifed in the stomach then pushed into the pool to die. Now, I saw him go into the Grotto about eleven o'clock this morning. Is it possible that he was killed then and could have been there all day?"

"It's very possible. Remember that the water in the basin is cold and that the Princess uses it far more in the summer than the winter. It is more than likely that the place was not visited at all during the day."

"Then I think he went in to meet his murderer."

Joe produced a pencil and paper from his pocket. "We must list everyone who was present both at Christmas and this morning. Now then, starting at the top, there's Princess Amelia."

"Oh surely not."

"You say that, Sir, but who is to say that she is not a homicidal Hanoverian?"

John grinned. "Go on."

"There's Lady Georgiana Hope, the Countess of Hampshire, Lady Theydon, Lady Featherstonehaugh, Lady Kemp and Miss Fleming. Any men?"

"Michael O'Callaghan could have come over from the farm and lurked in the Grotto. He had motive enough."

"What about Benedict?"

"Much as I dislike him," John answered, "I don't think so. He was serving me a drink when I saw Emilia through the window. Which reminds me; I found a piece of red material high up at the scene of her murder."

"What do you mean, high up?"

"Snagged on a branch at standing height. As if someone had been waiting in the trees. You don't think..." His voice died away as the full import of what he was saying struck him.

"That there were two people in red cloaks?" Joe asked slowly.

The Apothecary turned to stare at him. "Is it possible?"

"It certainly is, Sir. What easier way to disguise oneself than to dress in an identical way to the victim."

John looked sick. "Then the person I saw hurrying through the trees might not have been Emilia."

"Who's to say, Sir? Who's to say? Now..." He rubbed his hands together. "Who else for the list?"

"I can't think of anyone. Joe, you know that Michael

O'Callaghan and Georgiana Hope were planning to run away together."

"Yes, I do. Silly young fools. But it would certainly give both of them a motive."

"Indeed it would. But why kill Priscilla that first time? Because that's who the murderer thought he was getting."

"Um." Joe stroked his chin.

"What does that mean?"

"Nothing, Sir. Just um."

"Well, tomorrow I've got to question all the ladies, somehow or other find out what they were doing at the appropriate time." A thought struck John forcibly and he grabbed Joe's arm. "But I forgot. The Runners are due here tomorrow. They'll arrest me sure as fate."

"No, Sir, I don't think so."

"What do you mean?"

Joe flushed a little. "Mr. Rawlings, I haven't been entirely straight with you."

The Apothecary turned on him a puzzled face. "I don't understand."

"I wrote to Sir John shortly after you arrived here and begged him to give you time to solve the murder. He agreed to three weeks before he made an arrest. You have one more week to go."

John didn't know whether to laugh or cry. "You mean to say that my subterfuge has been for nothing?"

"Not for nothing, no Sir. You have managed to worm your way back in to Gunnersbury House. You are on the point of unravelling the mystery..."

"Some hopes."

"As I was saying, you are on the point of solving the entire thing. Another week is all you will need."

"But the Princess intends to pack up tomorrow and go the next day."

"Perhaps she can be persuaded to stay."

"But how?"

"I think, Sir, that you had better leave that to me," Joe answered, and touched his nose with his finger.

John's earlier feelings of tiredness had now vanished. Leaving the stables, plunging into a freezing night, he felt more alert and awake than he had for an age. Deciding to take another look at the Grotto, hoping that a torch would have been left in there, he made his way through the darkness towards the folly.

Despite the bitter weather the night was alive with sounds. The grass rustled with small wildlife and distantly he could hear the sonorous note of an owl. But another noise overrode these natural sounds. There was the crunching of feet on the frosty lawn as somebody approached. For some strange reason John's blood ran cold and he hurried for the protection of the folly where he hid in the deepest shadow, hardly daring to breathe. Silently, he watched the figure approach.

It was cloaked and it was difficult to tell at this distance whether it was male or female. Yet as it approached closer he could see that it was a woman who was drawing near to the place where he hid. Standing mute in the inky blackness, the Apothecary recognised the lugubrious features of Lady Theydon.

She paused at the entrance to the Grotto and looked stealthily around. She was only a foot away from John who could quite easily have stretched out his arm and touched her. However, he remained utterly still and quiet.

"Is there anybody there?" she asked nervously, her sticky voice tremulous.

The Apothecary did not move a muscle despite an overwhelming urge to cough.

She stared round a moment or two longer then decided that the coast was clear and entered the murder scene, from which a faint glow was still forthcoming. Dying to see what she was doing, John ventured forward a step, then another, until finally he was just able to peep within.

She was searching for something, that much was clear. Looking up and down the walls of the interior, then bending over the basin, peering frantically. But whatever it was Lady Theydon sought, her search was unsuccessful. For after a further look round she headed for the doorway.

The Apothecary drew back but not quite quickly enough. She had seen something.

"Who is there?" she called.

But he was off, haring up the hill to the garden behind, then racing through that in the direction of The Temple and Round Pond. She had seen him, of that much he was certain, but whether she had recognised him was a different matter. At least she had been too frightened to come in pursuit. Glancing over his shoulder, the Apothecary slowed his pace.

It was so cold that the Pond had frozen over and John looked with pity at the huddles of ducks and two solitary swans sleeping disconsolately on the shore. Suddenly he began to miss Rose, longing to show her sights like these, longing not to miss much more of her growing up. Determined that before the end of the week he would unmask the cruel murderer, John turned back to Gunnersbury House and the thought of a comfortable bed.

He rose at six o'clock and having washed and dressed made his way back to the Grotto. It was one of those misty mornings with a heavy frost, the sun blood-red behind the vapour. Determined to try and find what it was Lady Theydon had sought so frantically the night before, John entered the place of death and looked round him.

The torch in the wall-bracket had long since gone out and the place had a desolate air, the early morning light barely filling its corners. Not having an idea what it was he sought, the Apothecary began to repeat the search of the previous night. The walls revealed nothing except the bloodstain he had noticed earlier, so somewhat reluctantly the Apothecary turned his attention to the basin itself. It was certainly small, the water coming from a cascade, quite artificial, fed by a series of hidden pipes. Gingerly putting his hand in, John withdrew it again rapidly. It was freezing and only a fanatic would bathe in it of their own free will. Wondering whether Amelia organised a string of maids with boiling kettles to heat it up, John was just about to give up when he noticed something sparkle at the bottom of the basin. Hoicking up the sleeves of the Prince of Mecklenburg's stout cape, John put his arm into the icy water and pulled out an earring.

It was quite small, fashioned round a central stone, probably a topaz. Holding it up to what light there was, the Apothecary could see that it sparkled sufficently to tell him that it was not cheap and had been made for a lady of quality. Which gives me the choice of any woman in the house, he thought. Sighing a little, he slipped it into his pocket and went out again.

Breakfast was served at eight o'clock and John, making his way to the morning room, found himself following in the wake of the Ladies Kemp and Featherstonehaugh. Reminded vividly of his first visit to the house and his journey up the stairs when they had introduced themselves, he made sure that his eye-patch was in position before he spoke.

"Good morning, ladies."

They turned and bobbed curtseys simultaneously. "Good morning, Colonel Melville."

"Did you sleep well?" John asked, bowing.

"Very," said Lady Kemp but Lady Featherstonehaugh answered, "No, I did not. Couldn't get off for all that infernal whispering."

"Whispering, dear?" enquired Lady Kemp.

"Yes, wretched racket. In the corridor, outside my room. Went

on for ages. In the end I rose from my bed and went to remon-
strate with them. But it was too late, they had gone."

"Who was it? Do you have any idea?"

"I thought at first it was Madam Hampshire with one of her
pretty young fellows. But the voices didn't seem right somehow.
Anyway, there's no point in discussing it now. Whoever it was
escaped without me seeing them."

John bowed the ladies in to place at the table, seeing somewhat
to his surprise that the three of them were alone.

"I wonder where the others are," he ventured.

"The doctor has gone riding, young Naill is still abed. As for
the other ladies I expect they will join us shortly."

So this was to be his opportunity. With what he hoped was a
winning smile, the Apothecary addressed them both.

"Tell me, ladies, what was the most frightening experience of
your lives?"

Lady Kemp answered straight away. "Oh without doubt it was
the murder of that young woman last Christmas. I shall never
forget the sight of her, bleeding to death, her husband holding
her in his arms. He looked so wild, poor thing."

"Why do you say that?" John asked involuntarily.

Fortunately she misunderstood his meaning and said,
"Because it was so terrifying. I can remember the day distinctly.
We were all so excited about the masque. The cast had already
arrived from London and I must say that I was quite taken with
Michael O'Callaghan. Such a lovely voice, don't you know.
Anyway, I congratulated Priscilla on finding him but she said she
had known of him for some while."

"Get to the point, my dear." This from Lady
Featherstonehaugh.

"I am doing so," Lady Kemp replied with dignity. "As I was
saying, that husband of the dead girl came through the most terrible weather to be here. Quite frankly it was a miracle that he
arrived. Anyway, he must have followed her into the woods and

killed her because that is where we found him. But it struck me as odd at the time that he should have done such a thing in so public a place. I mean, why not murder her at home?"

Lady Featherstonehaugh snorted. "They presumably had an argument and he hit out at her in a rage."

"Well, despite what you say, I did not think him guilty. I think he found her body and stayed with it, grief-stricken."

"Tell me," said John, hoping he did not sound too inquisitorial, "did you step out for some air after the masque?"

Lady Kemp turned on him a puzzled face. "No, I don't think so. Why?"

"But you did, my dear," boomed Lady Featherstonehaugh. "I distinctly remember you excusing yourself and leaving the room." She turned to look at John. "I, too, took a turn round the Round Pond, very briefly because of the inclement weather. Do you know I glimpsed a man relieving himself behind a tree. Most unseemly."

"Indeed," echoed Lady Kemp. "Who was it?"

"I'm not sure, I averted my eyes immediately. But I rather think it was Mr. O'Callaghan."

Lady Kemp blushed. "I expect he was in a hurry to return."

"I can't think why. The performance had reached its end. Why could he not go to the closet like everyone else?"

"Perhaps it was occupied," said John seriously.

So both the ladies had left the house as had Michael. That meant all three could have hastened into the woods, wearing a red cloak, and killed Emilia. But why – if Priscilla was correct and it was her they were really seeking – did they do it? John felt that a frank talk with that young woman was long overdue.

The door opened and Lady Theydon came in, looking extremely careworn, John thought.

"Am I late?" she asked.

"A little," Lady Kemp answered, "but it is of no matter. How did you sleep, my dear?"

"Like a child," came the answer, and John stared at her open-mouthed, thinking that she lied with the ease of a professional swindler.

"Where are the other ladies?" he asked brightly.

The great dark eyes fixed themselves on him and she started to explain in her lugubrious voice.

"Well, the Princess is abed and breakfasts when she feels like it. And I think Lady Georgiana can be excused in view of the terrible tragedy. But Miss Fleming should be here to take her orders for the day. It is most remiss of her to be late."

As if that had been her cue, the door flung open dramatically and Priscilla, looking fractionally unkempt, came through it.

"Oh forgive me, Ma'am," she said, dropping a curtsey in the direction of Lady Theydon, "I overslept."

"Did that damnable whispering keep you awake?" asked Lady Featherstonehaugh.

"Whispering? No, I heard none."

"Then you were lucky is all I can say."

"And where is the Countess?" John put in brightly.

"Lying with her latest lover, I dare swear." Ignoring the hushes that came from the others, Lady Featherstonehaugh continued, "The lady married a very old man who was tickled to death to catch a respected actress for his bride. She is his third wife, incidentally. The other two both died."

"Of boredom?" asked Lady Kemp sweetly.

Lady Featherstonehaugh made a trumpeting sound but did not reply.

John silently congratulated himself on being right about Lady Hampshire. He put on his interested face. "So the old Earl is still alive, is he?"

"About eighty and on his last legs, but yes."

Priscilla spoke up. "If you can spare me for half an hour I should so enjoy showing the Colonel the grounds, Lady

Theydon. I have not seen him for a while and it will give us a chance to catch up on family gossip."

The heavy eyes rested on the Apothecary and for a horrible moment he thought he had been recognised. But having studied him they looked away once more as she tackled a serious plate of eggs.

"Yes, that will be in order. But first you must attend me in my rooms, Priscilla."

"Very well, Lady Theydon."

What exactly was the relationship between these two? John wondered. And why did none of the other women surrounding the Princess appear to have personal servants? Determined that the walk with Priscilla would provide him with answers, the Apothecary stood up.

"Ladies, if you will forgive me I have some correspondence I must attend to."

Miss Fleming looked at him meaningfully. "I will see you by the front door at eleven o'clock, Colonel."

"I'll be there," he answered, then bowed individually to all the women in the room before he withdrew.

Once outside he sped to the stables where he found Joe Jago brushing the coat of Eclipse.

"My friend, are you sure that the Runners won't arrest me?"

"Certain, Mr. Rawlings."

"But what about Sir John? Is it not his duty to see me behind bars."

"That's as may be. But as an old friend he is prepared to give you a bit of leeway."

"But I've been at liberty long enough by anyone's reckoning."

Joe stopped his brushing. "Sir, whose side are you on?"

John laughed despite himself. "You're right as usual. Joe, how are you going to persuade the Princess to stay a few days more?"

"Ah now, that's the question."

"Have you a plan?"

"I thought Eclipse here might give us the answer." John stared at him and Joe went on, "She adores this horse, does the Princess. If he were to develop a cold I think she might remain here until it got better."

"But how are you going to fake that? The horse looks healthy enough to me."

"Ah, it takes an expert to tell when a horse is under the weather, Sir."

"Oh, I see."

"Poor chap was off his food this morning."

"What a shame."

"Shame indeed, Sir," said Joe, moving round the gleaming chestnut of the creature's hindquarters. "Shame indeed." And he winked a spectacular eye.

Chapter Twenty

Priscilla, looking exceptionally pretty, quite tidied up from her slight dishevellment at breakfast, was waiting by the front door. She gave a small curtsey as John approached, then took his arm in a friendly manner.

"I've been so looking forward to getting you to myself," she murmured confidentially.

John was not quite sure how to reply, slightly startled by the warmth of her tone. Eventually he said, "I'm afraid that I've a lot of questions to ask you and I shall require truthful answers."

She flashed him a look. "I am always truthful with you."

"Very well. Let's get away from the house."

They strode out, walking deep into the estate where they were quite sure that no one could overhear them. Then Priscilla gave him a long glance, squeezed his arm, and said, "Well?"

"Listen, my dear, I've got to know what it is about you that people want to destroy. You told me on the night Emilia died that it was you the killer was after. Now you've got to tell me why."

Priscilla turned away. "I swore I would never disclose that to a living soul."

"But don't you see how desperate the situation is?"

"Yes, I do. I truly do."

"Then I beg you."

"Very well." She paused, then said, "Cast your mind back to when our present King was still Prince of Wales."

"I can recall it vividly."

"Do you remember there were those who hoped that he might take an English woman for a wife."

"I remember that he was very taken up with Lady Sarah Lennox, yes."

Priscilla made a contemptuous noise. "I speak of a time before that particular young woman came along. A time when the Prince was eighteen years old."

"Ah, you are referring to the rumours about a Hannah Lightfoot?"

"No, Sir, I am not." Priscilla paused and gave him a long stare. "It was I who was his secret mistress."

John stared, absolutely speechless. "You?" he gasped.

"Does that surprise you?"

"Yes, it does. How on earth did it happen?"

"We met at the ball given for him by Elizabeth Chudleigh. I was there with Lady Theydon. A mere nothing, a nobody. I remember that I wore an old dress of hers as I had nothing fine of my own to wear. Anyway, somehow in the midst of all that glittering throng he noticed me. Indeed he danced with me. And before he left he pressed a note into my hand asking me to meet him."

John was frankly astounded. Thinking that of all the beauties present on that wondrous occasion the Prince should have picked Priscilla.

"But that is not all," she continued, and suddenly she lowered her eyes and looked away from him.

"Yes?" said John, eager now to hear what is was she had to say.

"We did meet and we became lovers. We were both eighteen and it was the most passionate affair you can imagine. Oh John, how foolish I was. But at the time I dreamed of being Queen. But no, much as he adored me, his mother and her lover, Lord Bute, interfered. They saw to it that we parted. Damn them."

The Apothecary sat silently, overwhelmed by what he had just been told. He had indeed heard rumours that the King, then Prince, had lost his virginity to a certain Quaker girl called Hannah Lightfoot, that he had been in love with Sarah Lennox but ended up doing his duty and marrying the ugly little Queen, but this was astounding.

"And that was the end of it?" he asked.

She turned on him a livid coloured face. "Not quite," she said. "No, I'll tell you the reason why assassins are after me. You see, John, six months after the Prince and I ended our relationship I gave birth to a baby boy."

"The King has a bastard son!" the Apothecary exclaimd.

"At least one that I know of," Priscilla answered bitterly.

"What happened to him?"

"He was put out to a family as soon as he was born, poor little mite. I never saw him. As far as I was concerned he was forgotten. And then, at the age of six months, he died." She paused then continued in a low voice, "I went to his funeral. There was a stranger there, a man dressed entirely in black. I don't know who he was. I have never seen him before or since. But after that certain things started to happen to me."

"What?"

"A carriage tried to run me down; I was pushed when standing near a cliff edge; that sort of thing."

"But you escaped."

"Obviously, for I stand before you. But now do you see why the powers that be think I should die?"

"No, to be honest, I don't."

Priscilla moved closer to him, gazing up earnestly into his face. "Because I am the only person alive, other than for those from the King's court, who knows about Baby George."

Her lips trembled at this last remark and she started to weep, silently and sadly. Without really meaning to John felt obliged to put his arms round her.

"Oh," she sobbed, "it's so wonderful just to be able to tell someone of my sin. Yet at the time it did not feel as if I were sinning. I truly loved George, was glad to have his child. But now my secret grows dangerous. Oh, John, you do see now why Emilia had to die."

He supposed he did and yet he could not quite follow her argument. Kings had had bastards before and most certainly would do so again. So why was it so important that she should be removed? But whatever his opinion the poor girl was now weeping copiously and he felt duty bound to do his best to cheer her up.

"Come, come Priscilla," he said soothingly, reaching into his pocket for his salts. "I am sure everything will be all right."

She took the bottle and inhaled the vapours deeply. "Now that you are here they will," she answered.

The Apothecary felt vaguely uncomfortable but said nothing, noticing how quickly her eyes grew puffy, then feeling cruel for studying her so closely.

She smiled up at him tearfully. "Swear that you will tell no one, particularly Lady Theydon."

"But surely she knows. Didn't you say that she was at the ball when you met His Majesty?"

"Yes, I did. Of course she knew of our courtship in the early days but when I became pregnant I went away for six months. I lived in the country; a solitary existence. She knew nothing of it and still doesn't."

"I see." The Apothecary weighed his words carefully. "Tell me, what exactly is your relationship with Lady Theydon? You seem very close in some ways."

Priscilla fluttered in his arms. "How clever you are to guess. She is my aunt, my mother's sister. She actually brought me up. You see Mama died when I was twelve."

"When you were at school with Emilia?"

Priscilla nodded. "Yes. I can remember the day the news came. Emilia was so sweetly kind."

Her words made John's heart wrench and he turned his head away.

"Oh, my dear, have I upset you?" she asked. "I wouldn't do that for the world."

He looked down at her. "No, I'm all right. Thank you for telling me your story. Is there anything else I need to know?"

"No, I can't think of anything."

"Tell me one last thing," he said.

"What?"

"Have you known Michael O'Callaghan a long time?"

"I met him years ago, yes. Then I didn't see him for an age."

"Oh. Where did you meet?"

"In Ireland," said Priscilla, "where I went to have the baby."

By the time John and Priscilla returned to the house the Runners had arrived from London and were questioning everybody who had been present on the day Lord Hope had died. According to their records Colonel Melville, Dr. Phipps and the Honourable Gerald Naill had presented themselves too late to be counted as suspects. Nevertheless, they were called in to see the Runners to state their hour of arrival at Gunnersbury House.

Gerald went first and came out looking rather pale. "Damn fellows gave me a rough time," he said, quite crestfallen. "Didn't seem to believe my story that I came to play cards with the Princess. Asked me if I knew Lord Hope and I had to admit that I had met the fellow once or twice."

Dr. Phipps stood up. "My turn, I dare swear."

But at that moment Runner Nick Raven, who in company with Runner Richard Ham comprised the mainstay of Sir John Fielding's mobile unit, two Brave Fellows with a carriage ready to leave for any part of the kingdom at fifteen minutes notice, put his head round the door.

"The Colonel, if you please, Sir."

Suddenly very nervous, John stepped into the small ante room that the Princess had said the officials might use for questioning people. Once inside he stood, waiting to see how they would greet him.

Runner Raven, as dark and birdlike as his name suggested, fixed him with an avine stare. "Well, Mr. Rawlings, this is a fine how dee do."

"It is indeed." He looked Nick straight in the eye. "I didn't kill her. I swear it."

Runner Ham, a big genial chap, came over. "We know you didn't, Sir. Why should you? But we've got our duty to do. Another week, that's all that Sir John will allow. Then we have to arrest you."

"I know." John looked hangdog. "I've got to find the guilty party who, I think, lies somewhere amongst the Princess's ladies-in-waiting. Unless Michael O'Callaghan is the one. But the trouble is I am totally confused. And today I heard an odd story."

The words were out before he had time to think and he instantly regretted them. "Oh, and what was that, Sir?"

"I'm afraid I can't repeat it. It was told me in confidence."

"And does it have any bearing on the present case?"

"It might," John answered lamely. "It just might."

"Well then, let us hope it triggers something off in your mind, Sir."

"I pray with all my heart that it does," John answered as he made his way from the room.

Sitting outside while Dr. Peter Phipps presented himself, he thought through the strange story that Priscilla had told him and decided that it could mean one of two things. Either an agent of the people who wished to keep the royal secret was present here at Princess Amelia's court or they had sent someone in, someone who had vanished again afterwards, to make sure that Priscilla was silenced. But in that case who had killed Lord Hope? What had he to do with it all? Thoroughly puzzled, the Apothecary attempted to think logically.

Emilia had been murdered because she had been confused with Priscilla, the mother of King George's little bastard. But Lord Hope, as far as he knew, was totally unconnected with that affair. And then a terrible thought struck the Apothecary. Supposing he had been wrong all along. Supposing that a mad killer was on the loose, striking at whomsoever he, or she, pleased. Supposing that right from the start Emilia had been the intended victim. That there had been no motive for the crime but it had happened simply to fulfill the depraved lust of a maniac. In that case they must all be on their guard – for there was a lunatic in their midst.

Somewhat shaken by his ideas the Apothecary made his way out, thinking that he must find Joe and discuss this latest turn of events with him. But he had not even got as far as the door leading to the garden when he heard a voice calling the name of the Colonel. Slowly he turned and saw Lady Hampshire waving her fingers at him and peeping coyly over her fan, which she was vigorously employing despite the freezing temperature. John made a deep bow.

"My dear Colonel," said the lady, remaining seated. "I've been sitting here thinking about you."

"Indeed, Madam?"

"Yes, truly. How unfortunate that you should arrive at such a horrid time. What can you reckon to us all, I ask myself."

"It is indeed bad timing, my Lady, but one can hardly choose to have a murder at a convenient moment."

She patted the seat next to hers. "Can you spare me a minute, Sir? I would so love to have your opinion of things."

John bowed once more and took a seat opposite. She leant close to him. "Do tell me," she said, and laughed shrilly.

In her day she had been a great beauty, there was no doubt about it. Fine boned and with luxuriously lovely eyes, it was easy to imagine a much-married elderly aristocrat wanting to make her his wife. Unfortunately the rot of years had now set in and what had been a small vivacious chin had now vanished into a second, the eyes had puffy bags beneath, and John saw as she smiled that she was starting to lose her teeth. He imagined her age to be two years either way of fifty.

She smiled winningly. "Go on."

John cleared his throat and tried hard to think himself into the role of the Colonel.

"Well, Ma'am, it is very much as you say. Poor Lord Hope has been done away with and it is up to all of us to be vigilant and keep our eyes open."

Lady Hampshire gave an excited shudder. "Do you think the killer is one of us?"

John paused, thinking. "It is certainly someone connected with Gunnersbury House in some capacity or other. Tell me in confidence, Lady Hampshire, do you have anyone you suspect?"

"Well at the time of the first murder I thought it must be as they said. That it was the husband. But now I don't see how that is possible. I mean, what connection is there between that nice little Emilia and Lord Hope? Unless, of course..."

"What?"

"Unless they were lovers."

For some reason this remark infuriated John but he managed to control himself. "I think that is pushing circumstance a little far, Ma'am. I should imagine that the only link between the two is their murderer," he answered quietly.

Chapter Twenty-One

It was a relief to get outside, away from Gunnersbury House, the atmosphere of which had suddenly become oppressive. Walking resolutely in the direction of the stables, John was pleasantly surprised to see Elizabeth coming towards him. She curtseyed as they drew level.

"Good morning, Colonel," she said, and smiled, her scar harshly apparent in the morning light.

"Good morning, my dear," he answered and, lowering his eye patch, gave her a knowing wink.

Her manner changed. "John, be careful for the love of God. We might be being watched."

"Then meet me in The Temple in ten minutes. I'll go straight there. You follow."

And before she could argue or disagree he set off in the direction of the Round Pond.

This morning was warmer and the recent ice that had covered the lake had melted, leaving it that mysterious deep blue that had so struck him when first he had seen the stretch of water. Now, having a few minutes to spare, he strolled round its circumference, glad to see the ducks and swans once more swimming upon its surface. He remembered then another occasion, close to another expanse of water. Remembered Emilia as she had looked that very first time he had seen her. She had been wearing a large black hat which all but hid the gold sheen of her hair. But beneath its brim she had gazed at him with those gorgeous eyes of hers and John had been instantly attracted to her. An attraction which had turned into love and which had resulted in the birth of Rose.

John pulled himself up with a jerk. He had hardly thought of his daughter these past few days and now he felt a violent desire to see her again and hold her in his arms. With her mop of curling red hair and her wiry little body she was the nearest thing to

Emilia left alive on earth. His urgent need to conclude this case and once more be restored to his family was like an actual physical pain which made him hurry the rest of his walk and enter the confines of The Temple at a brisk pace.

He had last been inside it at night and now he paused in the entrance while his eyes got used to the dim light. He looked round at a rectangular structure clearly erected as a summerhouse. However provision had been made for the vagaries of the English weather, for a fireplace had been built in the wall facing him. There were various pieces of statuary about and John looked again on the plaster faun together with that of a swan and goldfish. He recalled the last occasion he had been within and the attack on Priscilla. Whoever was responsible for these killings and for that assault, he thought, was either extremely clever or extremely mad. Or could it be that they were both? Suddenly he shivered and was glad to hear Elizabeth's light but determined step as she made her way inside.

"Well?" she said.

"I've questioned various people but I'm no further forward as to who went to the Grotto yesterday."

"I don't see how you're going to discover that. Because whoever it was is going to lie to protect themselves."

"There is one thing, though." And John told her about Lady Theydon's fruitless search for the earring and his subsequent discovery of it.

"Where is it now?" the Marchesa asked.

"Here." And John felt in the Prince's cape, then turned the pocket out, fishing the earring from its depth.

"And you say that Lady Theydon went searching for it last night?"

"Yes."

"Then is she the murderer?"

"It is certainly beginning to look that way."

Elizabeth was silent, staring out over the blue water, deep in thought. "There is no chance of her having known Emilia long ago, I suppose?"

John, too, looked pensive. "I don't think so but there's always a possibility." He sat down on one of the garden chairs. "Oh, I can't wait to get this business over. It is the worst case I have ever had to deal with."

Elizabeth came to stand beside him. "That's because you are investigating the murder of your wife. Now, stop brooding. There's much to be done. You must get Lady Theydon alone."

"And then?"

"Challenge her with being in the Grotto. See how she reacts."

John looked up and smiled crookedly. "How easy you make it sound."

"Nothing is too dificult for you," she replied, and turning on her heel she walked briskly away, out of The Temple and out of sight.

With a sigh John stood up and stared around him, remembering how the last time he had been in here he had found Priscilla stretched out on the floor, the victim of an attacker. He bent down over the place where she had been lying but other than for a slight shifting of the dust there was no visible sign.

Shaking his head, totally bewildered by everything, he once more removed the earring and stood silently staring at it, where it lay, glittering, in the palm of his hand.

As he left the summerhouse and headed back he saw the Runners leaving in their coach, behind which was being drawn a small closed cart. Immediately he knew its purpose. The last mortal remains of Lord Hope lay within and were being taken to the nearest mortuary, there to be examined by a physician working, no doubt, for the coroner. John's mercurial eyebrows rose at the sight and he hurried towards Gunnersbury House.

As he reached the garden door it opened to reveal Princess Amelia, dressed warmly for the weather and just preparing to stride out, accompanied by Lady Hampshire.

"Ah, Colonel Melville," she said without preamble, "you will never guess what new disaster has struck. Eclipse has a cough and is confined to his stable. I simply cannot leave here with him in such a condition. So you are welcome to remain a day or two more."

John bowed. "I am most grateful, Highness. And how are you feeling?"

"Terrible, thank you. Lord Hope's body has been removed by those wretched court officials, Lady Georgiana is in an high hysteric because apparently the coroner has yet to release him for burial, and to cap it all my favourite horse is ill."

"Difficult times, Madam, difficult times."

The Princess let out a gusty sigh. "I have never known anything like it in my life. Sometimes recently I wonder if a curse has been put on this house."

"Oh no, surely not. Not a Christian household like yours," John answered, attempting to look pious.

"I hope you are right, Colonel. Now I am off to the stables to see Eclipse. Are you ready Hampshire?"

"Yes, Madam." And the actress dropped a respectful curtsey before both women set off.

Alone, John hurried into the house, determined to find Lady Theydon and get the horrible task of confronting her over and done. Purposefully he made his way to her apartments and there gave a confident knock – a confidence he was very far from feeling – on her door. Then he stood hopefully waiting while the silence surged all around him. He knocked again, but again there was no reply and putting his ear close he could hear total lack of movement within. Gingerly, almost fearfully, he put his hand on the knob and turned it. The door opened quietly, revealing spacious apartments beyond. John's eyes rapidly roamed the room checking that nobody was present, then he slipped inside, closing the door behind him.

The place was the height of vulgarity, decorated well enough but ruined by the thousand and one little nicks and nacks that Lady Theydon had dotted around the place. The Apothecary gazed with horror on a dozen little toy dogs, each with a tongue lolling out, placed on cushions round the place. These cushions in turn had awful cross-stitch sayings upon them. Messages like 'Come Unto Me' and 'For Ever Thine' met his startled gaze.

Furthermore, the lady clearly had a fetish for tying ribbons, for bows of every shape and hue were affixed to practically everything. Over the mirror, gilded and adorned with fat cupids, frantically jostling one another in their fight to get to the top, a large bow of blue with ribbons attached, fluttered in the gentle breeze. John caught sight of his reflection, eyebrows ascending to his hairline, and almost laughed aloud.

But this was not the moment for contemplation of the horrors which surrounded Lady Theydon, rather for searching for something, anything, which might link her to the deaths of Emilia and Lord Hope. Hating what he was doing but filled with an iron determination, the Apothecary started to explore the rooms.

A bedroom led off the main chamber and after a moment's hesitation he decided to start in there. Steeling himself he opened the clothes press and reeled back slightly at the odour that came from it. Stale, unwashed flesh mingled with a strong perfume which she always wore, presumably because she bathed little and was trying to disguise it. John wondered if she had ever used the Grotto for its actual purpose and plunged into the icy water. He rather doubted it.

There were a great many dresses within, all over fussy and in rather poor taste. The Apothecary wondered about her husband, mentioned but never seen, and had a mental picture of him as rather elderly and preferring to remain solitary on his estates, wherever they might be. He went deeper into the press, rootling towards the back. And then he saw it and his heart skipped a beat. Thrown onto the floor, partially hidden by a hideous pink petticoat, was a red cloak. With trembling hands the Apothecary pulled it out and saw that it had a tear at the top, a tear which fitted the piece of material he had found perfectly. And down the length of the mantle, dried now but still recognisable, were patches of a dark sinister red. Inhaling deeply, John fought to bring his breathing under control but found that he was gasping like a child.

Then he heard it. Quite distinctly footsteps were making their way along the corridor and coming towards the apartment he was currently searching. He looked round frantically as the door to the living room opened. There was only one thing for it and that was to dive under the bed. Grabbing the cloak and shutting the press, the Apothecary did just that and lay there, smelling the dust with which the floor was thickly covered.

He was fairly certain it was Lady Theydon herself, for from a minute peephole between the bed cover and the ground he could see her shoes walking back and forth. Then there came a knock at the door and he definitely recognised her heavy voice saying, 'Come.' The door opened and somebody entered the living room.

"Oh, it's you," said Lady Theydon, and rising from the chair into which she had sunk, she partially closed the bedroom door.

Within his hiding place, John cursed silently. Any hope of identifying the visitor had just been firmly dashed.

The voice said something and he heard Lady Theydon reply, "Stuff and nonsense, you really have to get a grip on yourself."

There was a remonstrance and John unsuccessfully strained his ears to hear whether it was a man or woman who spoke.

"I'm sick and tired of you," Milady went on. "I've covered for you and protected you at every turn. Why, I've even lied..." Here her voice dropped so low that the Apothecary could not catch the words, try though he might.

The other voice rose slightly but not enough for John to hear it properly.

"I've had enough of your schemes," Lady Theydon answered

firmly, standing up and starting to pace the room. "Why, if it weren't for the..." Her voice faded again as she reached the far side of the chamber and delivered the rest of her speech there.

The Apothecary cursed the fact that he was out of earshot, sure that whatever was being said was vitally important. Then he suddenly became still as the bedroom door was flung open fully.

"Get out of my sight," ordered Lady Theydon thickly from the entrance. "I can't bear even to look at you."

There was the sound of marching feet crossing the living room and a loud bang as the door opened and closed. Then there was silence.

"Oh, God's holy blood," Lady Theydon said to herself, "do I deserve to be involved with a person so odious."

John couldn't help but think that anyone with such terrible taste in objets d'art definitely deserved all they got. None the less he felt slightly sorry for the woman.

An urge to answer a call of nature was beginning to make itself felt and the Apothecary prayed that Lady Theydon wouldn't remain much longer. As if sent by heaven a bell rang loudly at that moment, making John jump, and Milady rose from the chair into which she had descended with a sigh.

"Oh pox," she exclaimed crossly. "It's the Princess."

He heard her pause before the mirror and then, much to his relief, she stamped out of the room on heavy feet. Rising from his hiding place, the Apothecary brushed the dust from his clothes and hastened to the one and only water closet that the house contained.

That afternoon, just as the blood-red sun was starting to descend to the trees, the Apothecary walked to Bellow Bridge in order to clear his head and think. Once again there was a glittering frost which marked with white fingers everything it touched. The blades of grass were hard and harsh, the trees black and bleak, the sky filled with an icy veil which hung unmoving over the landscape. Only the little Bellow Brook tinkled over the stones that lay beneath the surface of the water. It seemed to John, then, that the whole world was silent, caught beneath the spell of this intensely cold winter, waiting and hoping for the return of spring.

He was just going to cross the bridge when he heard low voices and knew by their very urgency that their conversation was private. Instinctively he stood still.

Lady Georgiana was speaking, so low that the Apothecary could not catch what she said. But he heard the reply all right. The actor's voice projected loud and clear:

"Oh darling, I can't believe that he is dead."

"Can't you?" she answered more clearly, and John's heart sank at her tone.

"Well, it's an awful shock of course but we can't pretend that it hasn't removed an enormous obstacle from our path."

"Is that how you thought of Conrad? As an obstacle?"

"Well, darling, he was."

"Michael," she said, her tone as icy as the evening, "Conrad died a terrible death, stabbed in the stomach by someone or other then pushed into the bathing pool to drown. I won't hear anyone run him down."

"I'm not running him down," Michael O'Callaghan stated with a note of despair. "I'm merely saying that with his removal the path is now clear for us."

"Yes," she answered, "suspiciously so."

"What do you mean by that, pray?"

"You can take it any way you like."

"No, wait a minute," the actor said, an edge in his voice, "are you suggesting that I had anything to do with it?"

"If the cap fits," she answered, and John could have wrung the silly girl's neck.

"I take exception to that accusation," Michael said nastily.

"So?"

"Just a minute, young lady. I can assure you that I knew nothing about his death. I was safely in Bellow's farm, working."

"At that hour of the morning you would have been in the far field," she retorted with feeling. "And there would have been no one to see if you had slipped away for thirty minutes."

The truth of this remark struck John hard and he started to wonder at the Irishman's furious self defence.

"I'll have you know, my Lady, that I worked hard all the morning, staying close to you instead of following my chosen profession on the stage."

"That was a matter entirely for you."

"No it wasn't, by God. We decided to be together come what may, unless my memory is playing tricks. For that reason I stayed behind and got a job at the farm, and for my pains I'm accused of murder. Well, good evening to you, Madam. Now that you're a wealthy widow I presume I am no longer good enough." This was followed by the noise of Michael stamping off angrily into the frosty dusk.

To give her her due, Lady Georgiana behaved with dignity and did not run after him. Instead she started to walk back slowly towards the house. Behaving nonchalantly, John fell into step just behind her. Hearing him she whirled round with a little scream.

"Oh, Colonel Melville, you startled me. I wondered who it was."

John bowed elegantly. "Only myself, my Lady. May I offer you my sincerest condolences on the untimely death of your husband."

She turned to look at him, surveying him closely. "Are you sure we have never met?"

"One cannot be sure of anything in this life. Perhaps somewhere in London our paths crossed. Who knows?"

She stopped walking and laid her hand on his arm. "How long have you been at the bridge?"

"If you are asking whether I overheard your conversation with

Michael O'Callaghan, the answer is yes I did."

"I see."

"Are you sure that you really want to break with him? Is this not just a time of heightened emotion that has left you feeling uncertain."

"You are very presumptuous, Sir. In fact I would say that you're downright saucy."

"I apologise," John said, meaning it.

"I accept your apology." They walked on in silence, then she said, "I have something to tell you. Indeed I would like your advice."

"Please go on."

"You say that I was wrong to quarrel with Michael O'Callaghan but the fact is that I don't altogether trust him."

John silently quivered. "Why is that?"

"You know that my husband was murdered in the Princess's Grotto?"

"You will remember that it was I who found him."

"Of course you did. Well, early that morning – very early – I met Michael in that very place. It was a brief meeting but the fact was that I left first and he remained behind saying that he would follow me in a moment or two so as not to arouse suspicion."

She was being amazingly forthright with him and John wondered why.

"To come directly to the point, Colonel, it would have been easy for him to loiter there and do away with my husband."

"Do you mean that they had an assignation?"

In the light of the moon that was just beginning to rise she turned frantic eyes on him. "That had never occurred to me. But yes, they might."

"But for what purpose?"

"To talk about me, of course. What else?"

Chapter Twenty-Two

"Carte blanche!" Princess Amelia said triumphantly, and laid down her cards.

John, who had hardly been able to concentrate on his hand, said, "Oh well done, Highness, well done," and resumed his thoughts about the more pressing events of the day.

He was making up a four at Piquet and was effecting a poor showing of it, partly because his brain was buzzing with information and mostly because the Apothecary's skills at gambling were limited to say the least of it.

Princess Amelia, who had insisted on playing cards before supper, said irritatingly, "I pride myself on my skill, Colonel. In less stressful times I would gladly teach you."

"Your servant, Ma'am, as in everything. How is Eclipse, by the way?"

"Still coughing a little. That nice hostler, Jago, has some special liniment which he is applying to his chest."

The third player, the Honourable Gerald Naill, said, "I always give my beasts a damn good dose of liquorice. That usually does the trick."

Lady Theydon rolled her brown eyes and remarked plummily, "Of course my dear husband is a wizard with all animals but in particular horses. He treats them all himself, you know."

"Yes, but he is not here, is he?" the Princess answered snappishly.

"Where are your estates by the way?" This from John.

"In Theydon Bois in Essex. Of course my husband spends most of his time there. He is somewhat older than I and prefers a quiet life."

John could not help but smile crookedly at his correct assessment. "How wise," he remarked.

She shot him a look but decided the comment was harmless and returned her attention to her cards.

The Apothecary took the opportunity to marshal his thoughts.

The conversation with Lady Georgiana had been most revealing. It would appear that she was one of those extremely beautiful young women whose emotions turned on a penny. Passionately in love with the Irish actor, presumably because he was difficult to secure, she had now turned violently against him and considered him capable of murder. But was he? Could her protests made with much anguish be an extremely clever cover for her own crime. Could she have waited in the bushes until she saw him depart and Lord Hope arrive, then gone in and killed him?

John cast his mind back to the performance and the possibility of her having killed Emilia. In common with most of the other actors, she had been missing for a while before she had returned to the salon in which the masque had been enacted. She would certainly have had time to slip into the woods wearing the second red cloak and murder his wife. His thoughts went back to Lady Theydon. Whoever it was who had killed Emilia, she had been an accomplice after the event. By hiding the cloak for them she was implicated in the crime. Yet today she had tired of that game and rounded on the guilty party.

The Apothecary thought back to those moments lying under the bed, surrounded by dust, and wished that he had been able to identify the person to whom Milady had been speaking. At least their sex would have helped. Yet really there was no male in the case other than the Irishman. He resolved to get to Bellow's Farm and have a chat with Michael as soon as he could.

Lady Theydon laid a card and looked at the Apothecary expectantly. He stared blankly at her and was just about to state that he had lost the thread when a servant called from the doorway, "Supper is served, Highness."

The Princess clapped her hands. "Ladies, Gentlemen, let us go in. Leave your cards exactly as they are. We can return to the game afterwards."

John stood up, much relieved, and looked round the room. The only missing person was Lady Georgiana who, as was to be expected, had taken to her chamber. Lady Featherstonehaugh and Lady Kemp were playing with Dr. Phipps and Priscilla Fleming, the last looking extremly pretty in masses of pale pink. In fact she had quite caught the eye of the gallant doctor who was paying her marked attention which she was receiving all aflutter and much to the annoyance of Lady Hampshire, who was sitting on the sidelines occasionally putting the odd stitch into a somewhat tired looking piece of embroidery.

There was a general exodus following the Princess's announcement, all with one intent. Princess Amelia purposefully headed for the one and only water closet, the gentlemen made their way out of doors, the ladies vanished to their rooms. Only the Apothecary, feeling no wish to relieve himself, stayed in the warmth of the salon and wished for the hundredth time that he was a little closer to solving the crime.

Slowly the card players began to make their way back in, waiting for the Princess to lead them into supper. John was not pleased to see Benedict standing waiting to serve the cold collation. Adjusting his eye-patch he walked straight past the fellow, following closely behind Princess Amelia, and offered his arm to Lady Featherstonehaugh. She turned to him.

"My play is sadly lacking tonight," she murmured. "Grim thoughts keep crowding in."

"That is my case also, Madam," he answered. "I am finding it hard to concentrate."

She adjusted her features to their dourest expression. "I am starting to wonder whether this place is unlucky."

"I grant you that recent events have not been of the happiest."

"It is a pity about that wretched horse." John stared at her blankly. "Getting a cough," she continued with irritation,

"Otherwise I know the Princess would have packed her bags and gone."

"Quite," the Apothecary answered, feeling just a fraction guilty.

They sat at the long dining table which despite the simplicity of the meal had been laid to overflowing. John found himself placed on the Princess's left with an empty space on his other side, the Honourable Gerald Naill on the far side of that. Staring down the line of guests he realised that Lady Theydon was missing.

Cold cuts of venison, beef, pork, together with various joints of ham, pies and game were busily being carved at the mighty dresser and passed to the guests. There was also a dish of ox tongues shaped into glazed arches nestling amongst the salads of celery, endive and chicory, together with a selection of pigeon pies easily identifiable by the spiky feet sprouting from the crust.

The Princess had started to tuck in heartily when she suddenly looked up from her groaning plate and said, "Where is Theydon?"

John glanced at the empty space beside him and said, "No doubt putting the finishing touches to her toilette."

"She should have done that hours ago. Benedict, be so good as to go and summon her."

"Yes, Your Royal Highness." And the footman bowed and made his way out.

Lady Hampshire, who had been remarkably quiet as she had been excused from cards, said "I daresay she is comforting Lady Georgiana."

Princess Amelia snorted. "I doubt it. Lady Georgiana will recover quite quickly from this shock, mark my words. A fine, strong, healthy girl like that will soon be looking around for another husband."

If anyone else had voiced this there would have been a shocked silence but as it came from royal lips there was a polite titter.

"Quite right, Madam," said Dr. Phipps. "No one should live

alone too long. A year is the absolute maximum time that anyone should remain widowed."

There was a slightly uncomfortable silence as the Princess herself had never married, though she had indeed had several lovers, the most raffish of whom had been the married Duke of Grafton. However, the doctor noticed nothing and continued to attack his pigeon pie with relish. Nobody spoke and into this temporary lull in conversation could be heard the sound of some distant commotion; feet were running and a voice was raised. Everyone at the table looked up.

"Vot is happening?" asked the Princess as the door to the dining room burst open and Benedict appeared, looking white and haggard.

"Forgive me, Highness," he panted, "but I think someone should come at once."

"Why, what's happened?" asked John.

"It's Lady Theydon, Sir. She's...dead."

Dr. Phipps and the Apothecary sat staring at one another then both rose to their feet simultaneously. John, remembering at the last minute his role as Colonel, said, "Do you mind if I accompany you, Sir? Army training."

"Of course," the doctor answered as together they raced up the stairs, the Honourable Gerald, uninvited but determined to be in on any gory details, close behind.

Hurrying along the corridor John inadvertently opened the wrong door and temporarily the three men had a vision of the Sleeping Beauty. Lady Georgiana Hope lay on top of her bed, fast asleep, her golden hair flowing loose about her shoulders, her angel's profile etched against the faint light of candles. The gentle rhythm of the rise and fall of her chest showed that she slept naturally and deeply. Just for a second John lingered longer than he should have done. Then he closed the door quietly and they hastened on.

As if in contrast to the picture they had just seen, Lady Theydon lay on her side on the floor, an expression of fear contracting her face into a silent scream. Her arms were ouflung, her legs pulled up as if she had kicked her attacker in vain. The dress she was wearing was soaked with blood and she had hunched her body in an attempt to staunch the flow. She could not have been more of a contrast to the cool perfection of Lady Georgiana's childlike repose.

The large brown eyes were open and as Dr. Phipps drew back the folds of the dress to look at the wounds John went to close them, then remembered himself.

"May I?" he asked the doctor, who nodded, too taken up with his examination to speak.

Meanwhile Gerald was making revolting retching sounds in the background and the Apothecary turned on him a furious face.

"Oh for goodness sake, Sir, do take your hideous noises elsewhere."

Gerald, who had gone a whiter shade of ashen, scurried out through the door, one hand clapped over his mouth, the other to his privy parts. Hoping that he would find a chamber pot in time, the Apothecary turned his attention back to the victim.

She had been dead about twenty minutes, half an hour at the most, which would coincide exactly with the time when the assembled company had left the room. Thinking back, John recalled that they had all gone out, every single person present; even the good doctor.

"Well?" he said.

"Whoever killed Lord Hope did this as well. Look, exactly the same modus operandi. Fatal wounds delivered to the stomach, and with some force at that."

John thought back to this morning when he had lain under the victim's bed. Yet again he cursed the fact he had not been able to identify the name or sex of Lady Theydon's visitor because that was who her killer had been, he felt certain of it. Yet this information was not something he could share with Dr. Phipps.

"Did a man or a woman inflict the blows?" he asked, a little hopelessly.

Much as he had thought, the doctor replied, "Could have been either. A woman in a rage is capable of dealing a harsh blow, believe me."

"Oh, I do," the Apothecary answered heavily, "I do."

Dr. Phipps straightened up. "Do you want to have a look?"

"Yes, I'd like to."

The wounds were deep, slicing through the material of Lady Theydon's robe and making a firm incision in the flesh below. There were three, one less than Lord Hope had received, but the same amount as inflicted on Emilia. Seeing them with fresh blood still present sickened John, reminding him only too vividly of the death of his wife.

"We've got to catch this killer and catch him fast," he said, looking up at the doctor.

"You do realise that the murderer would have blood on him like as not."

"Yes, which should narrow the field."

"Except," stated Dr. Phipps, noticing something and picking it up from the floor, "for this."

John stared. "What is it?"

"A kind of coverall." The doctor held it out and John, straightening up, took it.

"The killer put it on over their clothes?"

"It would appear so. Look." And Dr. Phipps pointed to a blood-stained, shapeless garment which resembled a white cloak complete with hood.

"God's holy wounds," swore John with much feeling. "First a red cloak and now this. The bastard thinks of everything."

"Tell me, Colonel Melville, do you think the killer is amongst the card playing company?"

"Not necessarily. There's a side staircase that leads to this landing. Very useful for smuggling lovers in and out. The murderer could have come in that way, done the deed, dropped his coverall and fled."

"But that is not necessarily what happened. The killer could be sitting downstairs at this very moment."

John nodded. "Yes, you're right. Sitting and watching to see how much we know."

They went back to a scene of complete havoc. Lady Hampshire had thrown a spectacular and somewhat theatrical faint and was lying in a becoming pose on a nest of cushions. Priscilla had also been taken poorly and was currently weeping loudly and sipping brandy, attended to by Lady Kemp who was patting her hands to no avail. Looking ghastly in the corner was the Honourable Gerald, not quite as green as when the Apothecary had last seen him but for all that clutching his guts. Benedict, very white, was uselessly walking round with a tray, while the Princess and Lady Featherstonehaugh, appearing quite calm, were stolidly munching cake and drinking madeira.

Dr. Phipps went to Milady, leaning over her and administering salts; John crossed to Priscilla's place and sat down beside her. She looked at him tremulously.

"Is...is Lady Theydon..." Her voice trailed away and she wept afresh.

John said gently, "You must be brave, Priscilla. Your aunt is dead."

For answer the girl flung her arms round the Apothecary's neck and wept uncontrollably.

Feeling her snuggled so close to him, sobbing against his chest, John wondered at himself for remaining so aloof. Then he remembered the circumstances in which the two of them had met. Emilia had been alive then and Priscilla had been her great friend, so it was small wonder that he regarded the girl as nothing more than that. Yet it occurred to him that she might indeed harbour other feelings for him. She was clinging to him as if her very life depended on it and murmuring something inaudible in his ear. Very gently, he extricated himself.

"How are you feeling?" he asked.

She turned a tear-stained face towards him. "Wretched beyond belief. Oh John, who could have done such a terrible thing? Poor Aunt Agnes." She sat upright. "I must go to her."

"No, I don't think you should."

She stood up. "But I must. Who else will tend her body?"

"It should be left for the time being. Until the Runners have been informed."

"Runners?" Priscilla looked alarmed. "Why? How did my aunt die?"

The Apothecary realised with a jolt that no one had yet told the company exactly how Lady Theydon had met her end.

"She was stabbed," he said quietly.

Priscilla let out an eldritch shriek. "Oh no, oh no. I can't bear it."

Every head, except for that of Lady Hampshire who was clearly enjoying being tended by Dr. Phipps, turned.

Princess Amelia was the first to speak. "Miss Fleming, control yourself. What is the matter?"

"Lady Theydon died at a murderer's hand," Priscilla answered dramatically.

The royal lady fixed the Apothecary with a basilisk stare. "Is this true?" she demanded.

"Perfectly," John answered. "Whoever killed Mrs. Rawlings and Lord Hope has struck again. Lady Theydon died of stab wounds to the stomach."

"Are you trying to tell me that the husband was not guilty?" the Princess went on.

"Clearly he was not."

"Then he has been greatly wronged." The royal lady stood up and turned to the doctor. "Dr. Phipps, what should we do?"

"Yet again a rider must be sent to Bow Street, Madam. There's no help for it."

"Odds my life!" Princess Amelia answered. "Was ever a woman as unfortunate as I?"

"I rather think, Madam, that Lady Theydon might not agree with that statement," John answered drily.

An hour later some semblance of order had been restored. Benedict had been despatched to lock the door of the murdered woman's room and had given the key into the safekeeping of the steward. The ladies had been escorted to their various chambers with the exception of Priscilla, who had declared herself too nervous to sleep in a room which connected to the scene of the murder by a communicating door. She had therefore been given a little used room in the guest suite to which John had accompanied her.

She had flung her arms round him and held him tightly. "Oh, my dear friend I don't know how I would have got through this evening without you."

"But I've done nothing," he had protested.

"On the contrary, you have been my rock. I shall always be grateful to you."

"Priscilla, I only did what any human being would have done."

She had smiled at him slowly. "But, my darling, it was the way that you did it that counted."

And with that remark she had left him, standing in her doorway, watching him as he made his way back down the corridor.

Now he sat with Dr. Phipps and drank brandy while Princess Amelia imbibed port.

"Tell me, Doctor, is there a lunatic killer amongst us?" she asked, her large frame hanging over the edges of the dining chair.

"It would certainly appear so, Madam."

"Will the Runners find the villain and take him away?"

"Unless we find him first," put in the Apothecary.

The Princess suddenly looked amazingly shrewd. "Is there a chance of that do you think?"

"There's every chance."

"Madam," said Peter Phipps seriously, "I would take extra precautions until the villain is apprehended. Sleep with guards on your door I pray you."

Princess Amelia raised her brows. "I certainly shall." Then she let out a low laugh. "What a conundrum to be sure. I always suspected that poor girl's husband and now it is proved not to be him at all."

John literally shivered. If his disguise were to be penetrated now then heaven alone knew what a predicament he would be in. No doubt he would be accused of committing all three crimes and arrested.

"Well, I intend to sleep with a pistol under my pillow."

"Hear, hear," said the doctor.

This last remark was greeted with a distant groan and the three of them turned to see the Honourable Gerald Naill standing in the doorway.

"Highness, I had to go out for a breath of air and I must have lost consciousness," he said.

"Well never mind, Sir. Come and sit down."

"If you'll forgive me I think I'd rather go to bed."

"I'll get one of the footmen to light your way."

"Thank you, Ma'am."

He reeled out of sight, a pathetic apparition.

The Princess turned back to her two guests. "Gentlemen, I would like to propose a toast. Here's to the rapid discovery of the killer. And here's to the profound wish that he does not strike again."

"May he not strike again," John echoed as he drank his brandy in a single swallow.

Chapter Twenty-Three

He awoke instantly and his hand was beneath the pillow reaching for his pistol before he was even fully conscious. There was nothing, total silence, and the Apothecary was on the point of thinking that what had woken him were his wild imaginings, when it came once more, a scrabbling at the door of his room and someone turning the handle. Slowly he sat upright, then lit a candle. The shadows of the great room filled his vision, sombre and dark and heavy, making him feel more nervous than he already was.

"Who's there?" he called softly.

Nobody spoke but once more there came that faint scratching. With his spine crawling John Rawlings got out of bed and, pistol in hand, proceeded slowly to the door. Then he stood in the gloom and listened.

"Let me in," whispered a voice, a voice he did not recognise.

"Who is it?" he asked again.

There was a faint sob, then came the word, "Priscilla."

The Apothecary's legs went weak with relief, then he felt annoyed that she should have woken him up. This was followed by a rapid sympathy for her. After all, it had been her aunt who had been murdered just a few hours ago. Nonetheless, it was with a certain reluctance that he turned the key in the lock and opened the door a fraction.

Her face appeared in the crack. "Oh John, I can't sleep," she whispered. "I am so distraught. Poor Aunt Agnes. What am I going to do without her?"

"You'd better come in," he said, and opened the door properly.

She entered the room, a handkerchief to her eyes. Somehow wanting to keep a distance between them, John went to the dressing table and retrieved his salts which he put beneath her nose. She took a delicate sniff, then turned on him a nervous glance.

"Forgive my coming here but I couldn't think what else to do.

Oh John, with my aunt gone you are now my only true friend."

For no particular reason he felt more than somewhat embarrassed by the situation.

"Oh, come now. What of the other ladies? What of Lady Georgiana? You and she are of an age."

"I know but believe me I have less than nothing to do with her. I do not associate myself with husband killers."

John stared at her. "What are you saying?"

"That she murdered Lord Hope. She was having an affair with Michael O'Callaghan. Everyone knew it except poor wretched Conrad. They both wanted to run away together and now Lord Hope has been removed they are free to do so."

"Are you seriously accusing her of killing him?"

"Yes, I am," Priscilla answered with a touch of defiance.

"But have you any proof?"

An unreadable expression crossed the girl's face. "Yes, as a matter of fact I have."

John sat down rather suddenly on the bed. "Why didn't you tell me this before?"

Priscilla sat down next to him. "Because I wanted to be certain in my own mind that she was the guilty party."

"And now you are?"

She turned a tear-stained face towards him. "Yes." Her voice dropped to an almost inaudible whisper. "Not only that, she did for Lady Theydon as well."

"What? But she was asleep. I looked in on her."

"Yes, I know you might well have been deceived by that Sleeping Beauty act but I saw her walking down the corridor when I went upstairs during the break before supper. If only I had challenged her but she looked strange, as if she were in a dream. I realise now that she must have been heading for my aunt's room. Oh, sweet Jesus."

Priscilla wept afresh, leaning against the Apothecary for support. Somewhat reluctantly he put his arm round her shoulders and she snuggled close to him, her strange smell filling his nostrils.

"Oh John, what would I do without you."

Ignoring this as best he could, he turned to look at her. "But Emilia's death? What of that? Do you believe that she killed my wife as well?"

"I can only presume so. I have no proof. But I know that I saw her creep into the Grotto on the morning of Lord Hope's death."

"Did you see her come out?"

"Oh yes. I hid behind a tree. She was in there half an hour or so."

"Was she covered in blood?"

Priscilla frowned. "No, I'm sure she wasn't. But how could that be?"

"Perhaps she washed it off in the bathing basin."

"Perhaps," Priscilla answered with a cross between a laugh and a sob, "she even took a bath."

A terrible picture had come into the Apothecary's mind. A picture in which a cunning woman bathed naked in the bathing pool to remove the signs of a murder before leaving the Grotto and her dead husband behind her.

He turned to Priscilla. "Thank you for telling me."

"She'll deny it of course. But the evidence is too strong."

"Indeed it is. I've asked you already but I'll ask again – why did you not speak to me of this?"

"Because I intended to set a trap for her. Use myself as bait. But now the trap has been set by Lady Theydon herself, God rest her soul."

John stood up. "Do you wish me to escort you back to your room?"

"Oh please do so. These corridors are so dark and ghostly at night."

"Very well." He picked up the candlestick and crossed to the door, waiting for her. She slowly rose from the bed and went to stand beside him.

"Thank you," she said quietly.

At that moment, her face softened b the candlelight and wearing only her night shift, she looked young and vulnerable and in need of protection. John felt immensely sorry for her.

"Don't worry, Priscilla," he said, "I am sure that everything will turn out well for you."

She gave him a tremulous smile. "I do hope you're right, Sir."

It occurred to him at that moment that she might be more than a little in love with him. There was something about the way she was looking at him, something about her manner that planted the idea. Then he wondered if she were putting the wrong construction on seeing Lady Georgiana go into the Grotto. If perhaps the woman had gone there to speak with her husband and was in fact quite innocent of the crime. If these could be the ramblings of a grief-stricken girl.

He took her arm as they walked back along the corridor. From downstairs came the faint glow of candles but these threw little light on the stairs so that on the landing itself large shadows formed pools of darkness. Passing by the door behind which Lady Theydon lay dead, John saw light and realised that someone had left tall candles burning. The thought of the corpse lying so still and white with solemn light being thrown over it made him shudder. He would be so glad, he thought, when he could leave this doomed house behind him forever.

As if picking up his thoughts Priscilla said, "I think I will leave here soon. There is nothing to stay here for now that Lady Theydon has gone."

He smiled at her. "Yes, I believe that would be for the best. But where will you go?"

Priscilla sighed. "I don't know. Perhaps I shall find a place as a governess. Something like that."

"Well don't think about it now. You have been under a great strain. You must try and get some rest."

"I'll do my best."

They had reached her room and Priscilla stopped at the door. "Goodnight John – and thank you."

He bowed. "I'm glad I was able to offer assistance." And having said this he turned away, anxious to return to the comparative safety of his room.

The rest of the night passed peacefully and John slept, somewhat to his surprise, deeply and without dreams. But as he woke the next morning it was with a sense of foreboding. He knew that somehow he must tackle Lady Georgiana and discover what it was she did in the Grotto; murder or merely have a conversation. Yet before any of this he must speak to Joe Jago who was probably still unaware of Lady Theydon's death. Accordingly, as soon as he was dressed he made his way outdoors and to the stables.

Jago was up and about, whistling to himself, a piece of straw in his mouth. He looked up as John approached.

"Good morning, Sir. I hear there was trouble in the big house last night."

"You mean Lady Theydon?" Joe nodded. "She was stabbed in the stomach while everyone broke up from cards."

And John proceeded to tell Joe the details, sparing nothing, and including Priscilla's late night visit and her accusations against Lady Georgiana Hope. When he had finished speaking, the clerk looked thoughtful.

"If it's true, Sir, then your search is over."

"Indeed it is. But somehow I doubt it. I looked into her bedroom just after the murder had been committed and there she was sleeping peacefully as a babe. Of course that could have been an act but somehow I don't think so."

"And there is no possibility that there could be two murderers?"

"If so, one is cleverly copying the other."

"Which has not been unknown in the past, Mr. Rawlings."

"Indeed not. But somehow I do not think that that is the case.

I believe that this is the work of one person and I think that person is slightly deranged."

"Um." Joe chewed slowly on the straw. "Either that or very clever."

"Perhaps a bit of both."

Jago nodded slowly but said nothing further and John continued, "So meanwhile what do you advise me to do about Lady Georgiana?"

"I'd ask her what she was doing in the Grotto, other than spooning with Michael O'Callaghan. Speak as the Colonel and go all officious-like. Say you have a witness who saw her going in and coming out."

"And if she refuses to answer me?"

"Then I will have to drop my role as an hostler and speak to her as an official of the court. There's nothing else for it."

"You're right. Joe, tell me..."

"Yes."

"Have you learned much stuck here in the stables? Did your ruse succeed?"

"Surprisingly, yes. It's amazing what gossip one learns round horses. Did you know that the Princess visits Eclipse almost daily and rides him twice a week? And who should she talk to when she is here but the friendly hostler. Oh yes, I have learned a great deal. And what of you, Sir? How is Colonel Melville getting along?"

"Quite well. No one has recognised me so far."

"Good. Well, do your best with Lady Georgiana. Remember that I will assist you if you get into difficulties."

"It seems a pity for you to break cover."

"I'll have to do so one day," Joe answered practically.

It was a pleasant morning, not as bitingly cold as it had been, and John felt his spirits start to rise. Soon it would be March and the return of spring, and already in the gardens were the first signs of the earth's awakening. Buds were swelling and he beheld clumps of snowdrops amongst the trees. He thought of Devon's magnificent skylines in springtime and wished he could be there again, riding wild and free behind Elizabeth's horse.

He smiled to himself. He always imagined her like that, leading him into adventure, never the other way round. Yet she had followed him to Gunnersbury and taken the most lowly job on the servants' scale. She was indeed a truly magnificent woman and the Apothecary wondered what it was that stirred in his heart when he thought about her.

He put his hand in his pocket and felt the earring, drawing it out and looking at it. Then he had an idea and carefully put it back again. Quickening his pace, John Rawlings made his way determinedly to Gunnersbury House.

It was horribly hushed within, the servants speaking in whispers and everyone he could see in deepest black. John considered that they had donned mourning for Lord Hope and were now continuing for Lady Theydon. It seemed, however, that some of the quiet was caused by the fact that most of the party had gone out for a walk in the countryside, and that the house was pretty well deserted. His enquiry after Lady Georgiana elicited the reply that she was taking the air in the garden on the orders of her physician. Nodding discreetly, John made his way outside once more.

She was arranged in a bevy of cushions which had been placed on a metal seat, her very posture reminding him of a poem he had once read about melancholy; eyes lowered, head elegantly placed in a hand, shoulders drooping. Clearing his throat loudly, John approached.

She looked up at the sound and managed the faintest of smiles. "How do you do, Colonel?"

"Very well, thank you, Ma'am. May I sit down?"

She made no effort to move but indicated the seat opposite. "Yes, by all means. I cannot promise to be the soul of linguistic skill, however."

"Never you mind," John answered cheerily. "I can talk enough for the pair of us."

Georgiana rolled her eyes slightly but gave him a wan smile as he took a seat across the way from hers.

There was a short silence, then she said, "You must forgive me, Colonel Melville. I am so deeply saddened."

"But surely your path is now clear," the Apothecary answered firmly.

She looked up, startled. "I beg your pardon?"

"I said surely your path is now clear to marry Michael O'Callaghan."

Georgiana looked at him coldly. "How dare you say that? As I told you the other night, I no longer trust him."

"As you know, Ma'am, I'm Richard Melville of His Majesty's army. However, I undertake special duties on behalf of the government." John adopted a mysterious look from his range of facial expressions. "So now I am going to speak to you very frankly, if I may."

She made to get up and walk away but the Apothecary said, "It would be advisable that you remain, Lady Georgiana."

She sat down again and shot him a furious glance. "Well?"

"The fact is that your affair with Mr. O'Callaghan is known and spoken of. Therefore it is my sad duty to ask you why you returned to the Grotto on the morning of your husband's death, after your conversation with the actor. And do not pretend that Lord Hope was not within because I have a witness who will say to the contrary."

She looked at him and her eyes were icy. "Who is this witness?"

"I am not at liberty to disclose that information. Suffice it to say that they are reliable."

Lady Georgiana gazed down again, her hands in her lap, apparently wrestling with her innermost thoughts. Finally she gave him another cold stare.

"I went into the Grotto to meet my husband. I was going to ask him for a divorce."

John's mind boggled, knowing the enormous difficulties of achieving such an enterprise.

"Yes?" he said.

"He refused to give me one. Said I was his wife and so I would remain until his death. We quarrelled – did your witness tell you that?"

The Apothecary shook his head.

"Well, we did. Anyway, I flounced out and left him there, staring into the bathing pool. That was the last time I ever saw him alive." She moved impatiently. "I never loved him, you know. My father arranged my marriage. I never cared for anyone until I met Michael. And now I'm not sure I even like him."

"He's a feckless devil but for all that he thinks the world of you."

"Yes." She gave a humourless laugh. "I'm sure he does. But that does not stop him being a murderer."

The Apothecary became businesslike. "So you are telling me that you quarrelled with your husband but that he was alive when you left him?"

"I'm telling you the truth. It may look black against me but that is what happened."

John merely nodded, placing the ends of his fingers together. "Tell me, what did you do when you left the Grotto?"

"I went back to the house and then went for a walk."

"Alone?"

"Yes, quite. I wanted to think about the future, about what we were going to do." She looked John straight in the eye. "Tell me Colonel, do you think Michael is guilty of murder?"

"I don't know," he answered honestly.

"And me?"

"I don't know that either."

She nodded. "At least you tell the truth."

"I wish that everybody did the same." John reached in his pocket. "By the way, is this yours?"

She took the earring from him, holding it in her long pale fingers. "No. Where did you find it?"

"In the grounds," he lied, thinking how easy it was for someone who was meant to be honest. "It was lying in the grass."

Georgiana looked thoughtful. "It could be the Princess's, though I'm not certain. She has so much jewellery that it's difficult to know one piece from another."

John stood up, indicating that their interview was at an end. Then he kissed her hand.

"You have been most helpful, Milady. I wish you good day."

"Good day," she answered, and watched him, shading her eyes with her hand, as he went back towards the house.

Chapter Twenty-Four

An atmosphere of intense gloom had settled over Gunnersbury House. Despite the fact that the walking party had returned it was nevertheless so quiet one could have heard a needle drop. The footmen, complete with black armbands, were talking in whispers, while the guests, about to go into luncheon, had an air of enormous restraint. Only the Honourable Gerald Naill, who had apparently stayed behind and knocked back most of a decanter of sherry, was oozing cheerfulness to all and sundry.

"How do, Melville," he called in jolly fashion.

"Very well, thank you."

"Care to join me in a drink?"

"No, not just at present. I must freshen up before luncheon." And the Apothecary made his escape upstairs to the room which he had been allotted.

On the landing the silence was profound and the atmosphere terrifying. John, even though it was bright daylight, felt quite nervous as he made his way to his chamber past the place where the body of Lady Theydon lay, waiting the arrival of Sir John Fielding's Fellows. Yet even as he drew level with the door his footsteps slowed and for some reason he found himself listening intently. In fact he even went so far as to stop outside for a moment or two.

Within, the candles that had been lit must have gone out, for there was no light coming from beneath. But there was a faint sound, a rustling as if somebody were turning over items, looking for something. John's scalp seethed and he had a mental picture of Lady Theydon, complete with bloody wounds, risen from the dead and searching the room for an article she had once treasured. He steadied himself and gently opened the door.

The corpse lay where it had been placed on the bed, the sheet covering it starkly revealing the shape of Lady Theydon who lay beneath. There had clearly been no resurrection. But for all that, John could not help but draw back the cover and peer beneath. He saw to his horror that one of the corpse's eyes had opened and was staring at him with a baleful glance. He hurriedly drew the sheet back again, leaving the dead woman to wink in peace.

But opening drawers and searching light-fingeredly within, her back turned to the Apothecary who had entered noiselessly, was Lady Hampshire. John stood watching her in amazement, seeing the dexterity with which she riffled amongst the clothes, until eventually she made a little sound of triumph and withdrew a ring box. Opening it, still with her back turned, she took out a ring and placed in on her finger, which she twisted hither and thither in the light, lost in admiration. From where he stood the Apothecary let out a deliberate cough and the woman spun round, clutching her heart.

She gazed at him, a look of terror on her face. "Oh, Colonel Melville," she managed to gasp. "I thought..."

"That the dead had risen? No, Madam, it is only me. May I ask what you were doing just now?"

She clutched her throat. "Oh, I'm going to faint, I feel certain of it. Help, Sir. I'm falling."

John caught her as she went down, thinking to himself that she was a truly exceptional actress. However, he went through the motions of bringing her round, holding his salts so close to her nostrils that she coughed violently, her eyes opening wide.

"Oh my dear Sir," she said feebly, "be so good as to see me back to my chamber."

John suddenly felt irritated beyond belief, sick of being ordered around by foolish women. The need to find the killer was of paramount importance. Seizing Lady Hampshire by the upper arm he thrust her into a chair.

"First," he said, a definite edge to his voice, "you will tell me what you were doing in here."

She made a moue. "As a matter of fact I came to recover a ring

I had loaned..." Her voice dropped to a murmur. "...Lady Theydon."

"Why now? Why with the dead woman still in the room? I think the truth is that you had taken a fancy to something of hers and were determined to have it, paying scant respect to the recently departed."

Her once-beautiful eyes narrowed. "If you accuse me of theft then I shall accuse you of murder."

"Accuse away. I was the only one who didn't leave the room when Lady Theydon was killed. I stayed where I was and was visible all the time to the footmen."

"A likely tale," she sneered.

John took a chance. "I think you got the habit of stealing before you became an actress and that it has stayed with you ever since. I also believe that you have been pilfering from Lady Theydon for some time and the ring was one thing you were determined to have."

Her face took on a look of malice. "So what if I did? Lady Theydon would have left me the ring if she had lived to make a will."

"How do you know that she hasn't? No doubt her lawyers in London would be able to enlighten you."

She changed from spiteful creature to supplicant in the wink of an eye. "Oh, Colonel, I beg you not to reveal my shame. It is true that I longed for that ring – see, there it is on my finger. Don't you think it looks fine? But I would never have killed for it, I assure you. Indeed, Lady Theydon promised it to me, I swear it."

Until that moment it had never occurred to John that Lady Hampshire would go so far as to murder to obtain something bright and sparkling, but now the idea came with full force. Staring at her he could see a wild gleam in her eye when she spoke about the jewel. The wild gleam of someone who could not help themselves and who would go to any lengths to obtain their desire.

"Very well, I won't tell anybody about what you have just done. Now, put the ring back and we'll forget it."

She took it off, reluctantly, but he could see by the slightly crazy expression in her eye that she would be back for it.

Having escorted Milady to her room, John went to his own. There he washed his face and hands in cold water and was just about to go down to luncheon when his door opened. The Apothecary turned in surprise from the basin to see Elizabeth framed in the doorway.

"My dear girl," he said, "what are you doing here?"

She pulled a face. "I'm emptying the slops."

"Well, I haven't got any."

"I'll take your washing water."

"Of course." And he carried the basin and emptied it into the unpleasant bucket she was carrying. "Oh God, Elizabeth," he went on, "you shouldn't be doing this."

She raised an expressive shoulder. "My dear John, I could hardly get a post as a parlourmaid, now could I? But I'm afraid I've been of no great help to you, other than for finding out about Benedict."

John was agog. "I know that he has a passion for you. But what did you discover?"

"That he spies for Princess Amelia. Oh yes, I know she looks harmless but she hates anything – anything at all – to slip past her. So she employs Benedict to find out everything that is going on."

"And does he?"

"Mostly. He is very puzzled by you, incidentally, though he hasn't realised who you really are. Nonetheless he is certain you are not what you seem."

"Whatever gave him that idea?"

"He says you are too light-hearted to be an army man."

"The gall of the fellow. I'd be obliged if he took his notions elsewhere."

Elizabeth turned away. "But actually I've been of little practical help, have I?"

John stood studying her back, noticing yet again how straight and strong she was, how, other than for her firm high bosom, he was looking at a fairly masculine physique. And then he noticed the hollow where her neck met her shoulders and the most extraordinary sensation swept over him. It was a mixture of emotions: grief at losing Emilia, the age-old longing common to all red-blooded males, the desperate need for physical comfort. Coming up behind Elizabeth, he put his arms round her and kissed her neck again and again with a kind of frantic despair. She turned to face him and at that moment he desired her more than anything else in the world. He put his lips on hers and kissed her deeply, for a long time. Then he couldn't help himself. He started to press close to her and raise her skirts.

Elizabeth frowned. "John?" she said.

"I want you," he answered.

Her expression changed. "No, John, not until you want me for myself alone."

"What do you mean?"

"It's Emilia you are missing, it's her that you need."

"No, that isn't true."

"I'm afraid, my dearest, that it is."

"Elizabeth, I swear..."

"Say no more," she answered, putting her finger to his lips. "Just ask me when your sadness has gone."

"And will you agree?"

She smiled a witch's smile. "Wait and see," she said, and picking up the sordid bucket she left the room.

John stood, gazing at where she had been, trying to control himself, hoping against hope that she would reconsider and return. But after a few minutes during which his breathing returned to normal, he knew that she would not. Looking in the mirror he saw that his eyes were full of lust and longing, as was the rest of his body. Straightening his clothes and adjusting his eye patch, then sighing deeply, John Rawlings slowly descended the staircase.

He thought about Elizabeth all through the light meal, picturing her as she had stared up at him, her ugly beauty so close, the scar which she hated one of the most attractive things about her. In fact he was so rapt in contemplation that he said and ate little and sat deep in thought, picking at his food and leaving half of it on his plate.

Not everyone was present, the Princess having taken herself off, Lady Hampshire deciding to remain in her room, and those that did foregather were in no mood for conversation. Sitting silently in this way, it suddenly occurred to the Apothecary that the Beak Runners – Sir John's mobile unit – would probably be due to arrive that very afternoon. If so it was imperative that he absent himself quickly. Much as he had a good relationship with Runners Ham and Raven, he knew that their patience with him must now be wearing thin. They were bound to make an arrest. Consequently, as soon as it was polite to do so, John excused himself from the table, put on the Prince of Mecklenburg's sturdy cape and walked out into the winter sunshine.

It was a fine afternoon and John made his way to The Temple, determined to look round once more. But as he approached the door he heard two whispering voices and, flattening himself behind a pillar, listened carefully to what they had to say, determined that if it was nothing to do with the murders he would absent himself.

"My dear," said Lady Kemp, "do you think I should tell those court officials, the Runners?"

"Well, it really is up to you and your conscience," answered Lady Featherstonehaugh.

"What do you mean by that, pray?"

"Simply that in so doing you might be implicating yourself."

"I see."

There was a silence, then Lady Featherstonehaugh said, "You must agree that our actions are decidedly odd."

"Yes, but so interesting. Anyway you've made my mind up for me. I shall say nothing to Sir John Fielding's Fellows."

"Well, I've made up my mind. I think you should."

"Oh la, my dear, now you've sent me into a regular pother. I don't know what to do."

"Tell them."

"I'll think about it. That's the most I can say."

"Oh zoonters!" retorted Lady Featherstonehaugh crossly.

John moved away wondering what in heaven's name that extraordinary bit of conversation had been about. At the moment it meant nothing but perhaps something would reveal itself in due course. In any event, it was time he visited Bellow's Farm and quizzed Michael O'Callaghan. He set off at a brisk pace through the estate, not risking going by road. But as he proceeded into the trees he was aware of a coach turning into the carriage sweep and saw that the Runners had arrived and had brought with them the cart they used for transporting the dead. The grim thought that Lady Theydon had also been placed under the coroner's jurisdiction struck him most forcibly.

At this point in his perambulation Bellow Brook divided the grounds from the farmlands and, slithering down the bank, John crossed on the stepping stones and climbed up the embankment the other side. Then, shaking the water from his shoes, he removed his eye-patch and made his way to the farm.

To his astonishment he saw that Hugh Bellow was up, leaning heavily on his homemade crutches. Jake, meanwhile, looking amazingly good-tempered, was milking. Of Michael O'Callaghan there was no sign.

"Good afternoon, Sir," called John. "It's nice to see you up and about."

Hugh pulled a face. "I'm more of a supervisor than a worker.

But at least I've said goodbye to my bed."

"May I look at your leg?"

"By all means. Shall we step inside?"

"Gladly."

As he went into the farmhouse Jacob looked up from the milking shed and gave the Apothecary a black glare. John responded with a cheery wave and a bow.

They stepped into the warmth of the kitchen and Hugh hobbled to the dresser and poured two pints of beer from a stone vessel.

"Well, my friend," he said heartily, "it's good to see you again."

"And you Hugh. Tell me, how is the new hand getting on?"

"Well, he's a good worker, I'll say that much."

"But...?"

"But he mysteriously vanishes from time to time. Jake can't be everywhere and I can only hobble round the farmyard so he has a pretty free rein, of which he takes full advantage. Mind you, he's always back for his dinner. Never misses. And he has an appetite like an horse."

"Where is he now?"

"Heaven knows."

"Well, I'll have a look at your leg then I'll go and search for him. I want to ask him a few questions."

Hugh looked grim. "I hear the big house has become a place of death. Two more gone. Who can possibly be the culprit?"

The Apothecary shook his head. "I have no idea, I'm afraid. Yet the need to solve the crimes is imperative. The Princess will stay in the house for only a couple more days, three at the most. Then she will shut the place down and that will be that."

"You mean the murderer will get away unpunished?"

"Yes," said John baldly, recalling the minutes he had spent under Lady Theydon's bed, down in the dust, and yet been none the wiser about the killer's identity.

An inspection of Hugh's injury – which was healing slowly but soundly – over, John sauntered out and stared round the farm's considerable holdings, wondering exactly where Michael O'Callaghan had got himself.

"Come back to spy on us?" said a voice behind him, and he turned to see Jacob, milk bucket in hand, giving him a supercilious look.

"On the contrary," John answered smoothly. "I've actually come to have a word with the new hand."

Jake snorted. "Him. He's about as much good as you were. Soft like all you town folks. Work-shy."

"That's not what your father told me." The Apothecary paused, then said, "Look, Jacob, I know you've hated me since I first arrived at Bellow's Farm but there is no need, really. I don't want to take your place in your father's affections nor am I after usurping your position. Neither is Michael O'Callaghan. We are simply here to help during your father's disability. That's all."

Jake scowled at the milk bucket. "That's your story. I think you're a murderer."

"Then why," said the Apothecary, thoroughly put out, "don't you go to the constable in Brentford and hand me in?"

"Cos I've better things to do with my time."

"Nonsense. There's a substantial reward. Go ahead and claim it."

"And earn my father's wrath? No, it wouldn't be worth the money."

"Surely you could go in secret. Need your father ever know?"

"He'd find out somehow. He's got a bit of gypsy blood and nothing escapes him."

"That's what I could do with, a bit of clairvoyance. 'Zounds, what a tangled web this is."

Jacob put the bucket down. "I'll tell you this much, John Rawlings – that is your real name, isn't it?" The Apothecary nodded. "That Irishman spends half his time on the Gunnersbury

Park estate. Crosses over by the way you came in, judging by the state of your boots."

John looked down and saw that mud from the embankment had indeed stuck to his footwear.

"And what do you reckon to that?"

"I reckon that he's either mad for love or that he's killing people," Jacob answered succinctly. Then he spat on the ground, picked up the bucket, and strode into the house without a backward glance.

Half an hour later John was sitting on a bale of hay, telling Joe Jago everything that had happened that day, with the exception of his interlude with Elizabeth. For dear friend that Joe was, he could not bring himself to discuss the strange feelings that had swamped him when he had been in her company. Feelings that had been in his mind all day and which he had overcome by forcing them firmly away, only for them to come creeping back as soon as he relaxed.

"So, Sir," asked Joe, "what do you think of Lady Georgiana's version of events?"

John sucked on a piece of straw. "It's difficult to say but quite honestly I tend to believe her."

"You do, eh." Joe went very quiet, the light blue eyes gazing into the middle distance, and John knew from his look that the clerk was deep in thought. Eventually he said, "Tell me, Sir, what kind of woman she is."

"What do you mean?"

"Is she a foolish flap or does she have strength."

"A combination of the two," John answered. "She's fickle in her views but I believe she has a tough backbone."

"How tough?"

"I don't know, Joe. At a guess I would say she's pretty strong – I mean, she was considering running away with Michael O'Callaghan while her husband was alive, and that takes some doing."

Joe's eyes took on that faraway look once again. "I think I'd better speak with her," he said.

"Changing the subject utterly, how is Eclipse?"

"I can announce to the world that he is cured."

"Does Princess Amelia know?"

"She does. She intends to make public tonight the fact that she is packing up this house in two days time."

"Oh 'zounds and 'zooters," exclaimed John. "We'll never catch the villain in that short space."

"That's where I think you're wrong, Sir. I think his or her lordship is about to strike again."

"You do?"

"I'm certain of it. They must be flushed with triumph that nobody has suspected them so far. Now, what I want you to do is stay in the house and stay put. Keep your eyes everywhere."

"But the place is enormous, Joe."

"You'll find a way, Sir. I have every confidence."

"And what about you? What are you going to do?"

"Me, Sir? I am going to reveal myself for who I truly am. Tonight I am going to see the Princess herself."

"And what are you going to say to her?"

"I've no idea at present," Joe answered cheefully.

And with that the clerk turned away and started polishing some bridle brass, whistling to himself as he did so.

Chapter Twenty-Five

Leaving Joe in the stables, John walked back through the setting sun. The snow was not on the ground but in many ways the late afternoon brought the occasion of Emilia's death vividly to mind. Though not as cold there were so many similarities that he paused for a moment and drew a breath or two to calm himself. He only hoped that Joe was right, that the murderer would strike again and this time they would be waiting for him or her.

His thoughts turned to Elizabeth and just for a moment he was brutally honest with himself. He longed for her so much and yet she was so powerful a woman that he could not face the thought of anything permanent. He had been in love with Emilia and no one else could ever take her place. Yet, like a mighty river, his love flowed into tributaries, and in common with the whole of mankind he longed for company. So this was to be his dilemma. He was caught in the trap that enfolds all humanity.

He walked on, then for a moment thought she had come back to him. With the dying sun shining on the Round Pond, blinding him, he could see the shape of a woman, blackly etched against the sunset. She stood motionless, looking in his direction. John could not help himself; he broke into a run towards her. But as he got closer he saw that it was Priscilla who was standing there, smiling at him. She held out her hands.

"John, my dear, you look agitated. Is anything the matter?"

He felt like answering that the entire situation was enough to make anyone discomposed but decided against it.

"No, nothing. I didn't recognise you, that's all."

She dimpled at him. "Come, Sir, I would have thought you know me well enough by now."

"The sun was in my eyes."

"Oh, I see."

She slipped her arm through his. "John…"

"Yes?"

"Oh, nothing. This isn't the time. Will you walk me back to the house?"

"Of course," John answered, and headed off in the direction of Princess Amelia's residence.

Priscilla, who was becomingly arrayed in a soft grey cloak with a hood, must have sensed his mood for she said little as they progressed side-by-side. Finally, though, she spoke.

"I don't suppose I shall see you again after tomorrow."

He turned on her a look of astonishment. "Why?"

"Because Eclipse is better and the Princess intends to close up the house and return to London. She says she has had enough of death and despair and one can hardly blame her. I shall go back with her and then I shall have to find employment elsewhere." She looked at him from her small eyes, obviously expecting him to say something, but when nothing was forthcoming, went on, "John, will you be looking for someone to care for little Rose?"

So that was the way her mind was working. Hastily, John said, "You realise that I am still wanted in connection with my wife's murder. Until I am cleared I am not going to be in a position to employ anyone."

Priscilla slowed her pace. "I suppose you're right. But when you're exonerated, as you will be, kindly remember me."

He did not know how to answer her so he said nothing. But he knew in his heart that he would never employ her, convinced that she had grown fond of him and was probably after more than simply caring for his daughter. Keeping his eyes steadfastly in front of him, John walked on.

He entered the house to sense an air of excitement, which, he thought, had lifted the atmosphere completely. Lady Hampshire was in the large reception vestibule talking spiritedly to Dr. Phipps, who was listening politely. They both turned as John came in with Priscilla, and John saw a gleam in Milady's eye which made him realise that she was seeing them as a couple, albeit in his guise of Colonel Melville. His heart sank further at the thought.

"My dears," Lady Hampshire said immediately, "you will hardly credit what has happened."

"What, Madam?" Priscilla enquired.

"The hostler from the stables has arrived here, quite smartly dressed, and it turns out he was working for Sir John Fielding all along. He is presently ensconced with the Princess herself."

"Gracious! Are you sure?"

"Positive. Apparently she granted him an audience because he has been so good to Eclipse. Seems he knows all about horses too. A regular Jack of all trades."

"More like a Jack in office," Priscilla said sharply. "To think he's been here spying."

"He's been helping to find the murderer," John commented drily.

Priscilla fluttered in his direction. "Of course you're right, Colonel. It's just that his secrecy seems so intrusive somehow."

"I can't agree with that," he replied, looking straight at her, and as he could have predicted, she dropped her eyes.

Gerald Naill came in from the direction of the garden, looking rather flushed. "Seems the hostler was Sir John's man, by God. I wonder who he is going to arrest."

"What makes you say that?" This from Dr. Phipps.

"I don't know exactly." Gerald looked crafty. "But someone is going to get the chop up, I feel it."

"I'm not so sure," said Lady Hampshire. Then her expression changed as she remembered the recent incident regarding the ring. She gave John a guilty look.

He was wondering what to say next, literally changing his weight from one foot to the next, when the door to Princess Amelia's red salon opened unexpectedly and a footman appeared.

"Colonel Melville, would you be so good as to attend Her Highness."

So this is it, the Apothecary thought. For better or worse my true identity is about to be revealed. Aloud he said, "Certainly," bowed to the assembled company and solemnly followed the servant into Princess Amelia's private sanctum.

It was not a room he had been in before and he was immediately struck by its splendour. Wonderful red and gold wallpaper adorned the walls, which were finished with fine curtains, pale pink with deep red flowers adorning their length. Tied with bows to a rod above, they hung from ceiling to floor, swishing graciously downwards. Above the marble fireplace, picked out in gilt, was a panel with a beautifully painted classical scene. But dominating all was a glorious crystal chandelier, presently in the process of being lit by a servant. Bowing deeply to the Princess, John was solemnly ushered to a seat. He sat down in silence and waited for someone to speak.

Joe Jago, looking quite handsome in a smart suit of dark blue embroidered with silver, waited for the footman to leave the room, then he turned to John.

"Mr. Rawlings, you may reveal yourself to Her Highness. I have spoken to her in confidence and she has forgiven you your deception."

Feeling totally unconfident, John slowly removed his eyepatch, then his wig. Then he stood up while the Princess stared at him.

"So, Sir, apparently you did not kill your wife," she said finally.

"No, Madam, I did not."

"Then why were you found with the knife in your hand?"

"I did not know I even had it. All I do know was that I found her dying and held her close to my heart. I was not aware of the passing of time. In fact, I was aware of nothing until the search party came looking for me."

"You had the look of guilt about you."

"I can assure you, Ma'am, that I am not guilty of the crime, nor any of the others. I disguised myself as Colonel Melville because I was desperate to gain entry to the house and find the murderer for myself."

"He speaks the truth, Highness," said Joe. "I have known Mr. Rawlings for several years and I would trust him with my life."

For some reason John found this statement so touching that despite his resolution tears filled his eyes and he was forced to turn away and wipe them with a handkerchief. When he had recovered himself he turned back to Princess Amelia thinking that he must look a total fool. The red in his hair was growing out so that now, wigless, he looked like a child's drawing of the sun. Further he was certain that he had dirty streaks on his face. Swallowing hard, John tried to smile.

She gave him a surprisingly gentle glance. "So it would appear that I was wrong about you."

"Yes, Ma'am, I think you were."

"So who do you believe is responsible for these crimes?"

John shrugged expressive shoulders. "Highness, I have no idea. Someone in your household I would imagine."

"Vie do you say zat? Could it not be a person unknown?"

"But what motive would they have? Surely it has to be someone who is on the inside." Suddenly John found himself blurting out the story of his hiding in Lady Theydon's bedroom and the conversation he had overheard while doing so.

Princess Amelia listened in silence, eventually saying, "That would appear to prove it, though not necessarily."

"What do you mean, Ma'am?" asked Joe.

"It is possible that her visitor was not from this house."

"It is indeed possible but not probable," Joe answered firmly. "I agree with Mr. Rawlings. The killer lies within."

"With, of course, the exception of Michael O'Callaghan."

"But he has gone, surely," put in the Princess.

"No, Ma'am," said John carefully. "He is still around; working at Bellow's Farm to be precise."

"Oh the rascal. I suppose he could not leave the side of his beloved." A devious look came over her face. "The death of Lord Hope has certainly eased the path of that pair of thwarted lovers."

"It has indeed," replied Joe weightily. "I feel I ought to tell you, Highness, that Miss Fleming believes that the killer meant to do for her rather than for Mrs. Rawlings."

"Oh? And why is that?"

John and Joe exchanged a look, realising that they were treading on dangerous ground.

"Well, why?" the Princess asked emphatically.

Joe cleared his throat. "She tells an extraordinary tale, Ma'am. Namely that she bore the bastard son of your nephew, the King, and that since the child's death people have been out to finish her off."

The Princess turned on them a gaze of astonishment. "But that is utter rubbish. My nephew was a total innocent until he fell into the clutches of Sarah Lennox. But his mother soon put paid to that little plot hatched by the Fox family, and now the King is happily married."

John caught himself thinking that if there was any reality to Priscilla's story the relationship would have been conducted in the utmost secrecy.

It appeared that Joe was having the same idea, for he said, "Indeed, Ma'am, it is hard to know what to believe."

The Princess gave a snort. "The wish was father to the thought, I reckon."

John said, "But do we have an inkling who has committed the crimes?"

"Not as yet," Joe answered. "But we shall soon, believe me."

Feeling decidedly the worse for wear, John went to his room and there washed his face, remembering as he did so the occasion on which Elizabeth had come in unexpectedly. Now he felt slightly ashamed of the way he had treated her, holding her so close and kissing her so deeply.

He sat down on the bed and thought about her, remembering their first meeting when she had been dressed as a man. Yet despite her slightly masculine build Elizabeth was a true woman, a woman who yearned for love. A love which one day he would give her, he knew. He wondered then if he were starting to recover from Emilia's death but realised that, in common with all mankind, it was physical longing that made the Marchesa so very important to him. But was it just that alone? Thinking of everything that had passed between them, John knew that it was the woman herself who was so vital to him.

He lay down on the bed and closed his eyes, and must have briefly dropped off to sleep because when he looked at his watch an hour had gone by. Wondering what stage Joe Jago had reached, John struggled into an evening coat of the Prince's – altered by Priscilla – and went downstairs.

Everyone must have been changing for dinner because the place was deserted and John wandered amongst the grand chambers, climbing the stairs in his search and even going to the room in which Emilia had performed the masque. There was no one around other than for the servants.

"Do you happen to know where Mr. Jago is?" he enquired of a footman.

"He has gone to see Lady Georgiana, Sir. He has been in with her for almost an hour."

"Good gracious. Ah well, thank you."

He turned to descend the staircase again and then suddenly a door somewhere burst open and the frantic figure of Milady appeared running down the corridor towards John.

"Save me," she gasped.

"From what, Ma'am?"

"From that terrible man. He has been questioning me and now he is going to make an arrest."

John stared at her blankly. "Of whom, pray?"

"Why, of me of course."

But it was too late. Joe was marching purposefully down the passageway and had caught Georgiana up.

"Madam," he said, "I am arresting you for the murders of Mrs. Rawlings, your husband Lord Hope, and Lady Theydon. I would advise you to come with me quietly."

"But Joe..." John started.

The clerk turned on him a fierce look, closely resembling some mythical figure of vengeance with his coppery curls alight and his blue eyes blazing.

"Sir, everything has been given away by the fact that Madam dropped an earring whilst about her husband's murder. An earring which is still in your possession, I believe."

"Yes," the Apothecary answered faintly.

"Be so good as to fetch it."

John stared at them, wondering that such a simple piece of jewellery could belong to such a woman. Then he slowly made his way to his room and fetched the earring from its hiding place in his drawer, where he had placed it for safekeeping. By the time he returned Lady Georgiana had come downstairs with Jago one step behind.

"Well, Sir, be good enough to show it to Milady."

Reluctantly, John took it out of his pocket and offered it to Lady Georgiana. She gazed at it, then said, "No, that is not mine. As I have already told you, I don't know to whom it belongs."

"You will have to tell that to Sir John Fielding," said Joe firmly. "Now, are you going to make a fuss or behave yourself."

She shot him a look of pure dislike, then, with her head held high, allowed him to lead her out of the house.

Half an hour later dinner was served, it being six o'clock and somewhat later than was customary. News of the arrest of Lady Georgiana had swept the house like an infectious disease and everyone was agog with the gossip.

Princess Amelia set the tone by announcing in no uncertain

terms, "If Mr. Jago believes it is her, then he is right. That man is thoroughly sound. After all, remember what he did for Eclipse."

"Yes, but women and horses are different species, Ma'am," put in the Honourable Gerald Naill, and was given a series of black looks from the assembled company for his pains.

The Princess gave a contemptuous snort. "I am avare of zat, Mr. Naill. It is Jago's integrity that I was commenting upon."

"Quite so," he answered, deciding that discretion was the better part of valour.

Priscilla, pink in the cheeks, spoke up. "It's truly hard to believe it of Lady Georgiana."

"Believe it or believe it not," said Lady Hampshire, "it has happened."

"There are many things that one cannot believe," Princess Amelia commented, fixing Priscilla with a dark gaze.

John decided he must speak. "Jago must have had good reason to arrest Lady Georgiana. He does not do things lightly."

"But Colonel..."

"Allow me to interrupt," the Princess said in ringing tones, "the Colonel is a piece of fiction. It is Mr. Rawlings that you are addressing. He entered this house in disguise to find his wife's killer. And none of you recognised him," she ended triumphantly.

"Not even you, Ma'am," remarked Lady Featherstonehaugh quietly.

The Princess glared and Lady Kemp tittered.

John removed his eye-patch and wig and, rising, bowed to the assembled company, who applauded mildly.

"I am so sorry that I had to gain entry by false means but there was no other way for it."

It was at that moment a thought struck him so forcibly that he sat down again rather rapidly, smiling automatically, even though his mind was a million miles away. He was remembering an incident that had happened long ago. A night when a silent figure had stood in his garden and watched his house. A figure full of menace that had disappeared rapidly when it realised that it had been observed.

"How was Lady Georgiana removed?" This from Lady Hampshire.

"Those awful Runner people came in a coach and took her and Mr. Jago away. My God, to think she'll be clapped in Newgate."

John could have answered that he imagined that she would be kept in the cells below the court at Bow Street but could not bring himself to reply.

Priscilla caught his eye and she gave him a warm smile. "Of course, I knew it was Mr. Rawlings all along. I took a chance which, it seems, has paid off."

"Well you certainly looked guilty, Sir," said Lady Featherstonehaugh.

"As I have assured Princess Amelia, Madam, I most definitely was not."

While they had been speaking they had all been aware of a distant commotion, as if somebody or other was hurling abuse. Now the sound got louder.

"Whatever is that?" asked Dr. Phipps, who had been sitting silently listening.

"I really can't..."

But the Princess got no further. The door of the dining room burst open and there, with three servants clinging to him, dragging him to the floor, was Michael O'Callaghan.

"What has happened to her?" he bellowed, down on his knees. "What have you done with her in the name of God?"

John got up and went to the man's side just as the footmen finally got their way and floored him.

"She's been arrested," he said quietly.

"For the murders?"

"What else?"

"But I swear by Jesus, Joseph and Mary that she is not guilty of those crimes."

"How can you be so certain?"

"I'll tell you how. Because I did them. It is me they should be taking away."

There was a scream from Lady Hampshire who fainted, most conveniently into the arms of the doctor.

Princess Amelia rose to her feet. "Mr. Rawlings, take this lout of an Irishman into an ante-room and question him. It would appear that there has been a miscarriage of justice."

Chapter Twenty-Six

John entered the ante room to discover a scene of devastation. Michael O'Callaghan was struggling on the floor with four footmen, two of whose wigs he had succeeded in knocking off to reveal spiky shaven heads beneath. The third one was bleeding from the lip, while the fourth was clinging to the Irishman's leg like a terrier to a rat. The Apothecary paused momentarily, thinking that Michael's strength must be profound, then he shouted, "Stop it. Stop it, I say." And literally all five of them ceased fighting to gaze at him.

"Tell these bastards to let me go, John," the Irishman bellowed.

"Do as he says," the Apothecary ordered. "I think he'll behave himself with me. At least I hope he will."

"If course I will," Michael said, picking himself up from the floor.

He solemnly handed the servants their wigs back, bowing as he did so. They were snatched from his hand and thrust back on assorted heads, not altogether neatly. Then, amidst a bevy of black looks, the Irishman collapsed into a chair.

John took a seat opposite. "What made you confess to the murders?" he asked. "Was it to save Georgiana?"

"No, it was because I did them."

"Really? Why did you kill Emilia, may I ask?"

"Oh, that was a mistake. It was Priscilla I was really after."

"You no doubt are a member of the Secret Office and wished to remove her because of her earlier scandal."

Michael's jaw dropped but he kept his composure. "Yes, that's right."

John nodded wisely and steepled his fingers, a characteristic borrowed from Sir Gabriel. Then he laughed. "It does take a bit of imagining, doesn't it? Her intrigue, I mean."

Michael nodded. "It certainly does."

He was out of his depth but struggling gallantly. John looked at him shrewdly. "So you know all about it?"

"Not all, no."

"But instruction came from the Secret Office to dispose of Priscilla. Didn't you feel guilty because she had given you employment? Had been kind to you?"

Michael O'Callaghan looked as uncomfortable as it was possible to do. "I had to do my duty."

"Did you? Did you really, Michael? Now recount to me the facts as they actually happened? Go on, tell me the truth for once."

Suddenly the actor looked weary to the heart, as if the recent strain was at last beginning to tell on him. Seeing this, the ruthless side of the Apothecary's nature asserted itself.

"You've told me a tissue of lies, haven't you? Well, that won't suffice to get your lady love out of gaol. Do you know anything about the scandal in Priscilla's past? If so, I'd be delighted to hear it."

The Irishman lowered his head. "I don't know any facts, to tell you the truth."

"Indeed you don't," the Apothecary said softly, and O'Callaghan shook himself, rather like a wet dog, and remained silent.

"Very well, let us pass on to the murder of Lord Hope. How did you manage that?"

"Oh, that was easy. I just skipped over from Bellow's farm, caught the brute in the Grotto, then skipped back again."

"Dropping your earring as you did so, no doubt. No Michael, it's not good enough. Listen..." The Apothecary leant over the space that divided them and spoke earnestly. "I know that you would sacrifice yourself for Georgiana's sake and I think it is a truly noble gesture on your part. But believe me, your story is as full of holes as a baker's sieve. You'll have to think of something better than that if you are going to impress Sir John Fielding."

"To hell with him," the actor answered wearily. "And to hell with you too, John Rawlings. I thought you were my friend."

Some of the Irishman's fatigue seemed to transmit itself to John, who said, "Michael, I am your friend, very much so. But if Georgiana is guilty of three brutal murders would you really want her for wife and possibly the mother of your children?"

"Yes. No. I'm not sure."

"Listen to me. I am not certain that she is guilty. I think the killer might still be at large."

Michael raised his head. "Do you really? Or are you just saying it?"

"I mean it."

"But surely those officials wouldn't make a mistake."

"I know the man who arrested her. I think he is one of the most excellent people it has ever been my good fortune to encounter. But I believe that this time he could be mistaken."

The actor gave him a long stare. "Then in that case..."

"In that case your flinging yourself about, burdening yourself with guilt, is pointless. What we've got to do is trap the true killer, and we've got to do it fast."

"How can I help you?"

"This is how."

And in the small confines of the ante room and speaking quietly, John Rawlings described his plan to the Irish actor.

By the time he rejoined the dinner table it was to find that most of the other guests had gone to play cards. Wishing fervently that he had a quarter of his adopted father's aptitude for gaming, John was glad to sit down for a glass of port with Dr. Peter Phipps.

The physician was in pensive mood, clearly troubled by all that had taken place. "I can tell you frankly, Colonel – I beg pardon, Mr. Rawlings – that I shall be glad to get out of this house."

"When do you intend to go, Sir?"

"Tomorrow morning. I still practice now and then, and even the most querulous of patients will seem like a rest cure after the recent ordeal. D'ye know, I somehow cannot credit that Lady Georgiana should turn out to be the murderer. But there we are; stranger things than that have happened in life."

John nodded and his mobile brows twitched as his mind went haring down a million odd corridors. Supposing that Michael O'Callaghan had played the biggest bluff of his life by confessing to murders he had actually committed... Or supposing that Lady Georgiana, that ice cool beauty, had truly been responsible... Or supposing that, as John felt utterly certain, the murderer still lurked round Gunnersbury House, ready to strike again. He realised that the doctor was speaking.

"Lady Theydon has been removed?"

"Oh yes. The Runners have taken her to Brentford mortuary. The coroner will have to release the body for burial."

"What a way to end it all. What had the poor woman done?"

"She befriended the wrong people, that's what."

"Who do you mean, Sir?"

"I'm not sure," John answered him slowly. "That's just the trouble. I'm not sure."

"Have another glass of this excellent port to refresh your memory."

"I don't think it will do that, but I thank you, Sir." And the Apothecary held out his glass.

There was a distant knocking on the front door and the doctor turned to John. "Oh, not more disquiet. Surely that truculent Irishman was enough for one evening. What happened to him, incidentally?"

"I sent him back to Bellow's farm. He didn't kill anyone, Sir. He was merely confessing to try to save his sweetheart."

"Do you mean Lady Georgiana was having an affair with him?"

"I'm afraid, Sir, that I do."

The physician assumed an expression which John interpreted as 'it is impossible to shock a doctor'. In any other circumstances he would have found it amusing but tonight even his cynical sense of humour was stretched to its limit. There was a momentary silence interupted by a discreet knock on the door.

"Come in," called Dr. Phipps.

A footman entered the room with a letter on a tray. "This came by express messenger for Mr. Rawlings."

The Apothecary stared. "Who can it be from?"

But as soon as he cast his eyes on the paper he knew the writing. The letter was from Joe Jago.

It simply said:

Honoured friend,

I can say Little except Please Watch the Grotto without Cease. I Think All Will be Revealed there. Remain Vigilant. Your most sensibly Obliged and Humble servant.

The signature J. Jago was written with a flourish and the address at the top of the note was given as The Red Lion, Brentford. John reread it with a rise in his spirits. If his interpretation was correct then the arrest of Georgiana had been a ploy and the killer was indeed still at large.

His thoughts roamed over the suspects. The Princess herself could not be excluded though he found it really hard to credit that such a plump woman could have leapt nimbly through the trees wearing a red cloak or fought Lord Hope in the Grotto. Still, stranger things than that had happened and she could not be ruled out. Then came Lady Hampshire with her penchant for much younger men. Had her desire to obtain jewels that sparkled led her to kill for them? If she had mistaken Emilia for Priscilla could it have been for something that Priscilla had worn? Similarly with Lord Hope who had flaunted rings and snuffboxes and brooches.

His thoughts turned to those two strange women, namely
Ladies Featherstonehaugh and Kemp. What was it they got up to
in their private time? Could it be that they worked together as
murderers, one giving the other an alibi? He ran this idea over in
his mind and found a great deal to recommend it.

Finally he came to Priscilla who was, he felt certain, growing
extremely fond of him. The trouble with her was that she lacked
motive. Why should she kill an old friend and why on earth kill
Lord Hope? Lady Theydon had clearly been done away with
because she had refused to give the murderer any further assistance. But the other two? John mentally discounted Miss
Fleming for having no reason to kill.

This left him with the enigmatic Michael O'Callaghan. The
Irishman had confessed to the murders but surely only to defend
Lady Georgiana Hope. But could this have been a bluff, a bluff
which had fooled John completely. Well, almost completely.
Though he had included the actor in his plan to find the murder-
er, he had not told him everything.

"Was it good news or bad?" asked Dr. Phipps.

John dragged himself back to reality. "Neither, really." He
glanced at the handsome watch that Sir Gabriel had given him
for his twenty-first birthday. "Um, it's just gone eight. I think if
you'll excuse me that I might go for a stroll."

The doctor downed his port. "Do you mind if I join you. I
could do with some fresh air."

Wanting desperately to be alone, John replied, "It's still very
cold, Sir."

"Oh that doesn't worry me," the physician answered heartily.
"I always wrap up well."

There was no help for it, the two of them fetched their out-
door garments and marched out into the February night, John
thinking that he would take a brief walk and return later. But for
all that he found himself heading in the direction of the Grotto,
the doctor striding along beside him.

Spring was definitely on its way, the bitterness of January a thing of the past. But it was still chilly and the Apothecary felt himself shiver as they approached the building in which the Grotto was situated.

"Do you remember last time we were here?" John asked.

Dr. Phipps turned on him a bleak look. "Only too clearly. What a terrible expression Lord Hope had on his face."

Recalling those white features and the mauvish-blue lips drawn back in the travesty of a grin, John shuddered again. "Poor fellow. He must have been detested to have merited such an end as that."

"That, or simply in the way," the doctor answered.

Though he was longing to take a look inside, armed as he was with a lanthorn, the Apothecary forebore. However he did linger a moment to see if he could hear anyone within. But there was nothing except silence and he and Dr. Phipps continued on and past, down into the parkland beyond.

They returned an hour later to find that the card party had broken up, Princess Amelia leading the way through a bowing line of her fellow players. Seeing John, she bore down on him while he bowed low, wondering all the while what she wanted.

"Mr. Rawlings, a vord viz you, if you please."

"Certainly, Ma'am."

So for the second time that day he found himself in her private sanctum, alone except for the usual handful of footmen.

"I will come straight to the point," she said as soon as she was seated.

John carefully perched on the edge of the sofa opposite and smiled politely.

"I think you should consider remarrying," she said. "Now that an arrest has been made and the investigation concluded it is time you thought of yourself."

"But, Your Highness, it is only two months since my wife died."

"You should regard your child, Mr. Rawlings. You cannot leave her motherless."

Wondering how the elderly lady knew about Rose, John answered, "I am sure that my father and I can bring her up satisfactorily."

"Well, I beg to differ. A little maiden needs a woman's touch. Now may I suggest to you Miss Fleming. The poor girl cannot stay on in my household and I think it would be an ideal solution."

John thought how marvellous it must be to give orders and have them obeyed instantly, and reckoned it must be the habit of royalty's lifetime to do so. He further reckoned that to refuse point blank would place him in trouble. He gave an evasive answer.

"Madam, I will bear what you say in mind. Of course the welfare of my child must be paramount."

"Good. I am glad that you are seeing sense. I know that Priscilla is hoping to speak to you. I suggest you propose."

And if ever, the Apothecary thought, I should propose to anyone again it could only be Elizabeth. However, he smiled and nodded and wished desperately that he were away from Gunnersbury House with its intrigues and lies.

Bowing his way out, rather magnificently, he found that most of the household had retired to bed, exhausted by recent events no doubt. But just as he was making his way towards the great staircase he saw that Priscilla was indeed hovering nervously, looking very sweet in a pale blue open robe. He went to her and kissed her hand and she gave him a nervous smile.

"Oh John, my dear, I do apologise for the Princess." She lowered her voice to a whisper. "She is such a foolish old romantic and heaven alone knows what she has been saying."

"Well..."

"Do you know," Priscilla rushed on, "that King Frederick of Prussia, while he was still Crown Prince of course, was madly in love with her and that, to this day, she wears his miniature next to her heart."

"Really?"

"Truly. She intends to keep it there until she dies and then, I dare swear, it will not be removed but will be buried with her. So she is the most devoted of creatures and believes that everyone should be the same."

"I see."

Priscilla went very pink. "John, what did she say to you?"

He sighed. "My dear, she suggested that you and I should marry, but..."

She turned away from him. "I think it is a good idea, John. Only as a business arrangement, of course. You wouldn't have to pay for a governess for your child and you might grow to love me in time. I am utterly skilled in housewifery and would entertain your friends gladly. Oh, my dear soul, I do think I would make an excellent wife for you."

Just for a fleeting second it occurred to John that it might indeed be the answer to all his problems. And then he thought of riding free over the vast expanse of Devon's wild country with a dark woman by his side, a dark woman who could outride him and outshoot him if necessary, and he knew the direction he wanted his future to go in.

"Priscilla, it's too soon for me to make any decision," he said kindly.

"But why is it?" she persisted. "Surely Rose needs a mother quickly."

He became aware at that moment that he wanted his daughter to grow up as an extraordinary woman too; a woman who could make her own decisions and be her own person. A woman who would not be as compliant and sweet as poor little Miss Fleming.

"Rose will do well enough with my father for the time being. He will try to make her as good a person as possible."

Priscilla's small eyes closed and her face crumpled into

tragedy's mask. She clung to John, collapsing in his arms.

"Oh, why, why? I love you, John. I have for a long time now. Oh please, my darling. As a marriage of convenience only. I know you will grow to love me in time. I know it."

He forced her to look at him. "Priscilla, no. I could never love you. I still love Emilia. Can't you understand that?"

"No," she wept, "I can't."

He stood there helplessly, wishing himself anywhere but there, and then he was aware of a presence standing close by and watching him. Elizabeth di Lorenzi had just stepped out of the shadows.

Chapter Twenty-Seven

She smiled in the darkness and dropped them a deferential curtsey. "Pardon me, Sir and Madam. I didn't realise you were there."

Priscilla rounded on her. "What are you doing above stairs? Your place is in the kitchens."

"I came to put the candles out, Madam."

"Surely that is a job for one of the footmen?"

"The footmen are feeling a little unwell, Miss Fleming, after their mill with Michael O'Callaghan. I offered to take on their duties just for this evening."

"Oh very well. Get on with it then."

From the shadows John felt the acerbity of Elizabeth's smile. "Very good, Milady."

He turned to her. "Thank you, Elizabeth. It was kind of you to step into the breach."

Priscilla straightened in his arms. "Oh my dear, I am suddenly tired and must be away to bed. Will you escort me to my room?"

"I think I'll take a turn in the grounds. Perhaps the servant would do so," he replied most ungallantly.

Elizabeth curtsied. "If Madam would like to come with me."

Miss Fleming shot them both a defeated glance. She had been manoeuvred into a position where she could do nothing but accept.

"Very well. Lizzie go ahead with the candelabra. I shall follow immediately." She turned to John. "Good night, my dear. Promise to think about what I have said."

"I will. Good night."

He watched her ascending, thinking how short she looked behind Elizabeth's long lean body. At the top of the staircase she turned and gave him a tremulous smile and a little wave, then vanished from sight. Glad to be away from her, John donned the Prince's cape, which hung near the front door, and stepped outside.

Uncomfortable though it was going to be, he intended to watch the Grotto all night. He had sent Michael back home, which was perhaps as well in view of certain ideas that the Apothecary had. So, devoid of assistance, it was up to him to keep vigil. Walking briskly, John found a place behind an all-covering bush and sat down on a cushion which he had brought with him from the house.

He must have dropped off, despite the discomfort, for he was woken by a great deal of giggling – somewhat inebriated, he thought – and the sound of someone falling over. Despite his instinct to go and help, John remained exactly where he was and observed.

A couple of ladies of the night – at least that is what he presumed from their garish ensembles – were staggering across the lawn, arms linked, shooshing one another for laughing so much. Yet as he watched them John could not help but think they looked familiar. He stared closely as the moon came out and recognised, through the mass of face paint, the features of Lady Kemp. Beside her, staggering slightly as she went, minced Lady Featherstonehaugh in outrageously high heels. The Apothecary was so amused that he laughed out loud.

Lady Kemp drew to a halt. "What was that?"

"What was what?"

"That noise. It sounded like somebody chuckling."

"I didn't hear anything."

"That's because you're drunk, you bitch."

"Bitch yourself! So are you."

They put their heads together and cackled wildly, then wove their unsteady progress on in the direction of the side door.

So that, thought John, was their guilty secret. In the darkness of night they dressed up as whores and went off, presumably to the rouge route of Brentford, to seek a bit of excitement. Well, good luck to 'em, unless, of course, they had added murder to their need for thrills. Getting up in order to relieve himself, John thought carefully about the snatched bit of conversation he had overheard but could find nothing in it except some vague reference to seeing something. He decided that next day he would question the two ladies more closely.

Again he must have slept, for when he opened his eyes it was to see the first streaks of dawn threading the sky. An unbearable cramp seized his leg and he jumped up, unable to control himself, hopping about and rubbing the limb back to life. Then every hair on his neck rose and he crouched down again, staring at what he had seen through the branches of the bush.

A figure was making its way across the lawn, heavy with morning dew. A figure that moved slowly, seeming to glide along. A figure hidden entirely in a long grey cloak with the hood raised and pulled across, so that from where he was observing it appeared to have no face. Despite all he knew about phantoms – which actually was very little – John was utterly terrified.

He watched as the figure glided up to the Grotto, looked slyly over its shoulder to make sure it was unobserved, then slipped noiselessly inside. For a moment or two John remained petrified to the spot. Too frightened to move or make a sound. Then with an enormous effort of will he forced himself to cross the distance that separated him from the building, and enter.

It was pitch dark within but the figure must have concealed a lanthorn in the folds of its cloak for, as John peered through the gloom, a tinder was struck and the lanthorn blazed into light. He watched from the doorway, as silent as the grave, while the hooded figure started to search along the walls and crevices of the grotto. Then, going down on its knees, a bare arm was extended and fished in the black waters of the bathing basin.

John reached in his pocket and brought out the earring which he had removed from the drawer, turning it over in his hand so that its jewel caught the beams of the lanthorn and sparkled softly.

"Looking for this?" he asked quietly.

There was an intake of breath and the figure wheeled in fright. Then it lowered its hood and gave a tortured smile.

"Why, John," it said.

It was Priscilla.

He crossed the small distance between them and caught her bare arm in a hard grip. She winced but continued to smile at him.

"John, my dear, whatever are you doing here?"

"I might well ask the same of you."

"Me? Oh, I came for an early morning dip."

"In the same water in which Lord Hope breathed his last? I think not, Priscilla. I think you were looking for the partner to this."

And he held out the hand in which gleamed the earring.

She stayed very cool. "Oh, yes. I knew that I had dropped it somewhere. Was it in here?"

"You know damned well it was. Why try and hide it? You've been very clever so far in concealing your actions but you've just run out of time."

Still that ghastly smile lit her features. "Oh John, darling, why do you sound so angry? I know it was against the Princess's orders for anyone to use the pool but I so wanted to bathe."

"Stop playing games, Priscilla. Why don't you admit what you've done?"

For answer she turned away from him and when she turned back her eyes were sparkling. "Oh, you're such an upright citizen, aren't you. Haven't you ever wanted anything so much that you were prepared to kill for it?"

"No, never."

"Then more fool you. Oh, my sweetheart, if only you had an inkling of how much I love you. Together we could conquer the world, you and I. Do you know when it was I first fell in love with you."

He shook his head dumbly, afraid of spoiling her flow.

"It was when I came into your shop in Shug Lane with a doctor's note for physick for Princess Amelia. You don't remember, do you? But I did. I can picture it now." Priscilla squeezed her eyes tightly shut. "I can conjure up every little detail. What you were wearing; the way you looked at me. That was when I knew that whatever happened I would have you for my husband one day."

"But I was married."

"So I found out. I made enquiries about you and discovered that I had been at school with Emilia Rawlings, nee Alleyn. So I wrote and was duly invited. But even if I hadn't known her I would have found a way of getting into your household. I truly love you, you see."

John stared at her aghast, simply shaking his head. "Did you kill her?" he asked.

Once again Priscilla smiled her ghastly smile. "I removed her from our path, that is all."

"But how in God's name did you get her to go into the woods, on her own and in the dark?"

Priscilla actually looked smug and John's hand twitched, longing to wipe the smile from her face.

"I told her that you were there. Said that you had slipped out at the end of the performance and had a surprise for her. Only it wasn't the sort of surprise she had been expecting." Priscilla giggled.

He had sworn to put down the person who had attacked his wife but now he just stood there, gaping, unable to move a muscle.

"But why Lord Hope?" he asked.

She moved closer to him. "Do you remember me telling you about the child I bore?" John nodded. "Well, it was all true except the King was not the father."

"You mean Lord Hope...?"

"Yes, he. He sired my baby."

"And the attack on you in The Temple? You just lay on the ground and squeezed your own throat hard, didn't you, you evil creature?"

"Oh yes," Priscilla answered guilelessly, "I had to. If you knew how much I wanted you to touch me. I had to do something, anything, to get you to put your arms round me. Oh darling, you're frowning. Don't be cross."

John ignored her. "And Lady Theydon?"

"She refused to protect me any longer. She whispered as much one night, then threatened me in her room. She had to go before she betrayed me which, I believe, she was about to do."

"Poor woman," said John. "I think she would have kept your secret for the rest of her days."

"How aptly put, my darling. Most amusing. But now you know my little pretence, what am I going to do with you?"

"Priscilla Fleming, I am going to arrest you for the murder of Emilia Rawlings."

"But I killed for you, John. All I did, I did for love. Just marry me, my dearest, and let us forget all about these incidents."

"Incidents, you call them! Taking the lives of innocent people is nearer the truth. You bore Lord Hope a child years ago, so why kill him now? Lady Theydon had covered up for you to the best of her ability. But it was the murder of the woman who befriended you, the woman I adored, that is totally unforgivable. You are a monster, not a woman. Rather than love you, I loathe you."

She gave him a look of such sadness that momentarily he felt sorry for her, realising that she was crazy and that nothing he could say or do would penetrate her consciousness.

"Oh my darling," she sighed, then quick as a flash she produced a pistol from within the folds of the all-enveloping cloak.

"Priscilla, be sensible," John reasoned. "If you shoot me you are bound to be caught. You've done enough killing. Put the gun away."

"But you don't love me, you've just said so. And you know all my secrets. I have to kill you."

Behind her, from the top entrance to the Grotto, John detected a faint movement. He deliberately did not look, terrified lest she should wheel round and face whoever stood there.

"Well, if I must die, I must," he said, playing for time.

She came right up to him, so close that he could stare into those small blue eyes of hers. In their depths he saw madness but he also saw a great tenderness and, overriding all, terrible sadness.

"Let me hold you as you die, my darling," she whispered, and cocked the pistol.

The fluttering in the entrance turned into a whirlwind as a great voice shouted, "No, Miss Priscilla, for the love of God," and a figure hurled itself onto her, pulling her to the ground so that the shot went into the roof.

John went down instinctively so that his entire view was distorted. But wrestling on the floor like a pair of fighting dogs he perceived the saturnine footman Benedict and the girl who had just tried to shoot him. Realising that the servant was himself in danger, John reached into his pocket for a pistol but discovered it gone, looked round for a weapon, his eye alighting on a piece of wood. Scrambling towards it, he snatched it up and getting to his feet stood over the fighting couple.

"Priscilla Fleming..." he shouted.

She looked up at him, said, "Why couldn't you love me, John?" then, putting the pistol against her head, fired a single shot and fell backwards into Benedict's arms.

Chapter Twenty-Eight

He had vowed to put down Emilia's murderer and dance on their grave, but now that reality had come he could do nothing but stare at what was left of Priscilla's head and weep uncontrollably. John wept the tears he had fought back so gallantly for so long. Sinking down once more, he sat on the Grotto floor and sobbed. Then he heard Benedict disengage himself from the dead woman's embrace and scramble to his feet.

"Come now, Sir, don't take on so badly."

John looked at the footman, shaking his head and muttering, "I'm sorry. I can't help myself."

"Best we leave here, with her so injured and all."

The Apothecary stole a glance and his stomach heaved. Half of Priscilla's head had been blown to bits and had spattered itself on the floor and, ironically, was floating on the surface of the bathing basin. Staggering to his feet, he lurched to the door and inhaled the cold morning air to try and calm himself, then, almost automatically, John reached for his salts and took a good, deep sniff.

Benedict appeared in the entrance. "Come on, Sir. Back to the house."

John set out, but strangely his legs were weak and it was somehow comforting to lean on the footman and be helped back.

"I apologise. I never really liked you, more fool me."

"It's understandable, Mr. Rawlings. I am the Princess's spy — unofficially, you comprehend. I make it my business to know everybody else's, if you follow me."

"I do. But why does she need such a person?"

"I don't really know. Perhaps she likes to feel secure in her life devoted to pleasure."

"Yes," the Apothecary answered shakily, "I suppose you must be right."

"But she is a good woman, Sir, despite the fact that when she was young she was fairly free with her affections."

"As I imagine we all are," John answered, and gave the hint of a smile.

So, supported by Benedict, he made his way towards the house and the great explanation that lay ahead of him.

Almost as if it were a state occasion, Princess Amelia had surrounded herself with her women. Clustered around her chair were the Ladies Hampshire, Featherstonehaugh and Kemp. Not such a stunning gathering as when Lady Theydon had been one of their number and they had represented the Four Marys, John thought.

He had told his story simply and from the beginning, omitting certain details about the three women for the sake of diplomacy. Benedict, obviously a well-loved servant, had joined him and provided the rest of the information.

"But what about Lady Georgiana?" Princess Amelia asked. "How is she faring?"

"It is my opinion that she and Joe Jago were acting in collusion," John answered.

"Do you mean to say that she went through with the arrest as a kind of charade?"

"Yes, I do. Jago spent some time alone with her and I think he persuaded her to cooperate. She is probably lodging in some expensive coaching inn in London at this very minute."

"And what of her future I ask?"

"Madam," John replied, "that is a matter between her and Michael O'Callaghan."

"Who is Priscilla Fleming's cousin by the way," put in Benedict. "There were three sisters in Ireland. One did well for herself and married Lord Theydon, the other two remained penniless and never left. O'Callaghan is the child of one, Miss Fleming the child of the other."

"And to think the wretched girl killed her own aunt. Vicked, vicked."

"She was mad, Highness," said John.

"Obviously. But a good actress."

The Apothecary looked at the footman. "Yes, she was a very good actress," he said quietly.

Chapter Twenty-Nine

The following day Princess Amelia packed up the house and left for London. The Runners had come and removed the body of Priscilla Fleming, and the Princess – being a woman of strong stomach and stout heart – had ordered workmen into the Grotto to enlarge it and make it ready for the summer.

"I cannot help it if it was a scene of violent crime," she had announced. "I like it and that, I'm afraid, is that."

John meanwhile had returned to Bellow's Farm to say his farewells and to check on the progress of Hugh. And, most importantly, to speak to Michael O'Callaghan. He had found the Irishman in the barn, packing his simple bag before returning to London.

"So it was Priscilla all along," the actor said grimly. "She was always a strange girl, even as a child. We were cousins, you know."

"So Benedict told me."

"For some reason she didn't want that put about. Probably thought my penniless state would reflect badly on her. Something like that anyway."

"Tell me, Michael, did she have a child?"

"Oh yes, she bore a bastard all right."

"And who was the father? Do you know?"

"It was a local lad, just a simple fellow she lured into her clutches."

"Not the King? Not Lord Hope?"

Michael gave a laugh. "No, neither. Did she tell you that it was?"

"She said it was both of them. So why did she kill his lord-ship?"

"Probably to make things easier for me." Michael looked grim. "But, by Jasus, it's made things harder. I must go to town and woo Georgiana all over again."

"I wish you luck. Do you think she'll come back?"

"I've no idea, to be honest with you."

The Irishman slung his bag onto his shoulder and held out his hand. "Goodbye, Sir. It's been a pleasure to know you."

And with that he went off up the drive and out of John's life.

Staring at his retreating back, the Apothecary smiled wearily and went to see Hugh Bellow.

"Well, Will – or should I call you John? – the leg's coming along, don't you think?" Hugh had asked.

"It's excellent. You won't need extra help for much longer."

"Just a week or so and then I'll be walking with a stick. Thank you for all you did."

"I'm glad to have been of help."

"Oh, by the way, Jake asked me to pass on regards. He's at market in Brentford at the moment."

"Is he happier by any chance?"

"Aye, he is. Seems he's courting a pretty widow."

"Well I wish him the best."

Hugh cleared his throat. "So it was one of the ladies was the killer."

"Yes. Do you know I felt there was something odd about her after the so-called attack. I went back to the scene and got the idea that everything was not right. If only I'd acted sooner."

"We can all say that, John. I think you acted to the best of your ability."

After that conversation the Apothecary had gone out into the fields and stared at the spot where he had once seen Emilia walk. But there had been nothing. Whatever had been the explanation, it was over. He knew that he would never see her again.

He had caught the stagecoach to Kensington and so, somewhat dishevelled, had arrived at his father's house. As he walked up the street his heart had almost stopped, for there coming towards him was the tall spare frame of Sir Gabriel, as stunning as ever in starkest black and white, hand-in-hand with Rose. Just for a moment John had stood and observed them, relishing his child's beauty, her red hair and lovely complexion. Then he had broken into a run, hugging Sir Gabriel to him, picking up his daughter and whirling her in the air above his head. Finally they had gone into the house.

"So, my dear, you are returned to us, as I always knew you would be."

"Yes, the murderess has been caught."

"And did you guess correctly?"

"No, Sir. She kept me on a string till the very end."

"I believe she must have been in love with you."

John had laughed. "You will never cease to amaze me, Sir. Do you know she even stood in my garden in the dead of night, watching the house."

"Wretched woman. Well, now she's gone and there's an end to it."

The Apothecary had poured himself a large glass of claret. "And tell me about Shug Lane. Who is running the shop?"

"Nicholas Dawkins, of course. Along with Gideon Purle. I have put a local apothecary in charge at Kensington and let Nick return to London, which he much prefers. So, my son, if you feel like getting away, you are free to do so."

John had smiled crookedly. "I would rather like to take Rose with me. I feel that she and I should get to know one another again."

"An admirable suggestion. And where are you thinking of going?"

"To Devon," John had answered without hesitation.

"And how is Elizabeth?"

"I owe her an enormous amount. She took the most pitiful job in order to help me. The day the Princess moved on she hired a post chaise and went West to await my arrival."

"Then you must join her, my son," Sir Gabriel had said wisely.

John had got up and kissed his adopted father on the cheek, considering that he had been more than blessed that such a man should have chosen to make him part of his family.

There was one more thing he needed to do before he went westwards. Quite alone, not even with Rose for company, John went to Kensington churchyard and put a bunch of spring flowers on the grave of Emilia Rawlings. Sir Gabriel had arranged all beautifully, having a marble headstone erected with the words, 'Emilia, beloved wife of John Rawlings. 1738-1764. Asleep with the angels.' At the head of the stone was the carved face of an angel that bore more than a passing resemblance to Emilia herself.

John had knelt down by the grave and spoken to it. "I swore I'd kill your murderer with my own hand, but I couldn't, my darling. You see, it was poor mad Priscilla. You do understand that, don't you?"

There had been no reply but he had felt strangely at peace.

"I'm taking Rose to Devon," he had said.

And this time the breeze had whispered, 'Good.'

And now he reined in his mount, his daughter sitting in front of him, and thought about everything that had happened. Before him stretched the wild Devon landscape, the vast expanse of sky, the rugged turf beneath his horse's feet.

Rose turned to look at him. "What are you thinking, Papa?"

"I'm thinking about your mother and how much she loved this place."

"We won't see her again, will we?"

"Not in this life, no."

"I miss her."

"So do I," answered John.

Then he stared as into his line of vision came a black horse with a woman rider on top. Her hair was streaming out behind her and she rode with that easy confidence that told him it must be Elizabeth come to meet them.

He waved his arm over his head. "Hello."

His voice echoed round the hills and she heard him. "John," she called.

He and Rose trotted forward while she cantered in his direction. Then as she approached, she shot them a look full of fun and said, "Catch me."

Her horse wheeled and went off at a terrific pace.

"Hold tight, my darling," said John Rawlings to his daughter.

And so with Rose clinging on for dear life and the Apothecary's heart pounding in his chest, he galloped off into the wild, wild country that lay ahead.

Historical Note

John Rawlings, Apothecary, really lived as did Sir John Fielding, the Blind Beak. John was born circa 1731, though his actual parentage is somewhat shrouded in mystery. He became a Yeoman of the Worshipful Society of Apothecaries on 13th March, 1755, giving his address as 2, Nassau Street, Soho. Sir John was knighted in 1761, when he was forty years old. His work in assisting his brother Henry, the author, in founding the Runners, later known as the Bow Street Runners, needs no further description.

Princess Amelia, daughter of George II, was born in 1710 in Hanover. She purchased the 1663 Palladian Villa, known as Gunnersbury House, in 1761. She was the intended wife of Frederick the Great who corresponded with her until his marriage in 1733. At her death his miniature was found on her breast next to her heart. But she was also the mistress of the Duke of Grafton and, apparently, the Duke of Newcastle. Her parties at Gunnersbury House became legendary and Horace Walpole was a frequent visitor. Some while after her death in 1786, the house was demolished and the land divided into lots to be sold off. Thus Gunnersbury eventually passed into the hands of the Rothschilds. For local historians, Bollo Lane is situated on the site of Bellow Brook, and Bollo Bridge Road is where the old wooden bridge once stood.